AF484046

# HELL AND THE HEART

## PIPER CJ

*Hell and the Heart*
Copyright © 2026 Fawn Storytelling LLC



PRINT ISBN: 979-8-9998383-6-0
EBOOK ISBN: 979-8-9998383-7-7
AUDIOBOOK ISBN: 979-8-9998383-8-4

Orders or events by U.S. trade bookstores, wholesalers, and all other business inquiries, please connect with Madison Nankervis:
madison.nankervis@gmail.com

Cover Design: Helena Elias
Editor: Kathryn Wohlpart
Developmental Edits: Letty Mundt
Audio Narration: Luna Rey
Formatting: Zachary James
Interior Artwork: Alessia Iachini ( @pandyals_art )

*to anyone who called upon a god who didn't answer*
*to those who were told their faith simply wasn't strong enough*
*to all oppressed by a religion they didn't choose*

*here's to the fire it took to forge our own path*

# Before We Begin: A Note from the Author on Religion
## (and Blasphemy)

3,000 years, nearly fifty gods, dozens of pantheons, three years of research, hours buried in dusty tomes, a fortune spent on JSTOR academic texts, a psychosis-inducing spiral into trying to do justice to dead languages, and we have the labor that is Caliban's story: *Hell and the Heart*.

It's me, Piper, and I was raised devoutly evangelical. As such, while the Abrahamic religions share regions, certain religious texts, overlapping names and lore, and other such similarities in their Venn diagrams, it would be a mistake for me to portray this as a reimagining of other Abrahamic religions, like Islam or Judaism, though I am grateful for access to both Islamic and Jewish sensitivity readers on the topic. That said, Caliban (Amagi, or our nameless Prince of Hell), operates within Christian mythology. As such, even the way he views or interacts with other pantheons is intentionally through the filter of his allocated Christian mythology. This text begins with the use of the Gregorian calendar, marks Jesus's birth as a significant milestone, and uses tales as they're known and recorded in Biblical texts and the versions within said worldview, both cannon and apocryphal.

This portrayal of Christian mythos may be unsuitable for some readers, particularly when our protagonist (the Prince of Hell) uses problematic or antagonistic language regarding Christianity and its spread. The "god" in this text is a fictional character, not a God with a capital "G," and all told through the interpretive lens of a fantasy author. Irrespective of my religious background, theological education, and mythological research, it is ultimately, a creative reimagination. Within the focus of Christian mythology and accompanying my adherence to the studies you will move through a biased version of events. The *No Other Gods* series does not aim to tell a balanced defense between Heaven and Hell, but to deconstruct from familiar religious narratives as our protagonist roots from "the other side."

In Marlow's (Love's) cycles of reincarnation, we include lives born into pantheons across the globe, including closed pantheons. I hope you'll find those instances were handled with boundaries and respect, as they are not my stories to tell.

I'd like to specifically address occasions where you might find a god's name misspelled or mispronounced, and call awareness to its intentionality. I'm not the first to implement this tactic, but if we reference witchy classics like *Practical Magic*, you'll notice they pronounce their goddess's name as Heck-tate, rather than Hek-a-te. This is common so as not to invoke a god or goddess, particularly if you're going "off script" on what might be allowed in their representation. Despite my strict adherence to time-period accuracy and deep-dive into lore, I'm also a witchy practitioner, and have occasionally opted for intentional misspellings if the entity in question may not have been thrilled with their portrayal, which I'm sure you'll recognize when you come across them.

Of course, it is a work of fiction.

It's also an offering to the Other Gods, and I intend to do them justice.

# Chapter One

**900 BCE**

Heat and salt swirled off a pale blue sea.

Glass-like shards of sand bit into my flesh, or whatever it was that I wore as skin when we walked the surface. I pushed my toes to the sheer tip of the rocky edge. Endless desert stretched to my right while a statuesque woman stood still to my left, as though she'd been molded from the cliff itself. Her gauzy shift tufted around her, bringing with it the scents of cinnamon and wine, strong enough to drown the sulfur that lapped at the shores below.

I endured the discomfort of pomp and circumstance as my title demanded. I'd remain in the crawling mirk of the mortal crust until I'd fulfilled my duty. But if we could just get on with it...

I sucked in an encouraging breath, a gentle prod for her to start the meeting.

"Prince." She broke the uncomfortable silence at last. She

didn't look over her shoulder as I moved into the place beside her.

"Queen," I replied.

Of course, she was not my queen, nor was I a member of her royal court. The formalities were merely that. Her pantheon was one of many queens, all of whom wore the title proudly. When occasion demanded that Hell speak with the Sumerians, Gula was my favorite go-between. As the goddess of justice and medicine, among other things, she was reasonable and to the point. As Hell's royal emissary, I was sent between kingdoms only when the need arose. Meetings like this were blissfully shorter than they might be if I'd been sent to engage with a war deity.

Her gaze remained fixed at the base of the cliff amidst a crowd of humans. The sounder of strangers—a generous term for mammalian collections of pigs, regardless of the mortal beast in question—was close enough that we could make out each of their faces. As a reprieve, no matter how temporary, the stampede was not so near that we were subjected to the sweat, dirt, and death that clung to their breath.

"The humans...*these* humans...are they why we're here?" I asked.

Gula hadn't been in the first place I looked, or the sixth, or the tenth. I could have asked an underling, and word would have rippled through the realms in an instant, but I preferred discretion. It was a luxury not often afforded to us.

A full, dark lip pouted, the space between her brows puckering as she said, "Sometimes they make me feel..." Her words were directed as much to me as they were to no one. Her voice had a thin, delicate quality that I'd never appreciated. It gave an air of insincerity to everything she said. "I think I am sad," she decided at last.

"Empathy?" I prompted. I knew the word. I understood the concept. Still, it was surprising. She wasn't the sort.

She looked at me for the first time since my arrival. Gula's large, dark eyes had the clarity of tea. They flashed as she narrowed them at me. The space between her brows squeezed tighter as her lip fell, "No, nothing so primitive. Empathy clouds judgment. It is my duty to remain impartial."

"Pity," I said. "One of the humans belongs to you, then?"

"There, in the back," she lifted her chin to gesture beyond the crowd, where a woman trailed behind the frothing gaggle of filthy bipeds. "She's called Aea. Her cries held such fervor I needed to see for myself."

We weren't watching a crowd, I realized. It was a mob. Their cries were belligerent and unintelligible. A central male figure had thrown a young woman onto the water's edge, and others crowded around to watch. The accused and the accuser. The accused—a woman no older than nineteen—was raw and blood-ied, presumably having been dragged from the nearby city to this place of judgment. Her hair was matted with dirt. Vertical lines carved through her dust-caked cheeks as she sobbed.

Maybe I understood what Gula meant. Perhaps...perhaps this was sad.

"Have you had one?" she asked, though it felt more like a disinterested murmur than a true question.

"A human?" Now *there* was a thought. I knew better than to laugh at a goddess of her caliber.

"It's rather something to be loved by a mortal. They have so little time on their rock, and when they choose to spend their blinks of time worshipping you...everything is fleeting. All of it. Remember that, Prince."

The Sumerians had reigned Mesopotamia for two thousand years. With the help of their gods, their people invented the wheel, cuneiform, geometry, sandals, irrigation, chariots, harpoons, and even sea-to-sea trade routes that led to the cloud of cinnamon wafting off the goddess now.

The Akkadian usurpers were marked by their economy. Most notably known for agriculture, taxation, and conquest. They overthrew with fists, ruled with coin, and promptly fell in under two hundred years.

Her people remained; though, her patience thinned.

"Why have you requested my presence?"

She gestured with a single finger. "Watch."

I inspected the cluster of incensed humans to see a wailing woman—Aea, the goddess's practitioner—following from a distance. She had to be roughly the same age as the accused woman, though the others paid her no mind.

The wind moved the queen's night-dark hair and covered the space between us with the sweetness of fermented honey wine once more. It was a welcome relief to the blood, sand, sweat, and sorrow that lined my nose.

Gula said, "Aea knows the accused is innocent. She's the one they want. Her companion has taken the fall for her, though she has done nothing wrong."

The ember of an emotion pulsed, if only slightly. Yes. That did sound sad.

"I believe Aea feels guilt. It should have been her dragged to the sea by her hair. So, she followed, deep in prayer, petitioning that justice win the day."

Another pulse, however subtle. Another edge of an emotion. Sad.

"What is her crime?"

Gula tucked a knuckle beneath her chin, folding one arm over her chest and looking down on the throng in judgment. "Idolatry. Blasphemy. Witchcraft. Humans are so..."

She let her thought fade as we listened. I could just make out the crowd's words. One loud, male voice claimed to speak for his deity—the same deity both the accused and accuser served. We were familiar with the name and were already exhausted by his people and their bloodlust.

Still, neither of us expected such zeal this far outside of Jerusalem.

They were mortals caught playing the game of gods, and they played it oh so poorly.

"Will you intervene?" I asked.

Gula tilted her head as if the question was as flimsy as the wind-whipped gauze of her dress. "No. I favor Aea. Justice would require that she pay for the crime in the accused's place. For this reason alone, I believe she does not actually desire true justice."

I wasn't sure if I was satisfied with the answer. Uncertainty was uncomfortable, but then again, so were emotions. These were her humans, not mine. I wasn't sure why I engaged, but I offered, "Perhaps in justice's stead, you might offer healing to the accused. She could survive the sentencing."

Boredom colored her response. "The accused does not belong to me. If *her* god wants to spare her, he'll send his servants."

And we both understood her meaning. The god of Jerusalem was busy. He had better things to do than to answer the cries of his faithful. No one would come for the girl.

"You could use her, you know," Gula said.

My lip curled in distaste. "Is this why you've called a meeting?"

"In your war with Heaven, that is," she clarified. "The accused is one of Heaven's faithful, is she not? Perhaps, if you find a compassionate angel, they would not look upon today's events favorably. They might even be disappointed that their king had not sent one of them to intercede."

Distaste turned into something bitter on the back of my tongue.

"Empires rise and fall," she said. "Mine did. All do. But when will *his*? Now, it is small. Once, the Akkadians were small, until they weren't. Then the Assyrians were small, until they weren't. What is to come of this god as his people grow? What will our future hold? But, if Hell were to consider a few pawns..."

Gula wasn't wrong. That didn't make it right.

There was no propaganda quite like the unfeeling manipulation of one's tragedy for another's personal gain. Moments like these could win defectors to our side.

Humans couldn't fathom their roles in our wars—used, ignored, and punished all in a battle to which they had not consented. Perhaps the girl's death would not be in vain, unfair though it was. Maybe Hell would gain a few of Heaven's soldiers after today's events.

The victim screamed something as the crowd forced her to her knees. It was a declaration of faith to the very end. Even in the face of her demise, she refused to denounce her deity.

The ember pulsed within me for a third time, so this time I spoke the feeling aloud. "It is sad."

Unlike the goddess, I did not keep my eyes on the mob as they lifted their stones and carried out their punishment. Sympathy allowed my lids to flutter shut as the bones below began to break.

◆

I was alone beneath the unyielding sun. Gula's motives smoldered within me. We'd exchanged the necessary words to confirm the alliance of our kingdoms as pantheons renegotiated their borders. The warring humans changed territories often. While gods preferred to remain in their realms, the mortal plane was sliced like cake; some received generous portions, and others were offered slivers.

She had no right to call upon one of Hell's royal members to suggest manipulation. It was uncouth. It was unacceptable. It was downright unqueenly.

But the small, pulsing emotion didn't shift to anger, no matter how strongly I felt that it should. Pity took root within me, the choking quality of its vine wrapping around my throat until it was hard to breathe.

I should have gone home.

My head could have hit the pillows of my palace chambers hours ago. My realm had dukes and counts and marquises and generals of war and torture and violence. They wouldn't have flinched at this display, but perhaps that's why I was called, and not them. Why should I?

A thrum of my fingers. A twist of my lips. A squint as I peered between the baking sun and the mangled evidence of mortals and their ruthlessness at my feet.

It was cruel to leave something for dead without finishing the job. I did not delight in suffering. Even a dog would have been offered a kinder death.

Another tap of my fingers as I lingered by the woman.

After all, I was not born to need humans, nor they to need me.

Vultures began to circle, and I made a decision.

Unlike Gula, or Heaven's King, humans didn't source my power. The battered woman gave me no offerings or temples or books written in my name. But as I looked into her badly swollen face, I was compelled to offer this innocent mortal who refused to denounce her faith, even when her god did not arrive, the gift of death.

It was merciful. Perhaps mercy wasn't my first nature, but these impulses were intriguing, at the very least. Between Gula, Aea, myself, and the bloodied husk on the shore, no one would get what they wanted today.

In a step, I moved from my place on the cliff to the space above the human's mangled remains. To my horror, I saw that not only was she alive, but she'd remained conscious. Her cheek was swollen and split. Her jaw was broken. Buzzards descended, lower and lower with each pass, as they grew closer to the promised meal of twisted, raw meat.

"It'll be over soon," I murmured. I extended a hand toward her bruised, swollen face, kneeling to take her pain away.

Her eyes fixed on mine.

My hand froze an inch from her face as she looked not just at me, but into me.

She was so close to death that I could practically see the soul crackling beneath her skin, ready to escape. Its pretty, pearly quality would wink out shortly. Then, she'd be just another dead body without a grave.

Her lips moved silently at first, then with a crimson gurgle, as a small stream ran from her mouth down her throat. I remained immobilized in shock that the human had perceived me as she managed three slow, clear words.

"Don't leave me."

A black vignette swirled at the edges of my vision.

It was like I'd been punched with the fist that had forged time itself.

My lungs, my stomach, my heart dropped and twisted.

Fragile, broken, innocent, tragic, pathetic—the words assaulted me as another drop of blood escaped the corner of her lips.

This was unacceptable. What I felt was beyond pity. The words on my tongue were furious, hateful, downright demonic, but this human was not the target of the fury burbling within me.

She hadn't cried for me to take the pain away. She hadn't begged for help. She'd asked only that I stay with her. My hand remained frozen an inch from her face, as pale as the salt that crusted the water's edge against the sandy brown of her skin, the purples and reds of her wounds, the black of the hair plastered to her face. It was all I could do to keep a tremble from my fingertips.

"Don't leave me."

*No. No, no, no.*

For the first time since I'd been breathed into existence, I was at a loss.

*It's not your business,* gnawed the voice in the back of my head. If I was mortal, I might have called the voice a conscience. Duty was an irritating beast, and I didn't care for its intervention. I was a god in my own right, by mortal standards, and as such, duty could take a back seat as I did whatever I wanted.

Was this what Gula wanted? Could this be her doing?

No, I would not use this woman—scarcely more than a child —as a tool in the war. This pitiful human would not be a martyr for my cause. Gula be damned, I would not let her bones turn to dust as her shattered faith became the poster for Hell's cause.

*What are you doing?*

I didn't even know how to categorize these thoughts. Did these musings, these prodding questions, belong to me?

I may not know humans, but I knew anger. A new, potent wrath perched within me.

Rage alone told me that I would do more than stay with her. I couldn't make this right, but...I wasn't without ability. Surely, I could do more than feel. I could do more than stay, even if I'd never found a need to rise to such an occasion.

A small eternity passed between her simple request and the time it took for my world to shatter. It couldn't have been more than a second before I cupped her cheek with my hand. Her swollen eyelids fluttered shut as I urged a deep and healing sleep to course through her veins.

I took away the desert, the sea, the sand. I erased the hate, the zealots, the stones.

Dreams of flowers, of first kisses, of smiles and sunrises, and the taste of warm bread flowed from my fingertips into her being as I leached away the pain.

I didn't stop there.

One arm beneath her back, one under her knees, and within an instant I'd scooped her into my arms. The cloudless sky faded from blue to shades of orange as the sun dipped behind the rocky crags. Dead to the world of madness and men, her head lolled, settling against my chest as I carried her to the caves on the northern shore and set her down far from the cruelties of the humans who'd wronged her.

*What are you doing? Why are you here? What is your plan?*

I didn't know.

I could have departed when Gula left.

I could have abandoned the girl on the shore.

I could have returned to my realm now that she was mended and safely hidden in a pocket of shadow and sandstone. With the flick of a wrist, a blue fire set the cave alight. It hovered a few inches above the crumbling sediment, casting silhouettes on the young woman's face as the flames danced.

*Don't leave me.*

The words played on repeat despite the unfamiliar voice that attempted to shout within me. I'd made no agreements. There was no contract between us. I had no obligation to this human. Yet there I sat, unable to move as I watched her eyes move beneath her lids as she dreamed.

The moonless night was black, save for the silver stars burning through the cave's mouth. I stared at her over the blue flame, hoping the girl would be glad for its warmth when she awoke. When she stirred, I realized there would already be enough to startle her and didn't want to add to the panic. I waved a hand and the flame disappeared.

Her eyes opened and I watched her from the far side of the cave, hyperaware of how small she looked. Her clothes were simple rags, and after the day's events, they were little more than tatters. A scrap of cloth slipped from her shoulder as she struggled to sit up.

I held my breath, mind racing as I waited to see if she'd see me as she had before. The mortal mind did curious things in the moment between life and death, after all, much like the vibrant hue of her soul peeking through the veil. Perhaps I'd be invisible, as I should be to human eyes, and I could leave her knowing I'd done her a kindness.

She pulled her knees to her chest, hugging herself tightly as she examined me.

I swallowed. "Don't be scared."

The air in the cave evaporated as we remained caught in uncertainty before she spoke.

Her voice was quiet, but strong as she asked, "Are you an angel?"

With the question came the return of pity.

Her god. Her faith. His servants.

Heaviness filled me as I looked at the hope in her eyes, gazing at a human who'd been punished and left for dead and who still thought that her deity cared for her, even now. My heart cracked knowing that, of all the things that had accosted her today, my answer might be the thing that shattered her.

"No."

She shook her head as she tried to make sense of me. I saw each memory flash through her eyes, wincing as if each recovered thought was a slap across her face. To herself, she said, "I didn't denounce him. No matter what they said. I was faithful. I was good, and—"

"I know," I said. I wanted to touch her, to comfort her, but stopped myself. I withdrew slowly. I pulled in a measured breath of air, tasting the sharp scent of something like the essence just between cloud and sky.

The opalescent soul I'd noticed in her moment before death flared, and I saw it shimmer beneath her skin once more. There was an ozone quality to her pearl aura, something so pure, so beautiful, that I couldn't quite name. It made my words all the more painful.

"He didn't deserve your loyalty. Your refusal to turn your back on that which ignored you...it broke something in me."

I wasn't sure why I'd said it. She deserved more. Maybe my feelings toward the enemy kept my wrath smoldering at a low simmer. She represented so many facets of the war, without having any idea as to the role she played.

Her face scrunched against the pain, not of physical wounds but the memories of stones, of tears, of shattering bones and unanswered cries. "But I waited for him, and—"

And because I didn't know what to say, I told her the truth.

"The gods you call aren't always the ones who answer."

That was it, an answer stolen on the wind that whistled beyond the cave, over desert and sea.

I waited for her to scream, to cry, to run.

She should have been terrified. Humans feared the unknown. They villainized anything beyond their understanding. And she'd lived such a faithful life of servitude, that meeting an immortal being who wasn't her god had to be horrifying. I braced myself for the onslaught, but she said simply, "I'm Shala."

My lips parted at the gift. Her name. Such an innocent, powerful offering.

"What shall I call you?" she asked.

I hadn't been ready for this question. No version of my name had ever crossed a human's lips. "Whatever name brings you pleasure," I said.

I counted the space between her heartbeats as she looked up at the sky through the mouth of the cave, then back at me.

"Then, I'll call you Star," she said, "not only because you were chipped from the heavens, or because you were the guide that led me from the darkness, but because you burn as bright as the first star in the morning. And like the heavenly bodies, you are too wonderful for any word that belongs on earthly tongues."

Yet another new emotion in a day of firsts.

There was a tightness in my face, a warmth behind my nose, a sting on the inner corner of my eyes. I'd never felt it before, but I'd seen the faces of men and gods who walked topside as saltwater appeared.

Was I capable of tears?

Today, I would not cry.

I would feel. I would experience. And I would dabble in the risk of a promise.

I made a quiet oath to be worthy of the name she'd given me.

# Chapter Two

**895 BCE**

The realms shared an exhale at the advent of mortal calendars and their passage of time. The nebulous, tingly void that accompanied "forever" was tedious, without structure, lacking in purpose, urgency, momentum. The gods shared a collective, if unspoken, joy when humans evolved to seek the worlds beyond the veil, speak to their gods, and parse out the endless nothing into *something*.

Hell and its palatial ceilings, its vibrance, spices, columns, and costumes. A realm known for parties thrown in honor of truth and liberation was transcendent. Pleasure, power, oblivion, and timeliness spun pantheons and their deities into bliss so monotonous that it began to lose its luster.

With forever on our hands, many of the undying sought something that could only be found among the humans.

Mortals added a ticking clock to the concept of existence, and for that, the realms delighted in a collective newness.

Sleeves pushed to the elbow, hair slicked, posture as princely as I could muster, I sat through the perfunctory briefings on promotions, demotions, titles, and other royal necessities required of any kingdom's ambassador before my father stopped the meeting. The dukes and counts and elite such-and-suches had departed, leaving the two of us alone in the sparkling marble room. My father and I had moved from round tables and desks and tablets to the tufted cushions near a diamond-white fire while he went on about this and that and things that most certainly mattered, if only I could stop thinking about a salty sea, a cave, a mortal woman who'd asked me to stay...

His pale eyes lit, an unusual crinkle creasing his temples as he smiled.

Hell's agelessness could have made us brothers. Some pantheons favored beards and wrinkles and elders. Instead, I looked back at the tanned face, raven-dark hair, and thin, kingly circlet of a crown as he smirked at me.

"You're looking at the door like you have somewhere to be."

I couldn't help but steal another glance at the floor-to-ceiling double doors before returning my attention. "I apologize. I have...something on my mind."

There was a relief to the upward pull of his mouth. "I'm glad you've found something to do."

I straightened. "I've always had a purpose. You've given me—"

"A title, a crown, a kingdom." He waved it away. "You inherited a war. You were born after The Fall, and as such, have been spared encounters with Heaven. I want a better life for my son than I was given, and as such, pray you never meet an angel. Though..."

His thoughts drifted to an unspoken agreement we'd never discuss.

He was an angel, once.

He was Heaven's favorite, once.

He was cast out, once.

My father hadn't chosen to leave his realm. He hadn't rejected his brothers, his king, his pantheon. In an eternity together, I had yet to spy an ember of hate for those who'd rejected him, unlike the flame that motivated our enemy.

I was the son of a freedom fighter. It was a role I didn't take lightly.

"Go," he said.

I realized I was looking at the door again.

I hedged. "I'm here. I'm listening. It's just...there's something on the surface that..."

"Go."

✦

Five mortal years. I couldn't have anticipated what a month in Hell would cost me between the ever-shifting clocks and their terrorization of the realms.

The gods had sex and wine and power, but *nothing* felt like the worrying impermanence of mortality. My proximity to it introduced me to a new sensation: adrenaline. I stayed on the surface, hiding my face, as I sampled one emotion after another.

It was my first taste at what it might be like for deities to have worshippers; though neither term quite described Shala, nor me. I had no temples, no altars, no name on human lips, hers included. I was a prince of the shadows, a harbinger, a hope for my realm's future. I was a beacon for those within the immortal lands, not an entity for humans to seek.

Was this godhood?

It didn't feel like it.

Trailing her curiously from my place behind the veil, helping her find a new village, organizing opportunities, creating blessings—miracles, as she'd call them—so she might thrive.

I spent my days with the barest licks from one feeling after another on my tongue, asking myself the sorts of questions that had no answers. Is that what a human might receive from a god who cared for them? I'd never spent so much time among mortals, and I'd become addicted to the new, the unfamiliar, the curiosity of it all.

This couldn't be like this between all gods and their humans. I was sure of it.

I'd never encountered a mortal who buzzed with a crystalline soul like Shala. The same shimmering aura I'd watched as she wobbled between life and death had only intensified. Now, I spotted her pearlescence in a crowd of thousands. Despite the black hair she covered whenever she left the house, without the blush to her golden cheeks, free from the cadence of her laugh or seriousness of her dark eyes, the glimmer lingered.

Even the uneventful fascinated me.

Tonight, she was grinding barley into flour, and I couldn't look away.

The unpleasant scraping of basalt mortar and pestle mixed with Shala's gentle humming. Her tune dipped, climbed, then fell, over and over again. This low, fractured lullaby, twisted in some curious minor chord, belonged to no one but her.

Such a simple act: humming a haunting song of her own design.

She was a musician. A creator. A talent.

I stared, leaning closer than I intended, as I fixated on the crude, bare, hominess of what she'd made. Gods, kings, fae, and the lands of eternal were robbed of the profundity that lived in simplicity.

Utterly fascinating.

Her song was unbroken as she took a jar of fresh water and splashed it into the pulpy grains. She used the back of her hand to move her hair out of her face as she focused on her task, soft music never leaving her lips. She didn't need to do this herself. She had servants now. But she seemed to enjoy the labor, which I found fascinating.

A thin, glass-like fracture hinted at an ambush from my side of the veil an instant before I saw her.

"You're growing soft, brother." Izi. The taunting voice of my sister's humorless smile forced me to turn away from the human.

It took a flash before I understood who'd entered.

While the world was as much hers as it was mine, I didn't like her here.

"We can't all be forged from lust and shadow, Izi," I replied. I hoped she couldn't hear my thinly hidden irritation. "Some of us have other things to do."

I resisted the urge to ask how she'd found me, as there was only a fistful of options. More than likely, she had caught my scent when passing through the village.

I never knew where she was hunting, and to be fair, I rarely cared.

"Your rage is delicious," she purred. "A Prince who fights for his kingdom, his people, one whose diplomacy matches his wrath, shouldn't be so scrumptiously angry in a fishing village. I've never tasted it topside before. Do share."

"I don't like to be interrupted," I said honestly. "Your presence is often worth my ire."

Her chuckle diffused the blood-and-thunder storm brewing within me, if only for the moment.

It was possible that she'd asked around Hell for my whereabouts, but I preferred to believe that my ever-increasing absences had not yet caught the attention of the realm.

"Come now, Amagi."

She plucked the word for 'ice' from proto-Sumerian. Our true names were too powerful to be shared, even among siblings. Our chosen sibling monikers—Amagi for me, Izi as the counterpart word for fire—fit like bespoke gloves. She'd brought the words back like trinkets from the first mortal language etched into their cuneiform during one of our first visits to the surface, and we'd kept them between the two of us ever since.

I resented the intrusion.

She'd robbed me of a new marvel. How could I focus on bucolic minor chords when I was being haunted by a nuisance?

"Tell me, brother," she purred.

My lip twitched, souring against her familiarity.

Izi wasn't my full sibling. Though we shared a father, we neither looked nor behaved alike. She favored her mother, the Queen of Shadows, Weaver of Nightmares, and Mother of Succubi. It was quite the title to fill.

"I appreciate your interest, Izi, but I don't need your help tonight."

The First Daughter of Succubi lived and breathed topside. She thrived on mortal attention, sipping her power from their lives like wine from a goblet.

"I'm the expert among humans." She clucked her tongue.

Izi moved toward Shala and I bristled.

"I'd prefer that you keep your hands off of her," I said through my teeth.

My sister made a face as Shala continued about her task, face quirked in judgment rather than fascination, as if this visiting a mundane ordeal was below her.

"Why? Are you scared I'll do something?"

She took a few exaggerated steps toward Shala, dragging fingertips down the length of Shala's arms.

The human's lullaby paused. She shivered, shaking off a chill. Her brows pinched as she looked toward the door.

"Hello?"

Izi's hands clapped together in front of her mouth, face sparkling with excitement. "Oh, my is she perceptive. Is that why you've chosen her?"

She expertly baited a question that I refused to answer.

I had no knowledge of Shala's clairvoyance beyond her brush with death. Mortals pierced the veil in their moments before passing, and as such, she had asked *me*, not her god, not an angel, but *me*, to stay.

Her invitation remained an open door.

I had her permission to appear even now.

I wasn't about to work through the trepidations that kept me behind the veil with my sister.

Shala regained composure after Izi's frost dissolved from her arms, straightened her shoulders, then returned to her task. She no longer sang.

My sister strode the room as if claiming her territory. Her chosen figure was humanesque, though her proportions were akin to an hourglass in the traditional sense.

A human's vital organs would not support the pinched waist while pumping blood. A human's body had no need for supple curves and the pout of coal-dark lips and eyes the size of dinner plates. Her amber scent mixed with the heat of spiced pepper. A human's hair remained connected and static, not the shifting and changing black spill of coiling smoke that Izi wore. A human's skin ran in shades of brown and tan and pink, rather than the greyscale common to our realm, from the blacks and whites of shadow and light to the silver sheen of brandished steel that she bore.

The similarities were intentionally uncanny, if only to highlight what was, and wasn't, of this world. One was mortal. The other, a musing of womanly ideas.

I drove my anger into the back of my teeth, grinding them in an attempt to keep the rest of my face neutral. "Are you finished?"

Izi's eyes flashed, the candlelit glint of sharpened canines sinister in the humble room. Her voice was too loud for the space. "Of course not. Though I wonder...what are you getting in return?"

I balked.

What was I getting? The question was unfathomable.

Shala had rebuilt her life, and I'd been there to watch. She'd begun anew, and when she'd stumbled into their village in the middle of the night, I'd enchanted the guard at the city wall to believe any story she told. She was greeted with compassion, given food, water, shelter, and I'd given her the greatest kindness I could for an unclaimed woman of her region, and ensured that she married well.

Fascination. Satisfaction. Pleasure. Success. The joy in each minor victory as I chipped away at the marble of the world, each fleck of stone improving this human's life in the slightest of ways. Moment after moment I savored new after new after new.

Wordless sentries, the pair of us remained hidden as Shala sprinkled salt into the bowl and began to knead the sticky mixture. The home smelled pleasantly of the date and pistachio candy she'd made earlier in the day. I wasn't sure why she was still cooking well after sunset, but perhaps with an empty home and nothing better to do, she liked to keep herself busy. This was new, too, and my sister was ruining it.

Izi's lower lip protruded. "Talk to me."

"I have no answer that would please you," I said honestly.

My sister, as with all succubi, took lovers in the night. She lured men to their death, captivated hearts, and drank from souls. She walked through dreams and plucked what she desired from the mind. In return, her mortals were given the gift of unspeakable ecstasy. It wasn't the conventional relationship between god and worshipper, but our kingdom had never been one for convention.

"Should we touch her again? See if we can get her to do more than shiver?"

I pushed off from the wall, flat on my feet, as if ready to fight. It was more of a reaction than I'd intended.

It thrilled her.

Her move had gotten a rise out of me the first time. She seemed to take pleasure in heightening the stakes. An iron-sharp talon sprang from Izi's finger as she approached. This time, she went right for the head, watching my face as she ran a hand down her back, metallic-grey claws starting in Shala's dark strands and trailing down her spine.

I grinded my teeth. My jaw knotted. I watched my sister provoke the human—*my* human.

"I'd appreciate it if you keep your hands off her."

"She's pretty," Izi said.

Wrath took a protective shape as it flared within me. I didn't need to speak for my sister to see it.

She tutted her tongue. "If you're going to try your hand at godhood, you might as well live a little. The woman's husband is away. How often do two of you...worship?"

The clay home flashed crimson as I saw red.

I wasn't sure if Izi had filled the room with pheromones on purpose, or if it was an unconscious result of what she was. The onslaught of visions pulsed from her like she was the epicenter and thoughts of sex were the tremors.

Before I could brace myself, I saw Shala's dress puddled at

her feet, my hand slipped around her lower back, my fingers in her hair. Her eyes looked up into mine as I lowered my mouth for hers, feeling the blistering heat of her body against the cool skin of my corporeal form as we melted together. The gradient whites, shimmering pinks, and the glint of turquoise were opaline on my tongue, tasting that indescribable essence...

I blinked away the vision. I did my best to look unaffected but didn't have to look at the succubus to know I'd failed.

"I'm not an incubus," I countered, mind flitting to Izi and her full-fledged brothers and sisters. I had no idea if they were all like this. Izi may be one of many from her mother, but we were the only two from our father, the King. She was difficult enough as it was. I was grateful I didn't have to deal with more than one sibling. "Nor am I a god."

"Aren't you?" she made a contemplative face.

I didn't like to think about it. Not then. Not now.

"Go about your business," I waved her away, still working to collect myself from the involuntary thoughts of Shala's mouth, of her tongue, of how it would feel to have her hold me in return. How it would feel to have her press into me, for her legs to hook around my waist, for her—

"Stay out of my mind," I snapped, recognizing the renewed pulse of images for what they were.

She smirked as she moved toward the wall, then flittered toward Shala's door. "You're new to the practice, so let me give you a piece of unsolicited advice: if you're going to stake your claim on this one, you might want to ward her thresholds. There are far worse things than me prowling about."

I whirled on her to snap back at the threat, but before I had the time to rage, she'd disappeared to find her nightly meal.

I would have continued panting, teeth clenched, jaw flexed, poised to fight, if the humming hadn't resumed.

My shoulders slumped. I was alone with the human. *My human.*

Shala abandoned her half-prepared meal and walked slowly to the table. Her eyes traveled to the spot where I stood, unfocused. Perhaps she couldn't see me, but she sensed my presence. I chewed on my lip and settled into the seat beside her, touching her gently, almost gingerly. I wanted to be close, but...

She exhaled and closed her eyes. "I know you're here," she said.

She'd been stoned for her faith. She'd seen the face of the immortal. I hadn't left her side, nor had she left mine.

I squeezed her hand but revealed only my voice. "I am."

The skin between her brows pinched. She swallowed. "You felt...different. Strange."

A feeling—gratitude, perhaps—soothed the space between my shoulders. She was perceptive. She recognized when something beyond the veil didn't feel like her 'angel.' The demon she called Star.

I didn't want to scare her, but she couldn't make the mistake of being too trusting.

"Would it surprise you to learn there are others? More than me, more than the god or his angels that you once served, more than you could fathom."

"No," she said solemnly. "The day I accepted you, I accepted everything." She squeezed my arm in return. "I've seen the temples and those I knew to be heathens within. I've heard stories of sacrifices to foreign gods. Who was it tonight? A name I know?"

"It was someone...something...you don't want in your house," I said honestly. "But I'll fix that."

She chewed on her lip. "Fix it? How?"

I didn't want to explain the concept of warding. Not yet. I

just needed her to trust me. "There are three things I need you to do."

"Anything."

The uncomfortable tension that followed her proclamation was too much. I couldn't dwell on it, or I'd unravel.

"It's not for me, it's for you," I clarified. "There's a merchant from the distant south. He'll be in your village next week. He trades in fine golds and jewels, but he carries a black stone as smooth as glass. Make a trade for this stone and sleep with it under your pillow."

Her lips pressed together. "My husband won't appreciate gemstones..."

"You won't need to trade anything of value. I'll be with you even when you don't see me. Whatever you offer, I'll charm the merchant to see it as an excellent deal," I promised. "Second, there is a plant that grows just beyond the city walls. It has thick green leaves that grow in triangular spindles, with a thick, clear sap within. The sap is used for medicine against burns. Do you know the one?"

She made a face as if leafing through a book within her mind. "I do."

"Hang it, fresh or dried, over your front door. Take the sap from one leaf and wear it on your wrists. Will you do this?"

"What's the third thing?" she asked.

This was the most painful.

"Silence," I said. "I won't have you dragged from the city again. If someone asks you who you worship, you lie. If they question why you sleep with a stone beneath your pillow, you tell them it was a pretty gift from your mother before she died. When they inquire why you hang the plant, tell them it's an ingredient in broth from your home village."

"Denying one's god is an unforgivable sin."

My throat knotted. "Letting harm befall you is the only sin I won't forgive, no matter which of us commits it."

I didn't know where to start in the jumbled explanation of gods and souls and realms, or if I should at all. Humans had been given rigid binaries through which they viewed the world. Theologies helped us both, I supposed. Some more than others.

"I'm not a god," I said at last. And as far as she was concerned, this was true. I was nothing like the deities she'd been raised to know. "I won't ask the things of you that were once required. I don't have priests or holy texts or commandments. I just want you to live."

Her lips parted, caught on a silent question for a long while. After a quiet eternity, she said, "What can I offer you?"

The corners of my lips tugged up in a smile. "You've given me a gift already."

"Impossible," she said. "I take. But tell me what I could give you, and it's yours. From now until the end of my days."

The damned succubus and her images attacked me once more. Shala's lips parting as mine drew close. Her shawl slipping off her shoulder. Leaning against the wall, the window, falling backward onto the bed. Her hand guiding mine south as it slipped into something unspeakably beautiful, and curious, and new. Something hers. Something ours.

*No, no, no.*

Though she'd been poor in her previous village, I'd helped negotiate a marriage with a wealthy suitor. I looked at the three-story mudbrick home that I'd eyed a million times before. The garden beyond the courtyard was still. The gibbous moon filtering through the window was astonishingly bright. The candle flickered its yellow-orange glow, revealing her frown as she waited for my answer.

"You're my only human," I said. "Everything we do, everything we say...it's my first time experiencing these new, perfect moments. I've never had the opportunity to worry about anything beyond a cold war between realms and treaties. Caring for your wellbeing is..."

"Tedious?" she asked with a small smile.

Gods almighty, she *was* perceptive.

"In a good way," I replied. "Eternity is monotonous. Through you, for the first time, I've been able to experience mortality. The high stakes of eating every meal, of a cough, of bad weather, of everyday life. Anxiety is a new emotion. The responsibility is utterly unique. I'm grateful for the chance to taste it."

"There has to be something," she said. "Something you want of me. Some gift beyond my gratitude. Something greater than my heart."

I watched the sincerity on her face as she spoke and felt an interesting knot in my throat. It was an unfamiliar sensation. It was decidedly unpleasant, but in a way that I cherished, though I understood it for the oxymoron it was. I tucked a loose lock of hair behind her ear and reveled in the way her face softened as she leaned into my touch. There was a tingle somewhere behind my sternum, stuck just below my ribs, as something stirred.

"There is no gift greater than your heart."

# Chapter Three

**887 BCE**

It was a horror from which I'd never recover.

The frenzied cocktail of rage and helplessness were fiery, unseen flames beneath my skin as I scrambled to make sense of the nightmare from which I'd never wake.

It was as if Heaven had won the war, as if my father had been slain, as if Hell had crumbled and left me without a home.

I knew, *I knew*. I. Fucking. Knew. Better.

I'd known time passed differently, erratically, painfully, between realms. I understood the gaps in spaces and the movement of days, months, and years for the mortals. Izi claimed I hovered, but it brought me joy to be close. I was there when my human called. I answered in a way her god never had. Each smile, each glow, each earnest praise and piece of gratitude that tumbled from her lips, set pieces of me ablaze I hadn't known existed. I loved being around her so ardently that I struggled to remember a time before her and hadn't bothered to consider a time after her.

I'd been in Hell's palace for a little more than seven sleeps. I'd hated every night away from my human, but royal duties had called, and I could handle a few miserable moons away if my kingdom demanded it.

Ambassadors visited, and my presence wasn't negotiable.

I'd told her I'd be away. She expressed immense gratitude that I'd been present for as long as I had, and there wasn't a hint of disappointment as she urged me to go, to do what must be done, to return when I could.

I'd been topside so long that I'd forgotten how to fidget among gods. There was no skin to pick around my nails, no blood to draw as I clenched my fists until it broke through what would have been my flesh, had I been on the surface.

Dignitaries droned on, plans were made, treaties sworn.

I was here.

This was where I belonged.

The rest didn't matter.

Shouldn't matter.

Couldn't matter.

My father was a king and commanded the love and respect of our realm and its citizens. But he was more than that. His discernment, empathy, and attention weren't required of a royal, but they certainly fostered enduring devotion to all who'd followed him off the cliff beyond The Fall. It maintained the loyalty of those born after the catalyst between Heaven and Hell. These traits were especially acute between father and son.

"You're somewhere else," he murmured once the dignitaries had left.

"Hmm?"

A pearl of white teeth peeked between his lips. "Take a break. You're a tireless ambassador for our kingdom. You come whenever duty calls. And perhaps...duty calls you elsewhere."

I was a shadow of a prince, unable to focus as my anxiety remained on my human.

I tried to blink away the thought of her. My human was a fragile thing in a hard world. Seven nights were miserable, but negligible. She had a resilient heart.

I grounded myself on the glittering floor. "I'm sorry. I know my responsibility to the realm."

He gestured to the palatial ceilings, the columns, the enormity of what it meant to wear Hell's crown. "The kingdom isn't going anywhere. Whatever's on your mind...I'd like to hear the tale, when you're ready."

I'm sure I offered perfunctory smiles and bows. I probably signed my name and tipped my hat and shook hands with whoever lingered beyond the hall. Surely, I went through the motions, but my mind remained on a certainty:

Nothing should have changed. The world should have been exactly how I'd left it.

The moment the ambassadors left, I burst into Shala's house with incomprehensible exuberance. I was ready to make oaths of my own, swearing to never be away that long again, aching for our reunion.

Eternity was a long time, and Shala gave me a reason to *be*.

When she was absent, so was my purpose.

It took me thirty seconds of scouring the house to understand that Shala was not there. Her scent was no longer in the air, on clothes, or even on the bed. I leaped through walls and doors, floating between spaces in my haste to reach the servants' corridor where I heard them discussing the new lady of the house.

I knew the culture, the village, the people. If Shala's husband had taken another wife, she would have still maintained a position of honor as the first wife. This didn't make sense.

I returned to the house in search of said spouse and found a doe-eyed girl of barely marriageable age. I burned hot with rage and confusion—emotions with a sticky, unfamiliar tang—as I scoured the village for evidence of my human. I called on my legion of spirits who were stunned to hear from me on such a task, which was an interesting turn of events. I wasn't completely aware they were capable of the emotion.

A legion—each composed of two thousand—was more thought than entity. They were an extension of ourselves, a stretch of our will, a trick of shadow and light that raked the universe, spied for its leader, and enacted our will. Some members of the royal family manifested their legions as glittering accessories, shaping the clot and steam of action and will into color, into shimmer, into something blue or green or diamond.

I had no stomach for pomp and circumstance.

I'd never summoned my legions topside, but within moments, a wavering collection of condensed shadow, each with the vague, stick-figure shape of something bipedal, returned with news.

A high-pitched ringing replaced whatever the member of my legion was saying. His mouth moved, but I was incapable of comprehension beyond the initial message.

It was with a trembling voice and eyes to the ground as he told me that she'd passed in the years of my absence. The world became a static hum while the spirit described her burial site. There may have been more details, something about her earthly possessions, something about her last words, something that might have mattered or might not have, but I heard none of it.

She was gone.

"...Your Highness? How may we serve—"

Rage burned behind my eyes. "Leave me."

"But sir—"

Hatred frothed as I flung him back to Hell. "Leave *now* or you're the first I smite."

I stormed to the home that had once belonged to my human. I stuck my hand through the new wife's spine until she screamed in terror and bolted from the shelter. The moment the child bride's feet crossed the threshold, I set the place ablaze with the husband trapped inside. I neither knew nor cared if he was responsible. He was meant to be her earthly protector, and he'd failed. Whether she'd died of sickness or hunger or injury, he'd been meant to look after her, to call for doctors, to save her when I could not. His shortcomings cost him his life, and I sneered at his cries for help as he pounded against the door that would not open while he cooked within the clay oven of his home.

The wrath within me burned hotter than the inferno of her former home.

I stayed on the property until the fire cooled and his carcass was a charred husk of a man. I grabbed his ghost by the throat as it escaped his body and flung it into the middle distance, trapping it in limbo as it scrapped, clawed, and failed to reach its afterlife. I stood over the empty remnants of his body with a scowl.

That was it.

When I left the mortal plane, I vowed to stay gone for as long as it took for my hate to subside. The purple of my revulsion, the ruby of my fury, the gory urge to murder every man, woman, and child who walked the earth, would either fade with time, or it wouldn't.

There was only one way to find out.

One hundred earthly years went by in the timelessness of Hell.

On the hundred and first year, I told Izi that if she brought up Shala again, I would rip her tongue from her mouth.

Days and nights were a blur of violence and indifference, hate and pain, emptiness and sorrow. I mourned, I seethed, I became a hardened tyrant for a decade, a cruel dictator for another, and finally, a cold, distant remnant of the prince my kingdom had once known and loved.

✦

I'd had a human once.

She had brought me unspeakable joy. She had shown me depths and flavors and curiosities of emotions and experiences that I'd never known. I felt tenderness and want and curiosity and hope in a new and perfect way. I'd thoroughly savored every second together, until I'd encountered the hubris that came from believing I'd had it all.

I'd touched mortality. I'd brushed humanity. I'd nearly understood the frayed corners of an emotion, a feeling, a verb, a complicated four-letter-word that was practically an abomination on my tongue, so I held it in.

My human was gone.

Two hundred years, and I could take ambassador meetings topside once more.

I visited her grave site on the two hundred and sixty-sixth anniversary of her death to see if there was any trace, any remnants of her pearly soul, but regretted my fool's errand instantly. I had only painful memories where once she had lain. She'd done unspeakable damage to me by showing how full my life could be with her in it. And as much as I wanted to forget her, I knew I'd never be able to return to the life I'd once known.

Three hundred years, and I'd nearly begun to smile again.

34

Four hundred years, and the court could count on me to keep my level head once more.

Five hundred years, and I'd stopped saying her name before I fell asleep.

She'd changed me.

For better or for worse, I couldn't know.

# Chapter Four

**332 BCE**

The rich bouquet of free-flowing wine, the firm squeeze of a supple hip perched on your lap with soft breasts pressed into your shoulder, the rise and fall of music and laughter; the Hellenic pantheon knew how to throw a party.

Hell's Royal Court, nearly a third of its Infernal Court, and at least a few members from the Court of Nightmares, including Izi and her mother, the First Succubus, were in attendance.

Bacchus kept the wine flowing. Between Demeter's wheat, barley, olives and grapes, and Artemis's hunt, from common animals like boar and antelope, to something roasting on a spit that I was fairly certain was a leopard, there was a cornucopia of succulent dishes. Aphrodite was living art, and an honor to be around.

I drained my goblet and smiled as one of Bacchus's shapely Maenads refilled it. I guess, Bacchus, Bacchos, Βάκχος—were linguistically competitive to the neighboring Roman pantheon and its counterpart. A demon told a demon who had blabbered to another demon that a soothsayer had told a soothsayer: we'd one day refer to our host as Dionysus on this side of the cultural divide. But today was not that day.

Hades and I picked neighboring seats during the eight-day festivities, if only to toast to misunderstandings of antagonists and the afterlife.

A pink cloud of flowers and hair plopped into his lap as his bride lifted a silver goblet to join the toast. "To misconceptions."

Hades wrapped his arm around her waist, and she planted a kiss atop his head.

"And to your controversial love story," I added. When they both hesitated to lift their cups a second time, I amended, "Because fuck what's written, and fuck what others think. You're happy, and that's rare. What a beautiful thing to be so in love that a tale like yours is too complicated to be understood."

Hades met my toast, but Persephone's face softened.

"You speak like someone who knows what he's talking about."

Five hundred and fifty-five years, and I still flickered when I picked the scab where her memory remained.

I slapped on a grin. "We're not here for love stories."

We shared a belly chuckle as we looked toward the head of the table.

It was Ares, god of war, who had invited Hell, regardless of who supplied the wine and merriment.

The King of Macedonia, a human man called Alexander, was ready to be Ares's sword arm as he marched his empire east.

Hell knew the area well. What once belonged to the Sumerians, then the Akkadians, then the Assyrians, now belonged to the Babylonians. Hell had a front row seat to all that went on in the Cradle of Civilization, particularly as it watched the King of Heaven move from Canaan outward, thriving as far west as

Egypt, east as the Tigres, and trickling north as a war deity called Yahweh marched his rule onward and upward, conquering territory well beyond Mesopotamia.

Ares thought that Hell might be interested to hear how his people would conquer Heaven's people and proposed an alliance between Hell and the Grecians.

He was right.

Between plans, they did what they did best.

Eat, drink, dance, fuck, discuss, sleep, repeat.

I stayed present for the first week of festivities and negotiations, but a nymph—one of the Naiads, called Nai, for short—had brushed past me at the table. She bent at the waist to whisper how I couldn't make any decisions about allegiances without seeing Greece for myself.

Persephone leaned across her husband to give my bicep a squeeze. "Go. Get out of here. We'll catch up when we aren't conquering the world."

Her husband threw me a wink, and we emptied our cups before I extended my hand to accept the invitation.

The nymph's cheeks pinked as her hand disappeared in mine.

"Lead the way."

Maybe I wanted to escape the monotony of meetings. Perhaps I was just emboldened by the mix of curious and jealous looks as others at the table carried on with their talks while watching to see how I'd react. But I let her take my hand, following the woman made of little more than air and water whose loveliness rivaled...I stopped my mind from comparing the nymph to the goddess as I caught Aphrodite's sharp glare from my peripherals.

Could the goddess of love hear my unspoken words?

Of course not. She had to be speculating. I'd heard tales of her vanity and jealousy, though most immortals had an inscrutable list of intermingled fact and fiction to their name. Some were victims of the rumors. Others had started the tall tales themselves.

In a single step, the clouds and marble and scents of Olympus evaporated. No torchlight muddied the silver night. Moonlight washed the pale stones as we moved through the metropolis.

The earthly silence was deafening.

The city was awash in silver light. Rolling hills elevated half of the houses, the flickering candles in their windows doing little to rival the stars burning overhead.

"I thought nymphs preferred the forest?" I asked, both to get her talking, and because I truly didn't know why a forest deity would bring me to the heart of Athens.

"Isn't it neat?" Nai winked. She dropped my hand and gestured to three intricately carved fish and the liquid that burbled from their mouths into a marble pool below. "The humans have brought fresh water into the city."

I approached the pool and ran my fingers over its cool, clear surface. "To drink?"

"And for beauty," she cooed.

I knew a bid for attention when I heard it. I was meant to compliment her. To tell her that water was beautiful, as was she. I was no stranger to the words whispered to women, to tumbling into the beds of gods and fae and things that lurked in the shadows.

I'd even attempted my hand at the title of incubus and set out to meet a human in their dreams in recent centuries, but only once. The mortal had opened up for me, had invited me so willingly, and I'd hated it. I'd vanished before reaching their bed, never to return to their home.

I could tell Nai whatever she needed to hear now. I could slip my hand over her hip, tilt her chin up toward mine, pin her against the wall between two of the softly murmuring fish-shaped spouts.

But we weren't alone. A woman's gentle hum carried over the fountain's gurgle. The tune was almost familiar. Simple, minor, haunting. A humble home. The dead sea. A human grinding barley into flour.

My heart stopped.

She bit her lip, following my gaze to the sound of footsteps.

I swallowed. "We're not alone."

She relaxed. "It's a human, Prince. The two of us remain behind the veil. She can't see us."

I didn't meet Nai's eyes. I watched the darkness become a shape. She approached with footsteps so light I wouldn't have heard them at all if I hadn't been looking into the space between buildings. It was a young woman. There was something odd about her shadow. It should be inky in the alleyway, but it had a stark quality that I couldn't quite articulate.

Nai followed my line of sight. She waved the silhouette away. "That girl comes to the fountain often. As I said: she can't see us."

I remained immobile.

"What's she singing? That song, is it from your people? Do you know it from your pantheon?"

Nai flashed annoyance. "The girl just sings. Pay it no mind." She reached for my hand again, feeling the uncomfortable tension that stretched between us.

"You haven't heard the tune? The lullaby isn't Hellenic?"

"Do you...not like an audience? If her song bothers you, we can go somewhere else."

Silver moon. Silver buildings. Silver heavenly bodies.

I couldn't control my tone. My words came out husky. "You said this human comes here often? Why?"

Nai's irritation was palpable. "Women can't study beneath the Teacher. Even in Hell, you had to have heard of our great thinkers. Socrates, then Plato, then—"

"Aristotle," I finished for her. I was impatient as I said, "Yes, I know of him. He's giving the humans words for many of the constellations."

Nai fidgeted impatiently while the human settled onto the fountain's marble lip. I couldn't be certain of the woman's age, but she couldn't have been more than sixteen. She procured a slim papyrus scroll and began working, looking up at the night sky, then back to her paper every few seconds.

Something was wrong with her skin. Her hair. Her eyes. I couldn't look away.

"She's studying the stars..." I wasn't sure if I'd said the words out loud. It was a night with no breeze, and yet my breath was stolen by the wind.

I didn't have to turn to see Nai's expression. She made her feelings clear while I remained glued to the mortal.

"Listen," she said somewhat curtly, "I'm meant to show you a good time in Athens. Can we at least get on with the tour, or—"

I didn't care about whatever she said next.

So what if Nai had been an intentional plant to gain our favor and win us over? Wars and alliances were met in a number of ways, and I wouldn't fault the Hellenic pantheon for using everything in their arsenal.

"You did well," I said quietly, and I meant it. She relaxed slightly, some of the irritation slipping from her shoulders. "Trust me. You showed me a..." Could I say it was a very good time? Was that true? Instead, I said, "I'd like to be alone. Thank you, Nai."

She might have said something in return. I wasn't listening.

There was a pearly glow to the human's skin, and I couldn't look away.

I stayed behind in the veil, staring in slack-jawed amazement at a human woman with an aura that glimmered like tourmaline, who'd snuck out in the middle of the night to look up at the stars.

◆

Five hundred years: wasted.

I was adrift once more. I had no plan. No care for royal duties. No dignity.

I remained behind the veil as I followed her home that night, scouring her home for any other sign that *this* could be my human.

I fought to manage my expectations.

Even if her soul had returned to the human realm, she wasn't mine. She wouldn't be the same. After how many hundreds of years transpired in the mortal kingdom since Shala had passed? I argued with myself that *per chance* this was the same soul. *Maybe.* But this woman—no, this *girl*—would have lived a different life. She would have a new name, a new culture, a new identity. She wouldn't worship the same gods, or have the same traumas, or have the same man who'd bent to grant her mercy on the shores of the Dead Sea. She hadn't spent a night in a cave with me. She hadn't driven me mad when she'd gone. She was different. She was new.

This girl was wealthy. She'd been born into a good home. She knew little of labor, of strife, of pain. Her parents appeared to treat her well, though I didn't fully understand humans enough to appreciate certain things that were said or done.

She wasn't the same.

This wasn't my human.

That was it. Curiosity sated. Adventure ended. All could return as it were.

I returned to Hell, but my homecoming was met with silence, as I couldn't open my mouth to explain where I'd gone or what I'd done. My lips remained sealed when my father demanded an explanation as to why I'd abandoned negotiations. I had my legions intercept my sister the moment I learned she was en route to taunt me, refusing to give her the chance. Word had drifted through the realms that my attention had been caught by a human. There were no secrets.

Izi claimed to love humans. She said that, of anyone, I should be able to talk to her about my affinity for the creatures. But I knew she was the last one I wanted to talk to.

But this... This was...who was this? What was her name?

Two days in hell, a month in the earthly realm, and I returned.

I crossed the threshold into the human girl's home like a phantom in the shadows, drawn to her like a magnet.

I learned her name was Eleni, though I wasn't sure if it suited her.

To be fair, Shala hadn't suited the shimmering soul of my human, either.

They were mortal sounds on the tongues of men, quite like Amagi and Izi, flimsy attempts to name something utterly immaterial.

A person. A being. Something more. Something other.

I followed the iridescent opaque whites with flashes of pink, blue, and green that sparkled around her. Yes, it had to be her.

Her aura was the same kaleidoscope of hues amidst mortal seas of one-note blues and reds and oranges and whatever other colors were in the boring human palette. There was that same not-quite-a-scent to her soul. It was the lungful of pure air between the highest cloud and the cold sky. But most of all, lives and lives later, she looked up each night and remained connected to the stars. She, who had looked through the veil, into my eyes, and called me Star.

So, I waited.

And waited.

And waited.

I learned curious things about this new human. For example, she was fortunate enough to study beneath Aristotle himself, though it was done in secret, for her and for all women who deigned to study.

I continued to follow, numb to the years. As I did, compulsion took over.

Eleni was fortunate in discoveries, in money, in health. Her family remarked at how lucky she'd been in the past few years, and they, along with their daughter, made regular offerings to Athena to express gratitude for the work the goddess was doing behind the veil.

Right. It was the goddess who had taken an acute interest in Eleni's betterment.

Her family couldn't quite understand why her luck didn't extend to love, however.

For reasons unbeknownst to mortals, quite curiously, so mysteriously, most of her suitors ended up perishing of quick and mysterious illnesses. What can I say? I couldn't help myself.

One fell off a cliff. Another died from sepsis following a slice on the finger from a piece of parchment. As she stretched from sixteen to eighteen to twenty, her parents began to fret that their daughter had been born with a curse. My preventative solutions weren't creative, but my human had been married the last time I'd been around her, and the human male had failed her. I wasn't going to allow for that mistake again.

Her family remained diligent in their offerings for the first several years that I was in Eleni's life.

"You're welcome," came my deadpan joke as her father carried a silk tapestry to the goddess's temple.

"If you're fine with someone else taking credit for your hand-iwork, it's no skin off my back," Athena shrugged. "Her last few suitors were godless, but if you kill the wrong man, you and I will exchange words."

Our ribbing did more to bolster relationships between Olympus and Hell than any half-baked plan to fuck a nymph.

Women in Athens were not permitted freedom and education and autonomy unless they were protected under the goddess's banner. While Athena appreciated what I was doing, she cautioned me against my protective nature. It was poised to backfire, came her admonition.

But the days were lovely, the nights were bright, the future was perfect, and Eleni...well...she wasn't Shala...but she was mine. It wasn't logical. I couldn't justify it. But I had no intention of letting go.

Besides, what did the goddess of wisdom know?

◆

Everything, as it turned out.

Luck only took us so far.

An intelligent young woman was a blessing. A woman whose suitors mysteriously perished, on the one hand, delighted me, but these were not fates we shared. The very things that contented me were the curses that destroyed Eleni's reputation.

My brilliant, wonderful, tenacious human walked barefoot to Athena's Parthenon in the middle of the night, tears carving silent, salted lines down her cheeks all the while.

The moment she stepped onto the street without shoes, I knew what she had planned.

*No. Come on, Eleni. I've meddled, sure but...*

My heart fell into my stomach.

One foot in front of the other, the city's dust gathering beneath her, my veins turned to ice.

I knew she couldn't hear me. My years of silence shattered as I tried to grab her. "Eleni, stop. Please. I didn't... I wouldn't..."

She could neither see nor hear me. Darkened homes vignetted around her. Tears stained her cheeks. The windless night was barren, as if the metropolis had emptied so that no one could intercept her as she marched toward her demise. I was unable to articulate a single thought as I warred against the walls of her hopeless defeat.

I grasped again, a phantom passing through the veil, unable to touch my human. "I'm sorry! Eleni, I'll stop. Please, look at me. Eleni!"

I'd gone too far. I'd ruined her life. One she didn't intend on living for much longer.

"No, please, no," I grabbed for her hand, but we had no connection through the veil.

"Hey, look at me. Eleni! See me!" I put my body between her and the temple with every movement, fighting her every step of the way. Shala could see me at will because she believed in me. Shala had asked for me, specifically, to stay with her. My first human looked through the veil and saw my face. She'd opened the door between us that I could step through at will.

But Eleni?

This human had never peered beyond the line between seen and unseen that separated us. Even if she had, she'd opened her mind to her goddess and her pantheon alone.

Desperation drove me to frenzied repetition. Over and over, begging, "Eleni, no. Please, *please* open your eyes."

I'd pressed her throughout the cutting journey to open her eyes and look beyond the veil. I'd pushed and pulled as I grew hoarse in my desperation for her to see me, to sense me, *something*, but she did not.

Any civilian, any bystander, a single fucking candle in a single fucking house could have given me the barest of hopes that someone might intervene. The blue-gray night had no such plans.

Each step brought her closer to a day I couldn't stand to relive.

She marched to end her life, and it was 887 BCE all over again.

Raw, powerless panic overcame me just as it had I had when I'd returned to the surface all those years ago only to realize I was on the mortal plane without my human.

I didn't understand why I tasted salt until I smacked my lips mid-plea and knew, at long last, I'd discovered what it meant to cry.

"Please."

Washed in moonlight, kneeling on the foot of Athena's temple, Eleni procured her small blade and begged the goddess to lift the curse from her and her family so she might seek a peaceful afterlife.

"Stop! Stop. You can't! You can't—"

I couldn't watch.

I was out of options, and I was not her god.

"Athena!"

I'd never screamed a high deity's name with such turmoil.

My knees hit the stones with bruising force.

I couldn't watch my human as she lifted her blade.

I called out to the goddess as if I was a mortal, a mere man, a petitioner, desperate, helpless, willing to give anything.

The same word. Beseeching with the same broken, desperate word. I choked on my anguish as I pleaded with the Hellenic deity of wisdom.

"*Please.*"

She was on Athena's territory, and the goddess did me one, and only one, favor.

The world tilted on its axis.

The goddess opened my human's eyes.

Bluish cities, white columns, a silver night, the twirl of stars spun as we both reeled through the twirling nausea of a rip through the veil.

A sharp, strangled gasp escaped her lips. My fingers bit firmly into flesh as I dug them into her forearm. Eleni's eyes widened with panic, confusion, resistance as she gawked at my hands around her wrist, preventing her from plunging the dagger inward.

I squeezed harder, forcing her to lose control of the tendons in her arm, her hand spasming. The knife clattered to the marble steps.

She lost her breath, and her tears ceased. I saw myself reflected in her eyes: as ivory as the marble surrounding me, my teeth bared, my eyes flashed with a prayer of my own. But my devotion was to no higher being. It had been to her.

I was ready for her to faint. To stumble backward in fear. To scream.

Nothing could have prepared me for what she did instead.

The salt dried upon her cheeks. Her shallow breathing slowed. I released her wrist and her arm dropped limply to her side. Moonlight glinted on her hair, the fallen shift and exposed shoulder, her puffy eyes as she stilled.

"You aren't Athena," she said. Her voice was raw from a tear-soaked journey, but unmistakably calm. Distant, but not absent.

"I'm not."

We were us again. A woman of faith asking a demon if he was an angel.

I'd wanted to speak to her for years, and now that she could see me, caution tied my tongue. I didn't want to ruin this chance, to destroy our reunion with haste or fear. She knew nothing of my kingdom or realm in this lifetime. She might not have any negative associations with my world, nor the damning word used by the people of Shala's faith.

"Which god are you?" she asked.

*Did you spare her for the sake of a cruel joke?*

A useless thought tied to a painful memory of a battered woman in cave, wishing I was someone—something—I'd never be.

"I am..." What would demon mean to her?

Her eyes remained on me as she lowered to one knee in a rigid yet respectful display. My guts twisted at the gesture. "Who among the lords has been carved from the stars?"

I hedged. The word alone set my heart aching. *Star.* "You don't..."

There was a curious courage in the move. It was just enough deference to prepare herself for anything; yet there was nothing about her posture or reflection that relayed fear or worship or... anything. Shouldn't she be feeling something?

"I am..." I repeated the beginning with no thought to the

end. I didn't want to look down on her while we spoke. "Please, stand."

She hadn't shed a tear from the moment I'd appeared. Water had carved lines through her dust-stained skin from the barefoot walk to the temple, but her chest was no longer heaving. Breathing still, spine straight, she watched me for an answer.

"Your gods are not alone in this world." I searched and found the answer that would satisfy her. "There are other kingdoms. Other mountains beyond Olympus. Other deities."

I had no desire to lecture her on theology. I just wanted her to live.

Her head tilted, dark hair shifting to the side. "And when I've prayed to Athena...?"

I stopped myself from looking over my shoulder. I knew the goddess was not here, though given Eleni's faith to her deity, without Athena's permission, I would have remained unseen. This was my human, and the goddess had given us our time alone. That said, I was not about to disrespect the queen of wisdom, reason, and war in her own temple.

I was left with something I'd said to her more than five hundred mortal years prior.

My echo was a moment of honesty, of sorrow, of confession. This truth belonged to us, no matter how much time had passed or whose face she wore. From the Dead Sea to Athens, from one end of the earth to the other, I knew it wouldn't matter. This pearly soul would always be hers, as would I.

"The gods you call aren't always the ones who answer."

# Chapter Five

**326 BCE**

Fifty thousand pairs of feet stomped over rock, sand, and mud. The dust and sweat and unintelligible grunts of a conquering horde marched for the Macedonian Kingdom's expansion.

Mortals bothered themselves with battles, successes, unimportant wins and losses.

While I didn't have a gift for seeing the future, I, like many of us beyond the veil, learned the human king's plans long before the trembling public.

The calamities of war brought, with it, certain opportunities.

I remained on Grecian soil—a puppeteer plucking on invisible strings. I nudged a few humans and arranged an advantageous marriage to a high-ranking commander one short month before the man was, oh so tragically, forced to abandon his new bride in her upscale palatial home with no mortal man to bother her.

Her eastbound spouse took his armor, their best horse, a

clanging satchel of gold coins, and his culturally rigid performance of masculinity far, far away. My bright, intelligent, beautiful woman was all alone with only her friends, servants, and my ghost in the shadows left to accompany her.

So sad.

She'd taken to my presence as if I'd always been there.

Perhaps Shala had been my first human, but with Eleni, it was *my* turn to experiment with mortality. My residence on her side of the veil, among the frescos and mosaics, was for her eyes alone—skin stretched over muscle, the tingle of nerves, the sights, sounds and smells of a human. I wasn't the man of the house by conventional standards, but for her, a man I would become.

It was a marvel anyone wore clothes in this mid-summer heat. Eleni fanned her pinked cheeks, perching on the bronze edge of a woolen mattress, humming as she changed. She'd dismissed her servants early in the day, unpinning the bun atop her head and letting her long hair down all on her own.

"You've been quiet today."

I was grateful for every moment that I could look at her as two people might look at one another. Two humans. Two gods. Two equals. "That song you hum sometimes. Where did you learn it?"

She shrugged. "It's just in my head from time to time." After a pause, her expression changed. "Are you thinking of *him* again?"

I peered out the window at the city that baked below us as if I might peer through time and space and see the army. I shook off the image.

"You're asking if I'm thinking of that husband of yours?" A short, polite laugh. "I don't think of other men when I'm around you."

"He's not terrible," Eleni defended, lips quirking upward.

"And for that, I'm glad," I said. "I worked hard to find you an auspicious match." *Auspiciously absent*, but I kept that amendment to myself.

"Do you know of the war? I mean...the knowledge of the gods, that is. Where is my husband now? Does he live?"

My lips flattened to conceal my grimace. *Yes*, I'd had members of my legion tail the commander and report back to me on the expansion.

I'd prefer it if she didn't care.

I wasn't proud of the tar-like suction that lapped at me, nor how it soured my expression as I answered.

"His troops have crossed the snow-capped mountains. They lost men to the cold, but he lives."

She stepped out of her garment. "Try not to sound so disappointed."

I turned toward the window, watching the city as it cooked. I allowed her a semblance of modesty, feigning the role of a gentleman.

"Enjoying the heat?"

Past the clay roofs and monochromatic buildings, I fixated on the gilded sparkle of a far-off sea. I wanted to be near her, yet a thousand miles away whenever she spoke of her husband. I fixated on the glittering waves, one white and yellow speckle at a time as the water disappeared into oblivion.

"You're the closest thing we have to snow in Athens."

She pulled my attention back from the waves. "Hmm?"

"You and your ice, of course."

There was a sing-song quality to her joke. She'd found my hair, my eyes, the pale flesh I wore worthy of endless commentary. I was marble. I was porcelain. I was whatever frosty peak her husband had shivered over a fire to survive before the army descended upon Armenia.

Bathing salts and fragrant oils rolled off her as her dress fell away, which wasn't my preference. Wealthy Athenians were soaked, scrubbed, and doused in perfumes. Her servants drenched her long dark locks, soaking through her pores, masking that crisp, painful lungful of air that only she possessed. I missed the clean smell of her soul, but at least she was here. She was alive. She was mine.

I was better off staring at the sea rather than fixating on the ownership that consumed me.

*Mine, mine, mine.*

What was I doing?

*Water. Window. House. Human. Ground yourself, for fuck's sake. Pick something new. Be here. Be present. Control yourself.*

I focused on the way the gauzy curtains tufted in the wind, appreciating the pale orange of late evening over the sea. The rustling of locks of hair, sweat unburdened by florals, and fabric let me know she'd slipped into her robe.

I heard her steps before I felt the brush of her skin against my back. My jaw clenched involuntarily as she slid into the space behind me. I closed my eyes as she ran one hand down my arm, fingers interlacing in mine. She pressed her cheek into the place between my shoulder blades. Her heat soaked into me, warming whatever I had that passed for a heart.

"Eleni..."

This wasn't the first time she'd touched me, and I still didn't know how to respond. I had a human once before, but never like this. Not one I could touch. Not one I could hold. I didn't dare to take it further, as if my hands would stain her irreparably.

She was pure, and I was...me.

Eleni didn't see it that way and had spent the better part of two years winning me over to her logic.

Two years that I hadn't left her side. I'd walked home with her that night. I'd been her unseen sentinel, her companion, the center of her universe, as she was mine. I didn't dare return to Hell for more than the barest of moments, never knowing if it would be a minute or a day or a week that had passed in the human lands. For better or for worse, I'd told Eleni how I'd first met her soul, of our time together, and how I'd burned her home to the ground when I'd learned of her death. I hadn't known if honesty was the right decision when discussing our connection, but who else could I share it with, if not her?

Eleni had things to share of her own.

She'd likened our story to Eros and Psyche, though the human woman had lost her heart's love once she'd looked upon his immortal face. Maybe that was the cautionary tale that kept her from pushing for more, though she certainly mentioned Zeus and his human lovers whenever she found a way to work it into the conversation.

My sister had found me once in the days following my disappearing act from the Grecian party. Izi's amusement turned into something else when she called my attachment to this shimmering, opal soul what it was.

Obsession.

Telling her to go fuck herself was insufficient; so, I personally crafted wards to ensure that no infernal entity could cross Eleni's threshold. I had no interest in hearing my sister's opinion as I took up residence with the now twenty-two-year-old woman who studied the stars.

Hell would be fine without me.

But this soft, fragile creature with mere decades on the earth? She needed me.

Her betrothed, on the other hand…

Eleni's husband would be gone for a long, long time. Faithful members of my legion clung to him like a second dusk. The smokey extension of my will gathered at his shoulder. Shadows beyond the veil borrowed the outline of his fingers, guiding him toward the sweetness of the wrong wine, the confidence in a mistaken battle choice, a snowy passage, a carelessly held blade, and, fuck it, a wild jackal sprinting into the camp from time to time when things weren't moving fast enough.

If, rather *when*, I orchestrated the man's death, I could keep word of his passing at bay for decades. Eleni would never have to remarry, nor be forced to take on the social status of a widow, as long as her betrothed male was believed alive. It was an asinine system. The humans could learn a thing or two from the gods and the way we structured independence. But that, along with many of my uncontrollable feelings regarding mortal customs, changed little.

So, I controlled what I could. And for now, that meant being here with her.

The squeeze of her fingers returned me to the present moment.

I wished she wouldn't touch me like that. It rearranged my atoms in ways that made me feel out of control, which was so unfamiliar that it sent me into a spiral every time our bodies grazed.

"Have you stayed?" she asked. "Have you been in the house, I mean? When my husband and…" She looked over her shoulder at the woolen mattress and waited for my gaze to follow. My pulse quickened at the memory of her skin, the heat of her body, the shallow gasps as they joined.

Sex? Of course that's what she was asking. I wasn't sure whether to chuckle at the absurdity of the question, given the flicker of anger whenever I thought of someone else holding dominion over her. I loved the idea of my human grabbing the mortal realm by the scruff of its neck and taking it for a ride, if it brought her power or pleasure or joy.

"Did I stay to watch you left unsatisfied?" I asked, still facing the sea beyond the city.

"Well, Eros..." The moniker was a taunt, though not unkind. "I've been wondering..."

Blood flowed southward. I was no stranger to fucking. I'd shattered headboards from Egypt to Canaan. I once spent seven infernal months rolling around with one of Shaushka's daughters, until the highest-ranking members of Hittite pantheon turned her into an olive tree, if only to force her to take a break. Forever was monotonous, and holy shit were gods drowning in the debilitating endlessness of time.

These human souls, on the other hand, had no seconds to spare.

I was the one made of the ghosts that moved in the night. I shifted between realms in a step. I was not bound by the laws or physics of men. So how was it that this woman of flesh moved around me before I could blink? How was she in front of me with the bravery of the highest deity in any pantheon, touching the face of Eros like the Psyche to whom she likened herself? Maybe it was hubris that had kept me from expecting the movement, or perhaps I'd underestimated her spirit. But Eleni lifted onto her toes, bringing her lips as close to mine as she dared.

"Don't."

Her lips hovered unbearably close to mine. "Then stop me."

This was no fantasy.

This wasn't the impulse of an earthbound beast or the incubi beyond the veil.

This was where daydream met the moment upon waking.

She waited a hair's breadth from my lips as if she needed my permission. The radiant pinks and blues and greens that streaked and swirled amidst the opal of her spirit danced close enough to taste. The moment became a throb, became a need.

And that was it.

My life, or whatever I had that passed as one, ended and began with a kiss.

◆

If I had to define my existence, I would see it in three acts.

First, there was the time before humans.

I was Hell's Prince, bound by duty, moved forward by the idle days of beings and realms, without the infringement of mortals and their ways.

The last page of that chapter was written the day Shala's stoned and broken body peered through the veil in her final moments and asked me to stay.

In my second act, so brief as if it were a whisper, there was my lightning flash experiencing what it might be like to be a god with his human. Had I a semblance of apathy, as I might have with anyone else, perhaps I would have risen to godhood. I would have acolytes, worshippers, throngs of humans doing my bidding. I might have sipped from the cup of their praise, had the faithful among them etch my story into stone, become a name among men.

But I didn't make it past my first and only human.

Shala's death uncoiled the tightly wound pieces within me that took me a mortal century in Hell to rebuild.

Hundreds of years later, I achieved the impossible.

I put her behind me. I went on.

Act three began, not just with Eleni, not just her courage, nor her openness and acceptance, but from this moment.

Her mouth crashed into mine, and I was unmade.

The sharp, diamond essence was wet on her tongue.

I drank her soul into mine as if I truly might drain her dry.

I was no longer in control. I wasn't a god. I wasn't eternal. I was an animal, overcome with the desire to make her mine. Primal need had to be experienced to be understood. Until my fingers dug into her hips, until her breasts pressed into me until I dragged my teeth across her throat, tasting her, biting her, kissing her, the word went from a concept to my all-encompassing reality.

She tasted like the first thawed day after a long winter.

She was the flavor of hope, of a new spring when the world had been covered in snow. She was the energy of dawn's first light.

She was the heat that baked the earth and broke the seed as it forced its way from the ground.

I tore myself from her with a wild sort of gasp, as if I'd resurfaced from somewhere deep underwater, and looked at her with panic.

A word escaped her lips. "Please."

Her chest heaved. Her eyes were as wide as a startled doe's. She struggled to swallow, and I crumbled into myself thinking that I'd hurt her, that there were pieces of me that stole and sucked and drained, pieces I'd never explored. I raked both hands into her hair with the intent to heal, to apologize, to undo, to fix, and learned how wrong I'd been.

Eleni possessed the sort of fearlessness and certainty I had yet to see on the faces of generals on the eve of battle. "Please, don't let me go."

My breath escaped. She had not been panting from injury.

"Don't leave me."

Animal. Human. Primal. Mortal.

She moved before I could think as she jumped into my arms. Her legs wrapped around my waist, and I caught her, cupping her ass, holding her close.

She'd never fall again. Not while I held her. And I knew then, I wouldn't let her go.

"Never."

We weren't Eros and Psyche. The mortal woman, Psyche, had been punished for advancing things with Eros, but he—Cupid, by another name—had very particular ideas about being the final authority on love. He was the captain of their ship. The woman longing to be his beloved was its passenger.

But we weren't them.

She gripped the back of my neck, mouth never leaving mine, legs tightening around my waist as I carried her to the bed.

It was hard to know who was at the helm as I tossed her onto the mattress, descending on her with a masculine body that no longer belonged to me. We were at war to prove who craved the other more. Before this moment, I hadn't counted myself among carnal human lovers. My love for my human was different. It had been curious, protective, pure.

Then her head hit the pillow. Night-dark hair pooled around her. Her back arched. Her toes pointed, knees moving like the plates that shifted the earthly world as her robe fell open.

"I need you," she said between breaths.

I nearly laughed that she believed *she* was the one who needed *me*.

I'd never experienced this sort of ache, the desperation for two to become one. All thought drained from me, pulsing in a demanding rhythm to be inside her. I tasted her sweat, the scented oils of her realm, the sharp lungful of ozone, and above all, the shimmering opaline aura that belonged to her and her alone.

She tore the scrap of tunic from my corporeal form, flinging it to the ground with the sort of haste that told me she'd wanted it gone for a long, long time. My mouth moved from her navel upwards, between the bronze of her breasts, suckling her russet nipples, teeth and lips and tongue skimming across her throat, exploring every inch.

Her hands balled into fists in my hair. She moaned, "Let me worship you."

The words were poetry despite their absurdity.

She hitched her calves against the back of my thighs and held me in place—as much as she could for a human, anyway.

Clothes in shreds on the marble, bare in the secrecy of the world we'd created, we paused on the precipice. Her hips rolled, soaked lips brushing against the tip of my cock. A low growl escaped my throat, but I held back for as long as I could. She'd known carnal pleasure. I was no stranger to the concept. But the consummation between mortal and immortal? Tales were written of such things for a reason.

She dug the heels of her feet into my ass, bringing herself closer, wordlessly begging.

"Eleni..."

She pulled her face away from mine and peered into my eyes. "I will never want anything like I want this. Don't forsake me now."

While in my human body, I relinquished myself fully to earthly rules. I wouldn't have broken away from her hold if my life depended on it.

"This is it for me," I swore, terrified of the oath as it echoed through me. "*You* are it for me." I didn't know what I meant at the time, but the words wrapped their spell around me.

"Then let this be it," she replied.

And it was so.

If her soul tasted of pearl and sky on her lips, I needed to know its flavor in the deepest, warm parts of her. I wasn't ready to bury myself within her. Not with my final memory of her and another man being one where she'd been brought halfway to pleasure then ripped from reprieve.

I grabbed her legs and yanked her to the edge of the bed, kneeling as if I were worshipping at my own goddess's temple. She remained tense, eyes wide for three uncertain seconds.

One as she watched me, breath caught in her throat.

Two as she sucked in a sharp gasp the moment my tongue hit her sex.

Three as her head hit the bed behind her, hips lifting off the bed as she gave herself over.

I'd been right. There was no purer drink of soul in the world than the one between her legs. I wasn't sure that I'd ever come up for air. I would have drowned in her one thousand times over before choosing to breathe. The way the flavor changed while her muscles tightened elicited new, curiously primordial, responses from us both. These were sounds I'd never made, and ones I'd never heard from her. This was a rush of water, a scream, a spasm, then another, then another that each came with a taste of its own.

But I was left with something else.

In the glow of her glorious, holy orgasm, there was a choice.

I could drink her soul, and protect my human, and know what it was to be a god with a worshipper. I could carry on in this messy, interesting, piece of immortality.

*Or.*

I kissed my way slowly from her inner thigh upward. My throb had not ebbed. The thunderous pulse of need continued to claw through me. I could stop. I was no slave to urges. One thumb traced its way from her cheek into her hair as if it had a mind of its own. She looked up at me with a question as we were trapped in the moment before oblivion. I was poised so close to her entrance I could feel her heartbeat, as well as mine, along with the slick, ready tilt of her hips as her legs moved once more, urging me closer.

"If we do this," I said, "nothing will be the same."

"When has sameness served us?" she asked, pulling me closer.

I'd felt fear before. But the sheer lightning bolt of terror? Did it belong here?

I braced, arm flexing to keep myself in place.

She clutched me. "What?"

There was no route for me in the maze of confusion aside from abject honesty.

"I don't know what it will mean for either of us," I said. "For me, Eleni. Who I am. What I am. If we see this through...I don't think I'll be able to let you go. And maybe that sounds okay in this life, but is it fair to make that choice for you in your next life? Or the one after that?"

She touched me with tenderness as if I was the fragile mortal as she said, "There would be no me if it wasn't for you."

"El—"

"In the next life, too, right? And after that, and that, and that?"

"You'll always be mine."

"Let not a god speak my mortal name given by earthly parents. Don't call me Eleni, as I'm more than this name." She was quiet, solemn, and fierce as she dug her fingernails into my skin. "I'm her, too. The one you saved on those shores. I'm whoever comes after me. I don't want to exist in a world without you, in this life or the next."

Act three.

I slid inside her like a meteorite burning through the galaxy. Her iridescent aura became the thing from which stardust was made. We were the birth of the universe and its destruction all at once.

I was merely a star.

She was the universe.

# Chapter Six

**326 BCE**

I'd been gone for a wink. A breath. A sleep.

Incredulity was a shallow, icy coating in my throat.

A stickwork of smoke, a member of my legion, slipped between the cracks of her home to deliver an urgent message. I didn't like seeing any being from my side of the veil here in the mortal realm when I was with her but, given that my legion were fragments of myself sent into the world to represent my interests, its news bared listening. The misty filament insisted upon my return to Hell for a meeting. The faceless sketch of a body didn't deserve the wrath it received in response.

Smokey lines gripped the edge of the bed, unwilling to leave. Its relentlessness despite my ire convinced me that I was truly needed.

Eleni yawned, still half asleep as the earliest rays of dawn peeked above the horizon. "Come back to bed."

"I promise I'll be back before you wake," I'd said. "I have to return to my realm for the barest of moments. Close your eyes, and when you open them, it will be to your head on my chest. Sleep, Eleni."

Her eyes fluttered shut. "Not Eleni," she said, voice drifting as slumber called to her. "Not to you. Not to the one I love."

*Love.*

It was with angst and fury that I was torn from her side after the most important night of my existence, and the most magical word ever spoken by god or man.

I'd learned my lesson with Shala. Time passed differently. I wouldn't be away for more than a minute, that much I knew. I'd see what was required, then return. Though there was no consistency to time and its flow between the realms, sometimes gaining time, often losing it, I knew every moment counted.

I kept my word.

I was in Hell for less than a minute. I loved my realm, my people, my father, but they'd never pulled me in two like the ripcord my human had on me. I alarmed half of the royal kingdom and cut my father's decree woefully short as I counted the seconds before saying I'd heard enough. I was needed elsewhere.

The shock on his face at my dismissal was one that no entity living or smote had seen before, which was all he needed to know of my urgency.

But the sun's rays were no longer a fresh shade of orange when I returned to the surface.

I knew what had changed the moment I materialized in the room, but shock overtook me. I approached the mattress, fingers reaching tentatively for the neck where a pulse should be. I lowered my cheek to her lips, knowing I'd feel no hot puff of breath against my skin.

Eleni's body was still in her bed.

Her soul, however, was nowhere to be found.

"This can't…" I looked to the window, to the gauzy curtains, to the mid-morning light. I argued with the walls. "She can't have…"

Her long-cold corpse contained no shimmer.

"No. No! Wake up. Eleni, wake up! Eleni…Love…Love, please. *Please!*"

By noon, the servants would find it. Mortal ears couldn't hear the way my thunderous cries tore through the house, though they felt the earthquake as Athens broke and shattered. I would have raked it to the ground if Athena herself hadn't torn me out of her territory, revoking the kinship we'd shared.

Because we existed in the realms behind the veil, humans thought us omniscient.

None of us were.

If I were omniscient, I would have known who, and what, was responsible for this affront, this pain, this grievance worthy of every death, every plague, every disaster man or monster could fathom.

"You can't be gone. You can't."

Frigid tears lined my eyes. I clutched her lifeless body against mine. What deity could I call upon for necromancy? Athena had allowed her to see me once. Would the Hellenic pantheon allow me to chase her across the River Styx? What did Orpheus know of love if he turned back to damn Eurydice? If given the chance, I'd lay waste to the Charon, I'd slay Cerberus, I'd yank her spirit from Hades himself and give the gods a new story, a *true* story of what it meant to love beyond the limits of death.

For the first time since the universe exploded into existence and my atoms rearranged into their hellish form, I wept. Those of us who lived beyond the mortal realm were mighty, to be sure, but I'd never experienced such powerlessness.

I'd call in a favor on the realm's deity of pestilence if I knew who to blame.

I'd speak with our god of storms if I knew which city required fires and flooding.

I'd go in myself and break the necks and stop the hearts of every man, woman, and child if I were given a name.

But the sense of "omniscience" comes from our active legions—two thousand immortal servants per legion, one of whom we would post in the houses of the faithful, in places of interest, in war rooms of enemies—that report back to us. Our time flows in a river separate from mortal waters, and our underlings told us what we needed to know when we needed to know it.

Except, I had posted no legions.

I'd involved no immortals with my human.

She was mine. Not theirs for spying or prodding or touching. It was frustrating enough to imagine how unworthy any human in her presence was as it stood. The idea of an immortal being invading her space without her knowledge was unspeakable.

As such, I had no answers.

I hadn't even been able to ask her what she'd wanted to do with her soul upon her passing. Perhaps she might have chosen to stay with me, to join me in Hell's undying realm, to be one with the infernal. Even if she wanted to remain human, she should have been given the chance to decide as much.

To her, I was a star who took snow's form.

From this moment on, I proved my sister right. I was ice.

I laid waste to anyone who dared to exist between me and Eleni's memory—*Love's* memory.

Before I returned to Hell, I made my way through Granicus, Issus, and up to the Caspian Gates, slaughtering every member of the Macedonian empire I met along the way. I drained the blood of her husband and his men. Whether they blamed the inexplicable decimation of their troops on poisoned water or an act of any god on their dusty earth, I didn't care.

They needed someone to blame. So did I.

Blood dripped from my hands as I stormed from the deserts into Hell's palace. Shocked incubi, devils, winged minions, shadowed legions, and visiting dignitaries from the lower courts watched with lifted brows and wide eyes as their prince charged for the throne room.

I pushed past the outer chambers on my way to see my father, interrupting the trivial gossip of succubus courtiers as I pushed past the Soul Eater. My sister caught my tirade and scrambled up from where she'd been lounging, talking to some unrecognizable horror from the Nightmare Courts.

Izi's feet slapped against the black marble as she sprinted after me.

"Amagi, stop—"

My growl came from between my teeth. "Leave me."

"We have visitors! Hell is entertaining! You can't just—"

I didn't know anything about the company she'd kept and made it abundantly clear that I did not care.

"Please, brother, you need to calm down." A ripple of shadow trailed in her wake as she jogged to keep up with me. Amber and spice wafted around her, filling my nostrils, drowning out whatever had remained of the fresh cloud scent of sky.

My lips pulled back in a soundless snarl. "You have five seconds to get away from me."

"Your visits to the human realm are supposed to be fun," she insisted, bare feet slapping against the palace floors as she struggled to keep pace. Inky coils of hair, unbound by earthly gravity, pooled in front of us in a blackened pit in an attempt to stop me. I thrashed through it, pitch-colored smoke exploding at my sides as it rejoined the ever-shifting curls cascading down her shoulders. "No one blames your dalliances, brother! There's nothing wrong with playing with mortals, but you really need to—"

I spun at her at the insult.

"Playing?" The word came out in a roar.

She lifted her palms to pacify me. "This is what I'm talking about," she said. "You're gaining a reputation, and not the good kind. We can't have Hell with such an obvious weak spot. Imagine how easy it would be to topple the Nordic pantheon if Odin had only one human? Or how the Hindu pantheon would crumble if Vishnu—"

"Stop," I bit, pushing past her.

"You know I'm right!" she shouted, though this time, she stayed put.

Her voice became quieter as I marched.

"If you go to our father. You're damning yourself. You're damning us all." When it didn't stop me, she added three chilling words. "You're damning *her*."

I stopped mid stride.

"Her soul won't be permitted to return if she's this much of a distraction," Izi argued. I kept my back to her but hated the logic in her words. They were poison, they were hateful, they were a blight.

She made her final plea.

"Bend humans to your will far and wide. Love them, use them, leave them. But this fixation with a single soul is a mistake. Not just for you, but for the kingdom. Others are going to notice. You're putting Hell at risk, and no one in our realm will stand for it."

My shoulders remained tight, fists clenched, teeth together. "Izi..."

"You're going to have to let her go."

# Chapter Seven

**NINE MORTAL MONTHS LATER**

Asoul. An egg. A pale, wiggling, microscopic tadpole.
Once upon a time, I was an entity who swam with the glittering metals that burned between galaxies. I'd obeyed the obligation to visit the surface with its unpleasant odors, its ignorance, its blood and death and itchy, ill-fitting air. Then and now, I despised the crushing frustration of watching raving madmen rise to power and perpetuate the drama of the short-sighted.

Yet here I was begging for a clump of mortal cells. A womb.

Only the gods knew where. A soul yet to find its way back into the world.

She'd be back.

I knew it the way Shala had known her god would come for her. I knew it the way Eleni knew Athena would accept her sacrifice. I knew it in that... I knew nothing but trusted in a conviction that meant no matter how wrong I was, I had to see this through.

It was a faith that defied explanation.

Was this what it was like when human knees hit the ground, folded their hands in prayer, and took a chance on a god because *they* needed the entity to exist?

And if so, why did faith curdle at the sour intersection of hope and abandonment?

*Focus. This isn't useful. Any further down this path and you'll draw the sort of attention that lands you in front of the Soul Eater while Izi and Father debate the sacrilege of their heir, a Prince, an immortal, deifying the fleeting uncertainty of a woman.*

*Stop it, stop it, stop it.*

*These thoughts are useless once you've found her, and equally useless until you're certain she's nowhere to be found.*

The pursuit continued.

My human refused her mortal name when I'd spoken it. She'd insisted that I needed to see her—not Eleni, not Shala, but *her*—in this life and the next.

I knew there'd be a next.

But when? Where? Who?

Once, not so long ago, time had been a tedious, endless river of nothing. Between courtly duties, I'd dabbled in the Bacchanalian pastime of drinking and fucking to pass time's unyielding, tiresome progression. I'd play ambassador to courtiers, then sample the gory delights of Hell's Nightmare Court. I'd follow through with princely obligations before losing myself in the lawlessness of the primordial realm. And since eternity was a long time, and only so much could be asked of the King's heir in the span of forever, I'd spent more than enough of my existence in the chiseled stillness of nothing upon nothing, stone-still, apathetic, unfeeling, as days bled into months, bled into forever.

That was before Shala. Before Eleni. Before Love.

She'd be back.

Somewhere out there, she was taking form. Maybe I couldn't

feel it yet in a logical sense, but the part of me that latched onto her knew her return was in the making.

I stewed in rhetorical upon rhetorical, but what did this breadth of time mean for me?

I had to wait, but I'd call on the curses of every god known to the pantheons for the barest hint of knowledge on when I'd see Love again. After all, nine months in the mortal realm could be two weeks, two days, or two hours in Hell, for all I knew, and that was *if* her soul was reborn.

At any time, she could choose to leave her cycle, to follow the light that led her to the afterlife of her chosen realm, to join her gods, her people, the path laid before her.

But if...*if*...if she'd stayed...

Its inconsistency was of countless infuriating inevitabilities in our entanglement.

✦

A knock at my door, too loud to be a servant, too soft to be my father. "Open up, Amagi."

"Leave me."

The door cracked. We weren't full siblings, but her mother's status as Queen of Succubi gave her certain privileges that would have landed any other disrespectful citizen's head on a spike, royal or otherwise. She was the first daughter of her court, just as I was the first son of mine. Our relationship was equal parts siblings and ambassadors—Hell's Royal Court, and the Court of Nightmares. Our father ruled over Hell's other courts, from the Draconian to the Infernal, but only ours shared family.

At least, for now. Eternity was a long time, and the earthly world wasn't the only one that valued the blood ties of political allegiance.

Maybe the rumors of new siblings forced her hand, but for fuck's sake, Izi was newly unbearable in a way that would have ended in her banishment, had she been anyone else.

She slipped in and closed the door.

"Bite your tongue. I don't want to hear what you're about to say."

Izi's inky cloud of hair wafted around, defying gravity. "It seems you know why I'm here."

"I have a guess. And you being my sister won't stop me from killing you."

She caught me at the same desk I'd been at for the last six visits. My posture remained unchanged from her last however-many visits. She pressed her back against the door, saying her piece softly from across the room.

"You're making a mistake."

I pressed the tips of my fingers into my temples. "Your opinion is noted, unwelcome, and has been disregarded. Leave."

"Amagi—"

"Is not my name," I bit. "You don't know me, and I don't know you. Whatever advice you're about to give is to the sibling you want, not the one you have. Deal with your court as you must. Tell our father you tried your best. But the next time you weigh in on my human, you'll leave without a tongue."

There was a tiny squeak to her sound that caught me truly off guard. "Brother, you know not what you say."

"Sister." I gnawed off the word with as much venom as I could muster. "You know not to whom you speak."

I didn't look up when the door opened and the lock clicked as it closed.

I had nine mortal months.

It wasn't enough time to come up with any true plan, but it was enough to think about what Izi had said. I didn't give a fuck about relaxing or the *fun* to which she'd referred. I would throw my title to the fire over what mistakes I may or may not be making.

My sister was right about one thing, though I wouldn't admit such truths to her.

It was a mistake to let others know about my human.

The courts, the realms, the pantheons—immortals would have a reaction to the way I followed a human soul. I didn't care what it meant for the kingdom. My father could handle royal business. He could appoint new ambassadors. He could call upon our counts, our dukes, our duchesses, our marquises.

Legions awaited his command. His, mine, and all who served him.

As his only son, heavy was the crown, or so the saying went.

But my care was trapped with what this meant for my human.

Save for Izi and my blood-bound legion, the last immortal I'd spoken to of such things had been Athena.

I was confident the goddess of wisdom had not done anything so cruel as to betray Hell's trust by harming my human, but even the nymph, Nai, who'd been with me when I'd spotted Eleni's shimmering soul at the fountain, could have been a weak spot. She'd witnessed my visceral reaction that night. Nai could attest how lost I was the moment I'd seen my human.

The clock ticked inconsistently. It passed here. It passed above. But still, it passed.

Until I knew what this meant—until I understood my own stakes and motives—I didn't dare include my legions, no matter how loyal they were to me, knowing they served their king and kingdom above all.

I needed a plan, and I wasn't sure how much I trusted anyone to execute it, as I barely trusted myself.

I had nine mortal months before her soul would reenter the earth.

Eight now? Four? One? Had she already been born? What was this godsforsaken entanglement with time and my damned relationship to it.

I remained at my desk, writing nothing, reading nothing, unmoving, save for the mental tally I made of prospective enemies.

As it stood, two members of the Hellenic pantheon could identify my human's shimmering aura, if pressed. Was I ready to make an enemy of one of the strongest pantheons? I thought of Athena and the miraculous hand she'd granted in our moment of need, but I wouldn't let a moment of benevolence sway me if she had the chance to betray Eleni, Shala, Love.

As the first son of Hell, I had godhood in its own right.

Fae, cryptids, supernatural entities from all realms could live forever unless their life was ended by a god. Only gods could kill their own.

I thought of Eleni's barefoot, tear-soaked night bathed in silver moonlight in front of Athena's temple. The night she'd gone from a Hellenic devotee to mine.

My enemies were numerous, both real and imagined.

Age. Disease. Every human in existence. Nai. Athena. Izi.

If she was on Grecian soil again, would I fight Olympus for her?

*Tick, tick, tock.*

I had the ability to kill a goddess if I needed to, but it wouldn't come to that.

Athena would keep my secrets, not for me, but for wisdom's sake. Nai the water nymph, a minor deity in her own right, would have to go. As an immortal, they'd know a god-killer was to blame, but I couldn't risk the leak. Whether or not my kingdom had a fallout with the Hellenic pantheon as a result would be a problem for tomorrow.

I'd slay my own sister tonight, in this palace, if I thought it would serve my human.

Any moment now, Love would be reborn.

What I was going to do when that time was over, however, I had no idea.

# Chapter Eight

318 BCE

**D**ry, irritating, prickly, endless sand.

I scoured red mountain dunes of infinite desert and nomadic people atop their camels. I searched the caves of mountain tribes. I swept the rolling green hills of equestrians clad in furs with eagles for familiars. I went further south than any god had been. Every village, every city, every language, every, every, every, every.

Castles, rooftops, taverns, windows, villages, huts.

I verged on madness as my nine planned months bled into nine savage years before I found her. One would imagine it would be difficult to see diamonds and pearls against the blinding sparkle of never-ending snow, but I knew her the moment I saw her.

There were nearly two hundred million mortals wandering the earth, from baking deserts to lush gardens to mountains that pierced the heavens. Why, then, for the love of all that was holy and good and immortal did mankind ever spread to the desolate Arctic?

The last place I'd searched was an expanse of frozen nothing, lit by the shimmering green of northern lights, threatened by the ocean that licked at the sea floor underfoot. Of all the places my human could have been, why had these mortals chosen to carve homes from a never-ending misery of ice when there were lands where one could eat fresh fruit and walk barefoot year-round? I'd love to grab every member of her new people by the shoulders and beg them to return to a land with grass and crops and warmth.

There was an agoraphobia that came with the endless sky, the endless land, the flat blue in all directions above and flat white in all directions below. It was a purgatory of its own design.

Izi would have loved the irony of me being exiled to this barren wasteland.

Amagi—her proto-Sumerian moniker for *ice*—had nothing on the frost-bitten expanse where, at long last, I found a soul that glowed like the rarest of precious gems. She was clad in seal-skin furs, strips of leather holding her warming coat together. Her hair was as dark as it had been in past lifetimes, with wind-burnt cheeks, full lips, brown eyes and...

My immediate urge upon discovering her was first to weep for joy. Hope and light exploded within me, a magnet once more drawn to its purpose.

My relief was fleeting.

I spied the milky glitter shining around a young girl wrapped tightly in furs as if she were the sun itself. The excitement ceased before I could savor it. Shala—Eleni—*Love*—hadn't even seen me, and she was already terrified.

I had not arrived in a moment of peace.

The northern wilds and its people were unfamiliar to me, but I knew humans, fathers, and men.

I recognized a fist raised in violence when I saw it.

One foot in front of the other, I sprinted toward them, jaw clenched, ready for battle. I swung for the man, bracing for the crunch of bone, the ripple of flesh, the bloodied teeth that would stain the snow.

Instead, my hand passed through the attacker as if he were little more than smoke.

Panic wouldn't serve me.

I lifted my hands before me, wondering who I could call upon. What god would permit me to be seen? What form could I take that her eyes might perceive? How could I save her?

Another step back, rattled, frantic, desperate.

I understood from her cowering posture, and her place on the snow, that this was not the first time she'd been hit. From the hands raised to protect her face, her flinch, her meek cry for mercy, I knew she didn't expect this to be the last.

I needed to do something.

There had to be a way.

A weapon.

A loophole.

His fury goaded me into action. This man could be their king for all I cared. If he struck her one more time, I didn't care where we were, who she worshipped, or who this inferior mortal was. If he hit my human, I would savor the popping socket as I ripped his arm from its shoulder, salivating as his blood drained onto the permafrost.

Maybe her eyes were closed to *me*, but there were other things her people could see. Their totems, their guides, the animals that stalked the snow dunes...could it work?

Fuck. I was the Prince of motherfucking Hell. If I said it was, then it was so.

Fury took shape, and I let it overcome me. It ripped my clothes, it fractured my jaw, it turned my fingers to claws, it salivated with the threat of an apex predator as I unlocked raw, unadulterated power.

Time moved differently for me than I did for the mortals. I processed everything in the time it took for four distinct, thundering footsteps to hit the snow. I tore myself from the space behind the veil, springing forward with no regard for the consequence. With it came a lifetime of emotions.

I meant to shout, but a guttural, rumbling growl came out in its place.

Rage became me as I tore from the unseen land, snarling with the fury of a thousand monsters. This time, I knew before my corporeal form crunched against ice and snow that I was not landing on the frozen tundra with the feet of a man. I had no idea what shape I'd taken, demon though I was, there was nothing human about my build.

Shala—Eleni—*Love*—stood behind me.

My jaws snapped together, frothing with intent as I stared into the face of hate.

The man yelled something new, something I couldn't interpret, though it sounded like a stream of curses.

Biting wind whipped ice-sharp snow from the endless expanse, tousling hair in places I'd never felt before. The fur-trimmed coat of the man before me moved with the howling air as his eyes darkened, teeth bared.

Another lifetime passed for me in the heartbeat it took for the mortals to react.

Curiosity was my primary word for how I'd described each new experience with my human. I'd figured out the rest later.

Original pity over the death sentence she didn't deserve? Curious.

Sadness over her mistreatment? Curious.

Staying with her simply because she'd asked? Curious.

A desire to find her again? Curious.

Obsession and its evolution through lifetimes? Curious.

The speed with which I named it in truth—*love*—despite never before having encountered the emotion? Fascinating.

And now, a newly curious thing happened in my moment of explosive madness.

Fury solidified in a shape of its own in the most literal of senses.

The mortal male's hand was on a weapon in an instant, but the height of his brows, the drop of his jaw, his backward stumble, told me plenty.

A loud, angry accusation. The man shouted something I couldn't understand, but given his wide-eyed, slack-jawed horror, it may have been *Beast! Monster!* Or my personal favorite, *Demon!*

A snarl sliced through his shock.

I understood the heart of the exclamation, though it came in a language I didn't speak. I wasn't even familiar with the linguistic origins of the word. The horrified declaration that transcended translation.

His hand grasped at the weapon strapped to his hip.

My jaws snapped, frothing, lips pulled back an inch from his face.

I was too close for his harpoon to be of any use to him.

The girl—for she was not yet a young woman—plunged her fingers against me, into what must have been fur. With it came the clutch of inexplicable trust. Whatever I was, whoever she was, she knew I was there for her. I'd burst from the ether in a moment of torture. The bond was instantaneous.

The man's testosterone-fueled madness outweighed any wisdom. He took the two steps backward to create the room he needed to draw it from the leather holster around his waist. The light hit the serrated spike.

Whether for fishing, murdering beasts of the land, or just punishing cowering daughters, the thorny fin on one end may as well have been shark's teeth with saw-like ridges running its length.

The man bared his teeth, face contorting with hate as he hoisted his blade.

His hand was meant for her.

The killing blow was directed at me.

He brought it down with its full weight, cutting through a thick fur hide and embedding in my shoulder with a *thwunk*.

At least, he might have embedded it in my shoulder, had I been made of hair, blood, and bone.

After all, I was corporeal, but I wasn't.

Only a god can kill a god.

Maybe I deserved the title. Maybe I didn't. But one thing was for certain: this violent human male was not worthy to stand against me.

He waited for the embedded weapon to give me pause, to make me retreat, to so much as elicit a sound.

His panic came from my lack of reaction.

The whites of his eyes matched the ground around him. His face became a blanched mask as he fell, scrambling backward, rump hitting the ice as he clawed against the snow. With an animalistic *humph*, I shook the weapon from my shoulder. It clattered to the ground. Only then did I understand what he saw in the reflection of his wide-eyed terror.

A wolf, whiter than the endless winter, stood taller than the man's shoulder. Its diamond eyes looked back at me. Its lips peeled away from its dripping fangs as the rumbling snarl shook the frost upon which it stood. I looked back at the beast within me. Knowing it protected my human, I loved every hair and dripping tooth of my new, monstrous form.

I salivated as I imagined sinking my teeth into his flesh, bone bursting from joints as it ripped beneath my divine wrath.

I'd been a terrifying wolf for barely three seconds before realizing if I had caused the man fear, then even with the bond, the presence of an enormous beast may start to scare the girl. I hadn't spent much time around mortal animals, but I'd seen the domesticated cats, dogs, and birds that humans often kept as pets. With the man still scrambling backward in abject terror, I turned my attention toward my human. I lowered my ears, looked back at her with wide, peaceful eyes, and dipped my head as close to the ice as I could to try to win her favor.

The wind sang a song of its own, drowning out the whimpering cowardice of a male who failed to matter.

Like Shala in the cave, or Eleni on the steps, she should have screamed.

But she didn't.

She said something I didn't understand.

I'd learned seventy-seven Semitic languages, including dozens of Afroasiatic dialects. Indo-European languages, proto-Balto-Slavic languages, one at a time. I'd begun to learn the curious Germanic sound shift in the first millennium.

How many languages could humans invent? How many ways could I misunderstand my human? How could I tell her she was safe with me if I couldn't speak to her?

But...I didn't have to.

She asked me a question I didn't understand, but I memorized the sounds, knowing I'd learn her language and interpret it the moment I was able.

"Will you stay?" Her question, the cord that tethered our souls.

I didn't speak the language yet. It spoke through me, into me, all around me, and I knew.

This human did not fear me, despite the general terror.

Whether she had a death wish or no sense of self-preservation, the result was the same. She didn't recoil, nor did she panic in the life-saving way that had spared so many humans. She was meant to fight, fly, or freeze. I would have accepted the fawn of an extended hand to sniff her fingers, to try to win a beast.

I wouldn't have blamed her if she'd ran. Hell, I *wanted* her to be terrified, if only to know she had the instincts required to stay alive.

Coal-black eyes looked back at me with the sort of trust that cupped my heart in her two small hands, cracking it as she held it. She wore the weariness of someone far beyond her years as she stared through me, into me, despite my beastly shape. Perhaps she was too tired to be afraid. Maybe she was ready for it to be over. I couldn't say. All I knew for sure was that no man would touch her again.

✦

Myths had been started by less than what happened that day on the ice.

Dozens of witnesses attested to the otherwise unbelievable event.

A throng of her people watched as an enormous wolf forged of frost and fangs appeared out of thin air to defend an innocent.

A protector, a rescuer, a spirit who'd emerged from the realms beyond reason to put itself between a girl and her attacker. An ice-white monster, half the size of a mammoth, springing to a girl's rescue and staying by her side was the stuff of legends. I accepted my role in the tale, so long as I wasn't the story's protagonist.

She was the center of their story even before I knew her name.

She stuck her hands in my fur, threw a leg over me, and sat upon my back. I hoped she could feel my smile at her strange, brave gesture. I would have applauded if I'd had hands.

They weren't wrong to revere my human.

She was blessed, and they treated her as such. She may as well have been a god from the way her people revered her from that day forward. Unlike Shala and Eleni before her, I vowed not to leave her side, even for sixty Hellish seconds. Until her dying breath, she would have the resources of an immortal at her fingertips. I endured the blizzards and long nights and harsh terrain for as long as it took to bring her a spark of joy.

The frigid night of my arrival, a recently widowed woman took in the girl—my human—which was fortunate, as I would never again let her earthly father anywhere near her. I would have torn his jugular from its throat and left it freezing on the ice if I hadn't thought his blood would upset her.

The new woman received the blessed girl and became her world guardian as a surrogate mother, and as such, made her soup, lit her fires, provided her furs, and never spoke an ill word of the daughter she'd taken in.

My people called me Prince. Her tribe called me Hero. At least, I grew to understand that's what the word meant.

My human called me Fluffy.

I supposed I could be both.

It's worth admitting: Qawiaraq was a challenging language.

It took me nearly a mortal month to learn, which was a fact I'd lie about if ever pressed for an answer.

But when I learned that her name, Yuka, meant "Bright Star," for the third time in my existence, I was prepared to cry.

I was not an innate omnilinguist, but rather one of time and exposure.

I'd stolen a fish from a seal and dropped it at her feet on my second day.

"Thank you, Fluffy." She scratched behind my ears. Before knowing the language, it was something soft, something sweet, and something only for me.

I knew she could feel my smile.

This was my first time in the Arctic, and I had yet to adapt to the newness of the ways consonants and vowels met before they wrapped around one another. But I was able to communicate more than enough as a wolf. No man came near her, and she was given the sort of accommodations I could have only hoped for in Macedonia or along the Dead Sea. It wasn't the Grecian palace of yore, but the whale bones and animal hides and furs warmed with a bright fire were hers and hers alone. Yuka was revered as the girl who'd summoned a spirit wolf—respected as one who'd served as guardian and protector of her, and the village.

Here, she was left alone.

Despite a frostbitten land destined to slay the weak, she was the safest she'd ever been.

✦

Bright days filled with long treks, snow blindness, wind-chaffed skin were guided by the sun. We hauled the tents of hide and fur when we needed to move for shelter or food. The people bunkered down with the insulation of carefully crafted homes made of ice for weeks or months at the time, should we discover a prosperous source of fish and seal.

The ties that bound us tightened.

She'd speak to me during the day as if talking to herself, sometimes upon my back, sometimes walking beside me, sometimes wrapped up in my fur as I lulled her to sleep. "Where do you think we'll find game?" "The fire is getting low. If we don't find a new forest soon, we'll freeze." "My, the stars are bright tonight. Thank you for watching them with me." "Fluffy, come outside! The sky is singing. Green, pink, purple, blue...can you hear it? The colors sing."

That they did. There was an other-worldly sound to the lights this close to the Arctic Circle, though as someone other-worldly, I could attest to the phenomenon belonging to the mortal realm. Even for me, it was magic.

"It's time for bed, Fluffy. Cuddle with me?"

She slept against my fur at night, her head on my chest as five years passed, then ten. She marched with me during the day. We hunted together. We'd run under the daylight for moments of joy. She'd cry into my fur in moments of weakness. She was my world, and I was hers, though I'd never imagined it could take such a form.

Her people became my people, if by accident. I protected the nomadic tribe, as their pain brought her sorrow, and their victories brought her joy.

I didn't give a shit about the others, but I supposed my intentions were irrelevant, so long as I remained a guardian.

I would never forgive the tribe for standing by as a father beat his daughter in broad daylight. The only one I didn't hate, aside from my human, was Yuka's surrogate mother. That said, what was good for the many was also good for the one, and that's all that mattered.

I helped them hunt because it meant feeding her.

I offered warmth, healing, and led the way time and time again as they continued their south-bound journey, because it would keep her warm, keep her healthy, and get her someplace safe. I wasn't particularly fond of the howling winds, the white-out blizzards, or the grueling frostbite, but my human was here, and that made it all worth it.

✦

I'd felt love since arriving in the Arctic. I'd felt anger. I'd felt annoyance.

My first brush with fear came the day one of her gods came to see who had intruded upon his territory.

Despite my trepidation, Igaluk, their lunar deity, visited only twice with idle curiosity.

He treated my presence with indifference, which was neither good nor bad. It wasn't the camaraderie I'd felt with Athena, but it was better than any sort of territorial hostility. I was quite sure I was ready to take Hell to war with any pantheon if they challenged my claim to my mortal, and perhaps they sensed it wasn't worth the bloodshed.

I should have saved my apprehension for the true test of my mettle.

My guard was down when Nanook appeared.

In my tenth year, the god of bears, the apex northern predator, was not apathetic to my presence.

I smelled him before I heard him.

"Fluffy?" Yuka sat up in the middle of the night. She shot a look at her now-mother, and I shook my head. *No. Don't follow.*

90

The voice beyond the shelter challenged. "Face me."

She watched as I pushed the leather flap separating the warm tent with the great outdoors. I disappeared beyond the entrance, shaking my head one last time.

*Do not follow.*

The imposing presence atop the nearby hill cast a terrifying silhouette against the moon.

Yuka hadn't listened.

I understood the god's command, but to the village, a bear had arrived, and they were prepared for attack. Torches were lit. Weapons gleamed. Men and women waited anxiously as I took careful steps forward.

His lips pulled back from his teeth.

His people were afraid, and for the moment, he was the enemy.

Snow crunched beneath my paws as I scrambled for a plan.

I was a dire wolf, but Nanook was twice the size of an already-enormous polar bear. I couldn't fight him. Not if we were both in animal form. I had no right to his territory. I didn't belong among his tribes. One foot in front of the other, I knew I'd die before leaving Yuka.

The wind was particularly cruel that night, but it hadn't kept members of the tribe from bundling their furs around their faces to watch the standoff, hearts in their throats.

If I could hear their worry, so could Nanook.

"Name yourself," he growled.

Cowardice wouldn't serve me. I made my way to the top of the hill, close enough for him to reach me with teeth, claws, and weight, should it come to that. "I have no name that would satisfy you."

"What do they call you?" Nanook's voice was the powerful eddy of the rocks churning at the bottom of the sea. He spoke mind to mind in the immortal tongue, a booming voice inside my skull, yet threatening snarls to all who watched.

"Mortals have no formal name for me," I answered honestly.

Though I spoke into his mind, I felt the need to raise my voice above the howling wind. "I am a protector of one. I'm nothing more."

He planted his feet on the snow dune and sniffed the air around me. I did my best to keep still, though I knew the two of us took mortal shape, his body would be every bit as towering as the bear was now. Faith was alive and well in the north, and these were no idle gods.

A bluff charge accompanied his growl. "Half-truths."

"Hell," I sputtered. "Hell has no relation with the Adlivun pantheon, and with any luck, our paths may never cross again. I know of your gods—I know Sedna, your goddess of the sea, though we'd had no occasion to meet. I've met Igaluk, though he was disinterested, and that's all I can hope for. I mean your people no harm, but I also have no interest in them."

"Then you know you do not belong." He towered over me. "And you know you should leave."

"I have a human," I said, wondering if I sounded as pathetic as I felt. She was a secret to many, but I had no quarrel with these gods, nor did they deal with any of Hell's enemies. I could use an ally. "Only one. She's called Yuka at present, but I've followed her for several lifetimes, across continents, realms, and languages. I'm connected to her. Please don't send me away."

*Please.* I'd never prostrated myself before a god like this. But my title, my kingdom, my realm, meant nothing here. I was an intruder, and his word was final.

Nanook huffed, looking over my shoulder to where the villagers watched a wolf the size of a man face off against a bear three times its size. I could only imagine how our growls sounded to human ears.

I lowered my head in my best imitation of a bow. "I swear to you: I lay no claim to your people, save for the girl."

The people remained statue-still as Nanook descended from the dune.

I—the one they believed to be their protector—remained on the hill, unmoving.

I caught Yuka's eyes in the torchlight and shook my head once more.

*Don't move.*

Nanook looked even larger as he passed the nomadic huts. His hide alone would create an entire home, if not two, had he been a mortal bear.

Silver moonlight mingled with the shadows cast by flickering orange torches as the bear walked amongst the people, casting idle glances with coal-black eyes as he left enormous prints in the snow. The tribe knew from the exchange that they were on their own, and in response, they remained utterly still.

The night came and went. I had passed the test, at least for the time being.

Satisfied that I would not interfere with Nanook's mastery, he never challenged my presence again.

But he was not the only bear on the ice.

As if life in the Arctic wasn't hard enough, there is no predator more blood thirsty and dangerous than a hungry polar bear. In our years together, the tribe needed protection, and I threw my body between any claw, tooth, storm, or weapon that might put Yuka in danger. The predators were half the god's size, with none of his ethereal shimmer, but every bit as dangerous to squishy, vulnerable mortals. Each bear kept its life for all of three minutes from the time it threatened the village to its last breath.

I'd been Fluffy for so long that I nearly forgot I'd ever been anything else. I may have remained Fluffy if Yuka hadn't asked.

✦

Twenty years on this earth with ten of them at my side, Yuka stroked my fur as she did every other night. Her mother feasted with neighboring villagers, leaving us to settle by the fire. Meals with friends always resulted in her spending a familial night in their tent, as she'd become the village's mother. She knew Yuka was safe with me and deserved her own senses of companionship where she found them. Nights like these we knew we had to ourselves.

"You are no wolf," she said. "The village watched our protector appear from the air and we have believed in you faithfully. We've known peace. We've known prosperity. And never once have I asked you to reveal yourself."

I knew what she was asking.

For the second time in years, I felt fear.

"Surely, you'd open your mouth, and say your name," she continued. "One day, when you were ready, you'd show me what god walks the earth as a Great White Wolf."

I'd spent years scouring the earth to find her. Once we'd connected in this life, I'd had no occasion to consider stepping out of my lupine form. She was safe. She was happy. I was with her. What else could we need?

"Fluffy? I know that isn't your name. And I don't know what I've done that I've failed to earn your trust...but I'd like to fix it. Tell me how I may honor you, how I may become worthy of knowing the god who walks among men."

I got up from my reclining position. She pulled away, skin tight around her eyes, folding her legs stiffly as she watched me.

She'd asked. She was ready. She wanted this. What's more, she'd wrongfully shame herself if I refused.

And yet...I was terrified.

I hadn't thought of Hell in a decade. My kingdom was fine without me.

The true panic was here in the snow, wondering how Yuka would receive me. She'd only known a creature, an animal, a dog. I was respected as something *other*, but I was not a man. What's worse: I wasn't a god. At least, not one of *her* gods.

In this life and the past, I wasn't the god she'd called. Yet I'm the one who answered.

"I know you understand me," she said.

Yuka had spent her life being told I was a god who'd taken wolf form, and it certainly didn't hurt my case. She'd never treated me like a pet. But once we crossed this line, there was no going back. I wanted to be with her. *Let me cling to my wolfish form one moment longer*, I thought. *Let me stay right here, before your worldview cracks. Let me have one more heartbeat of you choosing me.*

"Please."

There it was again. That feeling. A twist in the guts. A fear. A longing. A complicated, strange, terrible, wonderful, altogether newness that a demon couldn't have experienced if he'd spent ten thousand years among peers in Hell.

This, here and now, was the appeal of gods adopting humans.

Black and white juxtapositions skewed my life in opposites. The cold war between Heaven and Hell defined our kingdom, drove our pantheon, and informed my every decision. And despite the stakes, gods, demons, angels, fae, and the like faced the monotony of foreverness.

Somewhere in the middle was a painful, beautifully, exciting, chaotic gift.

Immortals worry, stress, and donned responsibility when they took on a human.

Living among the mortals, caring for them, attaching ourselves to them, we were given the delicious, terrible rarity of agony, terror, and sorrow. And in this moment, on this night, I experienced a true, bone-chilling fear.

Beyond the tent, pink and emerald lights began to ring with the high, metallic hum of swords sharpened against one another, and I, myself, had become a believer. This was a sign from something bigger than me to treat the night as sacred.

"Please." That word again. She dipped her chin. "I'm ready."

I nodded, then left the tent, pausing in the antechamber of its insulated neck between the two leather flaps. It was a moment for myself and also to allow her the preparation she needed for my transformation.

The second flap of hides and furs caught the stray wind and snow, preventing the winter from entering the comfortable dome. With three deep breaths, I shifted into a man for the first time in nearly a decade.

I moved to pull back the fur and caught my hand's tremble.

Destructive, interesting, miserable, rare, fresh fear coursed through me, but this sensation was no mystery. I knew precisely what scared me. I was afraid that she'd grown to love the animal and would reject the man. I was scared that she would look at me and send me from the tribe like the demon I was. A wolf was one thing, but this form? Me?

Three more breaths.

I forced my hand to still and gripped the lip of the fur, startled by my own fingers, as if I'd forgotten how ice-white I was. I tried to move forward but was caught on the threshold by a note. She was humming.

It was no Qawiaraq song.

I'd heard their lullabies, their bonfire ballads, their histories sung for the better part of ten years. This was something else. Nine haunting notes rising, five falling. I listened to the fractured lullaby in a minor chord, over and over. I'd heard it before, covering the scraping of basalt as she'd crushed grain with her mortar and pestle. I'd listened to it in Athens as a student watched the stars beside a fountain. But in nine years, I'd never heard it from Yuka.

I moved forward without thinking. I'd never spoken Qawiaraq aloud, yet my first words to her were, "How do you know that song?"

Yuka had her back to the door when I entered. She'd been combing her hair with an ornate, ivory brush while she awaited my return—the only one in the village, as their tribe was not one for vanity. She looked at me with the sort of calm fortitude that told me she'd been expecting this for a long, long time. She lifted her chin in a sign of strength, the hand-poked tattoo running from her lower lip down her neck highlighted by the red-orange flame as she did.

She did not answer. She simply stared.

It was so strange to realize that while I knew her, she did not know me. "I'm..." I struggled for a name.

With the quirk of one corner of her lip, she supplied: "Fluffy."

The corner of my mouth tugged. "If it pleases you."

"And what *is* your name," she said, voice clear and even as though she were calmly addressing a crowd. "So that I might properly address you."

Her shoulders were too level. Her posture was too straight.

The formality hurt me almost as much as if she had feared me. I shook my head. "No, Yuka. I'm not seeking recognition. The only name I want is the one you give me."

She exhaled, brows pinching in the middle. She resumed brushing her hair.

"Interesting," she said. That was all. No argument. No questions. No fight.

"I suppose it is," I said, unable to keep the edges of a smile from my expression.

She set the comb beside the bed and turned to face me. "I sense that *you* might be able to tell me why I know this song."

The perception struck me.

I was so unfamiliar with being on two feet that it took a moment to ensure I hadn't wavered. I gestured to the furs on the bed, asking permission, and waited for her nod before I took a seat.

"This is the first time I've heard you sing it," was all I said.

She tilted her head to the side. Loose, freshly-combed locks tumbled over her shoulder as she listened. The high, metallic noise of the lights informed her of their presence even if there was no window in her home. "Perhaps it's a night for the spirits," she said. "Including ghosts of the past."

A sacred night. Yes, I supposed there might be something to that. I didn't know much of humans and their clairabilities. I knew of their lore and of days they'd gossiped and warned of spirits and demons, but as I had only paid mind to one human, I'd spared little time thinking about the veil being thick or thin. Athena, in her wisdom, created a crack in the veil for me to appear in the flesh to humans who belonged to another pantheon. Many gods could take the shape of men at will, but stepping into corporeal form was not an ability afforded to all of us. I was new to the practice, and had no idea how much of it was achievable without external help.

Could I take the shape of a man and walk through a city as a stranger, seen by all?

Would I always need to be chosen, or take a safe, accepted form?

Had I always possessed the ability, but never searched for the edges of my power until I was pushed to grow?

I suppose I had lifetimes to figure it out.

As it stood, I had to use the gift sparingly. Even when wearing the skin of a man, I could never truly blend in with humans. But on a sacred night such as this, perhaps my appearance wouldn't be so terrible.

Again, she spoke. "Truly, you come with no name? No message from the gods? No wants as our guardian spirit? Ask it, and it's yours."

This gave me pause. Perhaps ten years was a very long time for her, but it had been dust in the wind for me. I'd busied myself with keeping her alive and happy. This was my first time succeeding with my human for more than a few poorly-attended years, and that, in and of itself, was a victory.

"I have a singular want."

Her shoulders were too straight once more.

I realized my sentence was more horrifying than a strange man entering her tent unannounced. Then again, I was as pale as the white wolf, and she'd had no reaction. I was not dressed for warmth, but she hadn't been afraid. Maybe with her, I wouldn't lie.

"I want to succeed here, where I've failed before. The human life is short, and yours has been shorter than most. This time, my lone wish is to keep you alive."

"This time?" she repeated.

Wind, metallic hum, crackling fire, and the thump of my own pulse made a disquieting symphony between us.

I couldn't tell if I'd made an error.

I knew her people grew up with legends of the afterlife.

I knew animals were believed to have a soul, and that some souls could return to earth in a new body, should their soul be wholly claimed by the gods of their afterlife and consent to retiring into the endlessness of forever. I knew Eleni would choose me over any regional afterlife. With Yuka, I couldn't be sure.

I had no authority over this theology or their traditions. Then again, while their gods claimed them, I'd certainly made my stake to her clear. She'd come back time and time again. With any luck, the gods of her people would continue to leave her untouched.

"You're regarded as a spiritual leader, given your attachment to the guardian wolf," I said, delicately changing the subject while continuing to address her path in this life. "Is this life fulfilling? Are you happy?"

She didn't have to think for long. With a small, serene smile, she said, "There is no greater joy than knowing that your existence makes the lives of others better. I can uniquely help my people. With the wolf, or with you, as the wolf's spirit before me...I am happy."

I tried not to hold my breath while she was speaking, but my exhale relaxed us both.

"I'd like to help you," I said.

Unlike our time in Athens, I had no urge to touch her.

She was beautiful, to be sure. But Yuka had no interest, romantic or otherwise, when it came to the flesh. I'd never heard the pattern of her heart increase at the nearness of a human of any gender. She didn't swear, didn't grow excited, didn't blush the way mortals might. Asexuality did not deter her from joy, from community, from fulfillment. It didn't change a line of mauve or amethyst or white in the shimmering glow of her aura. I didn't have to taste her soul to know that my greatest pleasure was to be near it. "I'll be the wolf you need around the people. And at night, we can speak. Ask any question, and I'll answer, if I'm able. You can be an advisor for your people."

She considered this. "A line to the spirit world."

I nodded, though I wasn't sure I had the right to. I couldn't speak to the fallen, or give messages of the afterlife, as one might hope from a spiritual advisor. But we agreed. I would guide her. I would protect her. I would be there for her.

In return, I would not shatter.

"You'll become a man again? We can speak like this in the future?"

The smile might have reached my eyes, though I couldn't be sure. "If it pleases you."

Lines around her eyes crinkled, despite her youth. "It does."

My reward was the satisfaction of going as long as I could without my heart cracking like the ice beneath our feet, plunging us into the black, arctic abyss.

And, so, it was.

She was Yuka, Wolf Rider.

Under Yuka's role as anjatuq, shaman in another tongue, women made it through their pregnancies without issue. I tested my abilities to their limits and discovered new ones I'd never had occasion to access.

Anyone who fell ill was better by the next morning.

Her advice was sound, even without the wisdom of her spirit counselor, and never questioned by her people. Her leadership was sovereign and respected. She lived without harassment or threats. Neighboring peoples heard word of her leadership, and at each trading post, our tribe grew. Other nomads visited for medicine or advice, and in the form of the magical wolf, I would brush against them, gifting them with health before they left.

✦

Yuka was beautiful at twenty, and at forty, and at sixty.

Our lives were full, our conversations invigorating, our relationship as deep as the ravines that shaped the world.

In the years that followed, I did my best to explain my pantheon, but she had no need for categorizing enemies and adversaries. My kingdom and its wars were a far-off nothing, irrelevant given that not even the ghostly shape of my legion had laid its smoke upon the ice. She didn't need warding or protection from succubi and heavenly hosts out here.

I was from elsewhere, I was other, and that was all that mattered.

We spoke of time and soul and death.

I told her stories that she said were decidedly magical and fantastical. And we looked at the stars. *Fuck*, did we look at the stars.

She knew the Qawiaraq names for every constellation and recited the rich, passionate tales behind them. We'd wander as far from the village as we could so everyone would perceive a wolf and a woman—never the man he'd become—as they spent their nights on the ice as unlikely companions who stared at the stars.

And life went on.

Gods above and below, it was a *life*.

I experienced true, profound joy.

There was music. There was dancing and art and community, the likes of which I'd never truly experienced. I felt the days—*truly* felt them. The sun rose, it set, and sometimes in the long months, it would stay up all night or stay gone for months. My explanations of rocks and their tilts were boring, and rejected on the grounds of being uninteresting, which I found utterly delightful.

I loved her more now than I had in her bed in Greece, as if each day with her was more wonderful, more beautiful, more absurdly precious than anything the immortal realms might deign to craft, despite the ice and snow and winters.

This was what it meant to be alive.

Her bones began to creak, her hair turned silver, her skin sagged. No matter what I did to ensure she never knew pain, I felt the mortal clock ticking with every second that passed.

While few made it to her age in the wandering tribes on the ice, Yuka had no aches, no qualms, nothing that might trouble a human.

The woman and her wolf wrote their story until age eighty, one hundred, and by one hundred and twelve, my healing touch no longer sufficed.

I had no god to pray to as I watched the inevitable approach. There was no one to beg. I'd known loss before, but I was less prepared than ever.

Her cells wore off more quickly than I could fix. Her muscles fought me at every step. She kept her hand on my snout all day and I remained a wolf at night so she might lean against me, never bothered with the presence of a man unless we had sat for intentional conversation.

"What did you call me?" she asked one night. "In the other lives, that is."

I was the age I'd been the night I emerged from the neck of her tent. Holding my perfect, elderly human against the bed of furs, I hadn't aged while time had weathered her face. I stroked her hair, kissing her scalp as I breathed in the fresh scent of her soul.

"You were Shala in the first life," I said quietly, as if telling her a bedtime story. "You were Eleni in the next. And that's when you asked me not to call you by your mortal names."

The cavernous lines around Yuka's face deepened. Her eyes closed. "What were you to call me instead?"

It was the fourth time I experienced the situation in my endless existence: I wanted to cry.

"We didn't get the chance to pick a name, though there's only one that makes sense to me."

Her breathing slowed as she began to drift to sleep. "Mmm?"

"No matter who, or where, or what, you are my only human. To me, you are Love."

◆

The late summer sun had set on her one-hundred and thirteenth birthday before she'd turned to ask me a question. She didn't have time to ask before I saw the slip of her spirit. I was in a man's body in an instant, catching her, holding her body and soul as I begged her with silent, determined eyes to stay on this earth.

"Not yet," I insisted. "We have another summer. Give me one more year."

"My wolf, my star..."

I blinked back the threat of tears.

"Yuka, please—"

"Didn't we decide you're not to call me mortal names? You've found me in other lives, did you not? You haven't left my side in this one. How weak do you think my faith is if I wouldn't trust that you'll find me in the next? I won't be Yuka then."

"I'm not ready."

"Call me by my name," she said. "And let me follow the North Star home."

A chilled tear fell. "Please, Love."

"You have to let me go," she whispered.

The weather seemed to agree. The edges of the tent trembled as a late-season storm moved the sealskin furs. The first drops of rain threatened to turn our peaceful night into something else. "My beautiful wolf. My savior. The star who became a man. My time has come."

I shook my head. "You don't have to die. You can finish your mortal cycle. Come with me. We can go to my realm together. You won't grow old, or tired, or—"

"No," she said quietly. "I did good in this life, and I'll do good in the next."

"I don't think you understand." I didn't care if it was insulting. Call it denial, call it bargaining, I wasn't ready. "I'm not telling you to remain one hundred and thirteen on the ice. I'm saying you can join immortality. It's not the afterlife humans describe. This would be us. You and me. It's like...it's like becoming a god. It's like—"

I couldn't think of a time I'd rambled before this moment.

Tears were still unfamiliar to me. I wasn't sure as to the sensation when uncomfortable heat spiked along my eyes. I grimaced against the pain as it slithered into my chest. "Please," I said quietly. "I've asked so little of you. Yuka—"

"Three names, yet none of them feel honest on your lips. In each life, you call to my body, but not my soul. Look at me," she smiled, wrinkled lips cracking, eyes crinkling. "I was beautiful once, perhaps. But you aren't here for my body. Name my soul. It's her you seek."

My lip quivered. "I'm supposed to be the one who gives advice."

Bent, papery fingers brushed against my face as she cupped my cheek, wiping my tears. "I have a plan. We'll play a game, you and I."

My hands slid over hers, tender against knobby knuckles and thin, loose skin as I tightened her hold against me.

"Shh, shh. This body's time has come. You were wolf, you were man, you were spirit, you were god. You remember all things, but perhaps I remember, too."

I didn't want to tell her that no, humans did not remember.

She would forget me the moment her soul passed. I would be left to grieve, to mourn, to be abandoned once more the moment she escaped my hold. She would be on to new things, and I would be trapped for one hundred years more in my desperate cycle.

"I've always liked snow hares," she said. "Peaceful, curious. They look like messengers from the underworld, don't you think?"

"Hares?" If I hadn't fought for her healing, I would have been worried she was battling confusion.

"The game." She smiled. "Pay attention."

"Snow hares," I repeated.

I wrapped my free arm around her, cradling her as she began to drift backward. Raindrops began to pelt the tent with methodical beats. It wasn't a fall, not truly. It was more like sleep called her name, and she listened to its soft voice.

"A wolf would be too easy," she said, voice growing softer as her lids flitted shut. "A hare, however. That would be quite the trick."

"Yu—" I bit the name off. I couldn't bring myself to dishonor her wish. "I'm as old as time," I told her. "I didn't begin to number the years until I met you, for they were meaningless. I didn't know what it was to be mortal. I didn't know what it was to love."

I wasn't finished with my speech. My chest ached with unspoken words. I had so much to say, to confess, to hope and demand and beg, but her muscles slackened.

"Love," she repeated, echoing my final word. "Only Love, from this life until the end."

It was the last thing she said on the earth before her ghost joined the pink and green slashes of the Northern Lights, another spirit in the Arctic to dance above the ones who'd lost them.

When I wept, the sky joined me.

# Chapter Nine

**NOTHING**

Teach stillness to the ocean.
Describe cold to the sun.
Explain mercy to the blade.
When they learn the impossible, perhaps, at last, I will know how to express what it means to see the face of love, and then lose that love again...
And again.
...and again.

# Chapter Ten

**184 BCE**

Men and immortals had more differences than likenesses. Each juxtaposition was stark, jarring, and when it mattered, godsdamned infuriating.

Priorities blatantly contrasted, to be sure.

Their wink of a life expectancy made their choices, their priorities, their driving force incompressible to those of us who could see the bigger picture.

Gods found pleasure in dissimilar things.

The woes that plagued mankind were vapors, murmurs, and dust compared in the eyes of the Divine.

We received our energy and sustenance from astronomically different sources.

And of grave importance, when the gods procreated, it was a big deal.

The population among gods, angels, demons, fae, and the like changed so seldomly that each death and birth was etched into a tablet and echoed through the lands.

But *fuck* did humans reproduce.

There were at least thirty million more lives to sift through between the time I'd found my human in the Arctic Circle and the moment she took her last breath on her one-hundred and thirteenth birthday. As an eternal being, three lives with my human were little more than bubbles and froth in my timeline. It was hardly enough time to establish a method on how best to discover her soul, in whatever body it had landed.

Combing the earth was my all-consuming frenzy.

✦

Decades passed as I scoured every town, village, home, for my opalescent soul. I spared the minutes, an hour at most, to visit my kingdom and check in with my duties.

I was frequently met with a, "What the fuck are you doing?!" from Izi. "You can't keep this up. People *know*, Amagi. Father knows of your weakness."

Her dark form faded against the black marble as I shot her a fatal glare. Venom dripped from each word. "Are you that desperate for his approval? You have to try to undercut his relationship with his only son?"

But her threats landed. I trekked across the palace, past the Soul Eater, straight into my father's worried gaze.

Before the door closed behind me, I asked, "How may I assuage your fears?"

There was a gentleness to his eyes as his lips turned down. "Before I answer: I suppose asking you to detach from this obsession with a single mortal is off the table?"

My expressionless silence was answer enough.

"Then...I trust you know what you're doing."

There would be other visits, other days, other talks. Now, I needed to return to the surface. I offered the stiffest of shallow bows before pushing through the double doors.

Izi was waiting just beyond the Soul Eater when I exited his royal hall. I flipped my sister a vulgar gesture at her goading over the war, the stakes, my role, the metal-on-metal screech of her endless harping, and then returned to my search.

Hell was doing fine without me. Our war had been stale, political, and operated in the shadows long enough to go on whether or not I wasted my time in Hell. But my human? How fine would she be without a protector?

I had no strategy, save for the process of elimination, but no message from my legions, no infuriated tirades from my sister, no concerned interceptions by deities as I trespassed on their lands, deterred my pursuit.

How had the mortal world changed so much in such a short time?

I began to seriously reconsider my stance on involving the legion under my command. There was no helpless feeling like watching the mortal hours become days become years knowing that she could be anywhere—that anything could have happened to her.

Had she changed her mind once she crossed over, and gone to her people's afterlife?

Had a new, earthly mother died in childbirth, starting the nine-month-search over again, and again, and again?

I didn't know if she was happy, if she was suffering, if she needed me. No, I didn't like the idea of other immortal beings around her. Yes, the thought of word spreading as to my affinity for my human made me hostile. But if humanity continued expanding at this rate, how was I supposed to shuffle mankind through a sieve until I found my one, precious gem?

I was determined to find her, and find her, I did.

In the twenty-ninth mortal year of my hunt, my search came to an end just before giving up on yet another continent and crossing the mountains into kingdoms and peoples I had yet to discover.

The sharp smell of the air above the clouds. The pearly glow that emanated from below the skin. The essence of the one I loved.

It was worthy of a parade, of a feast, of a mandatory holiday to which each of Hell's citizens should dance in the streets if only to share in my joy.

I hadn't taken a breath in decades, and there, in a seaside town in chilly Britannia, my lungs filled for the first time since Yuka's passing.

But there she was, just outside of Durrington, the farm of the deer people, sloping on the edge of a riverbank.

*Breathe.* It was that voice within myself that I hadn't heard in a long, long time.

*She's here. She's alive. You're together.*

I can't be held accountable for how long I stared in slack-jawed awe.

*You found her, you found her, you found her.*

It was superficial to be sure, but the moment I moved past her soul, I realized that for the first time, her hair was not black. Her features had changed over names and ethnicities and centuries, of course, but until now I hadn't fully embraced how everything could change. I'd had no cause to come this far north, and from pale-haired reindeer herders in the north, to the rich umber of the southern deserts, to the glossy chestnut of the mountains, I wasn't prepared for how many different kinds of humans there were.

I'd never seen shades of red in human hair.

It was as if a few precious drops of blood had been squeezed into a water basin, then dribbled atop her head. The pinpricks that remained colored her chill-pinked skin. Quite like the deer for which her people were named, she had the dotting of a fawn sprinkled over her nose, her cheeks, her forehead. She looked nothing like Shala or Eleni or Yuka, but she looked everything like Love.

Her pearly aura might as well have been a halo. It stole the breath from my lungs, filling them with the crisp cloud and sky quality that I hadn't tasted in nearly thirty years. I was so excited to find her, to see her, that I hadn't done a moment of research on her, her people, her village, her culture, her beliefs.

Unlike Yuka, Eleni, or Shala cycles before her, she was in no danger from which she needed saving.

I was the danger.

I burst from the veil with the sort of uncouth elation that, understandably, nearly gave my human a heart attack. I knew my mistake the moment I'd made it. She was my human to me, after all, but to her, I was a stranger.

I stepped backward into the veil the instant her scream tore from her throat.

*Fuck, fuck, fuck.*

I could have ripped out my own hair.

Of course, she didn't know me. Of course, I was not only a stranger, but an apparition where a moment prior only freshwater and grass and solitude had been. She would have screamed even if it had been a bucket of puppies and gold coins that appeared unannounced to ambush her.

It was a fool's mistake.

I was humiliated by my blunder and unbelievably irritated with myself.

So much so that I couldn't bring myself to follow her home. Not that first night. Or through the mist and wind and raindrops of the second. I sat in scowling, smoldering self-loathing over what I'd done to terrorize my human until a new presence arrived in the wet gloom of my third day on foreign soil.

It would be a mistake to say a woman spoke, for a goddess was no mere woman.

The sodden earth beneath me trembled with the gravitas of her voice.

"Are you going to haunt my lands and prey on my people, or will you introduce yourself?"

I looked into the unflinching face of a being made of sunlight, fire, and earth. Flame-red hair cascaded to her feet. Our realms had yet to formally meet, but her reputation preceded her. I recognized her instantly.

She forewent the immortal language. The scattered temples in her home, the woven mementos to her on the hearth, her name on the tongues of her people, flowed into her as a power source. She outranked me here, on her land, and forced me to speak on her terms.

I was rusty in Goidelic languages but fell into cadence as we spoke.

"Brigid," I responded with a dip of my head. She outranked me, and I was trespassing. This was not how we were meant to meet. "At long last, I'm grateful to make your acquaintance."

"Is this how Hell sends its emissary?" she asked, folding her arms over her chest. The red-orange flames of hair showcased a life of their own. Her strands licked around her neck, her chest, tumbling down to her waist as she glared.

"I'm not here as an emissary, though you are owed one," I replied. "Honestly, perhaps I shouldn't be here at all."

"Perhaps not," she agreed, expression hardening.

The glow of her hair refracted off the burbling river. I hoped the light hit my face well enough to convey my expression.

"I'm here for a human."

She was unmoved. "Keeva. I'm aware."

I corrected the lettering in my head, scrambling for my Gaelic knowledge. Caoimhe. That's how 'Keeva' would be spelled.

I swallowed, trying to remember Brigid's numerous gifts. A high-ranking deity in her pantheon, she was the goddess of so many things, it was hard to keep track. Her dominion over fire was a given, and even if I'd forgotten, her hair certainly would have reminded me. Childbirth, metalworking, healing, home-making, poetry, and...

*Oh.*

"You're a goddess of prophecy and divination," I said, more for my benefit than for hers. Of course she knew why I was here. "My human, Caoimhe, doesn't know who I am or why I'm here."

While her posture remained unchanged, I noticed the slightest relaxation in her face. "Because in this lifetime, she's not your human."

I shook my head.

Her brows lowered. "You've come to foreign lands to cower on Celtic soil? Act your station. Speak your piece, Prince of Hell."

Perhaps it was the years of solitude, or the repeated heartbreak, or maybe the emerald grasses and the cauldron-dark sky had churned me in peculiar ways, but my lips parted, and given that she had a heart for ballads, I offered her my tragic tale.

I told the goddess the story of how a human had caught herself a Prince, and how that Prince had spent hundreds of years following her from body to body. I told her of our tumultuous lives, and of the long, healthy story of Yuka and the White Wolf. She offered a single, humorless laugh when I shared how the twenty-nine-year hunt had ended on her land only for me to frighten a married woman.

The mist stopped, leaving us alone in the cold dew as she examined me.

"You are on my land," she said, "so you will listen to my advice, whether or not you desire it."

My single, low laugh was sincere, however brief the moment of levity may be.

I'd shirked my ambassadorship with the other gods for so long that I'd nearly forgotten how to interact with one.

"It seems to me, Prince," she said at last, "you're trapped between humanity and godhood. Gods are freed from mortality by our detachment from it. I may favor a practitioner. I may even love one from time to time. But I balance affection while maintaining my sovereignty. You, however, appear to lend yours."

I made no attempt to conceal my expression.

"On your journey to accepting your godhood, you must first learn what it is to be mortal. And for that, you have appointed a girl to teach you the lesson."

This time, my chuckle was humorless. "Perhaps."

"Let's hope that's the reason."

I raised a brow.

Her laugh was equally dark. "No other justification would satisfy you," she said.

"It doesn't need to be satisfactory if it's true. Do you have a prophecy for me, Brigid?"

She cast her eyes to the water, but it wasn't in avoidance. I watched her contemplation as the threads of fate wove behind her eyes.

"She's been born female in each life, has she not?"

I balked at the question. I hadn't even considered it. "Yes, I suppose she has. Is that...unusual? I haven't spent enough time with mortals to be familiar with their soul cycles."

Brigid's eyes unfocused. "Her ability to bear children may be a sign of things to come."

I moved closer, if only by a fraction. "Tell me what you see when you peer into our future."

"The thread is on the loom. It may be nothing. Your fates are undecided."

I'd broken so many rules already, what was one more? I pushed my luck.

"What aren't you telling me?"

The hardness in her gaze returned. She had finished playing along. "Find your human. Learn what it is to be human. Pray that is the fate between the two of you. For any other path would mean something grand, something powerful, something bigger than you or me or your mortal. But one doesn't see the story until it's written."

My lips parted, head shaking in my silent question.

"You may remain on my land, as I hope this human is merely a tool for education..." Her eyes returned to the water. The last part was more to herself than to me as she said, "What a tragedy it would be if the two of you were crafted to create history."

She'd already begun to wobble as her form stepped from the mortal soil to her own pantheon. I caught her just before she disappeared. "Will my presence be challenged in your kingdom while she lives?"

"Do what you must," she said. "And for all of our sakes, I hope this lesson is your last."

When she left, so did the light.

The mist resumed, abandoning me to the gray silence of damp moss and chill.

I lingered on the riverbank and stared at the trout swimming upstream, wondering as to how they kept their fervor even though it meant battling the current, struggling day in and day out to fight against the very environment for which they were made. Were the trout born to learn a lesson? After which they might relax, they might find a pond, they might rest and join the idle slumber of freshwater fish?

Their answer echoed my own.

One could refuse to learn a lesson, but they could not deny purpose. Trout were the way they were because they had no other choice.

I was a phantom, unseen on the fourth day as I walked into her village. I planned to find her, but didn't have to search far. There she was, a wooden pail on her hip as musical Gaelic rolled off her tongue, chatting with someone near a well.

My human had been more or less solitary in the lives I'd been her guardian, and I wondered as to the friendships I'd kept her from, the human experiences I'd limited by being in her life. The question burrowed into me as her face lit.

For a second, I thought she'd seen me.

She looked right through me, the sun shining from her on the overcast day as if it belonged in her chest. Caoimhe set the pail atop the well's stony ledge and opened her arms wide when something scurried into the space that existed between my world and theirs, directly through my legs as it ran to her.

Not it. He.

*This* was genuinely surprising.

A boy no older than four, with hair the color of strained peaches. His fat cheeks glowed with his mother's light, with health, with joy.

Love, *my* Love, had a child?

And a happy one at that. This plump boy grinned without his front two teeth.

I almost hated the child as his mother scooped him into her arms. She squeezed the boy, spinning him in a quick circle as he giggled, kicking and squirming to be free.

Jealousy was an unbecoming emotion, and it wasn't one I was prepared to handle.

I'd arranged marriages, fought off fathers, and killed husbands.

But a son?

I turned away, though I wasn't sure where I planned to go. I couldn't spend twenty-nine years searching just to leave because she was fine without me. Unless it was the kind thing to do. The noble thing.

And then she spoke.

"How is my love today, Little Rabbit?"

My head whipped back as if she'd spoken my name—my true name. Fuck nobility. I looked at her through the veil knowing she couldn't see me. She had no idea I was there. And yet...

*"We'll play a game, you and I..."*

Yuka's eyes had sparkled at the prospect. She'd been so certain that her soul would recognize me, just as I did hers.

Hares.

Snow hares, to be exact.

It wasn't exactly evidence, but...

She'd looked at her son—the extension of her soul—and called him her love, her Little Rabbit.

And maybe this is what it was like to survive as a mouse who fed on crumbs. Perhaps this was why birds roosted where once grain had been spilled. It wasn't a clue, not exactly. This wasn't a password. But...I was an addict, and she was my drug. I clung to the word with indescribable desperation.

So, I remained.

It shouldn't have sustained me, but I'd cling to the dagger's sharpened edge of hope until it sawed my fingers to the bone.

She didn't know me in this life, and I could use that to justify tending to some long-neglected obligations. I forced myself to strike what passed for balance, since I'd had none with Yuka. From the moment I'd met her in her last life, I hadn't given her a single moment alone. Yuka hadn't had the peace to receive a papercut, even if she'd wanted one.

This version of my human had already walked the earth for nearly three decades. She'd made it this far without me. Perhaps I could wean myself from my addiction by finding the barest of moments to leave her unprotected, as I had in lives prior.

I had obligations to my kingdom that I'd thoroughly abandoned for some time.

Visits to my realm were in minutes instead of days—half an hour, on average. Forty-five infernal minutes if I was pushing it. It would give my human time alone in the human realm and offer me the chance to stay abreast of Hell's activities. My father was pleased with reports that I'd made contact with indigenous deities and at least one high-ranking member of the Celtic pantheon. He was less pleased with my reputation for tearing through unknown territories without doing my princely duties, and we reached a compromise that satisfied us both.

I could continue my station topside, but from this moment forward, I would introduce myself as Hell's representative and establish positive relationships with the land's entities, whether or not my human was there. In return, he would hold his tongue about my obsession—one that drew Hell's only heir far away for centuries at a time in the heat of war—and we would share an excuse for why I spent so much time away from our realm.

I was the traveling face of Hell, and I was to conduct myself as such.

"After all," he'd said, "you've been with this human of yours on and off for...what is it? A grand total of less than two centuries, when you combine her lifetimes. That's an excusable drop in the bucket. I'll defend you, my son, if anyone says otherwise."

He meant well, but my human was no drop in the bucket. She was a storm.

I'd abandoned my citizenship, as far as I was concerned. Returning to her side felt like coming home, whether or not she knew I was there. One lungful of painfully clean air, a single pearly shimmer, and I was where I was meant to be.

It didn't hurt my sense of belonging that her body moved every time I entered the room. She responded to the preternatural shift each time I arrived, whether consciously or not. Another crumb in my nibbling diet: she knew my energy. Absence made the heart grow fonder, or so I was told.

And fonder I was.

From our fourth day onward, Caoimhe was eternally healthy, her family was unnaturally prosperous, and fortune seemed to befall the woman, her son, and her husband at every turn.

I introduced myself to the Dagda, leader of the Tuatha Dé Danann, god of strength. I greeted Lúgh in passing, but his deep tie to oaths made him rather quiet, lest he say something he didn't mean. Balor, Aengus, and Donn were as welcoming as one might hope, though we had no plans for wine, feasts, or chumming anytime soon.

I contemplated taking the form of a white deer and walking amongst their people, but it would serve no purpose, save for my vanity. Besides, I was relatively positive Cernunnos, the antlered god of the forest, would not appreciate the gesture.

I was holding up my end of my father's bargain, and in

return, I was left in peace to lurk in the shadows, lovingly guarding my human as she ate, as she traveled, as she slept.

I'd contented myself with remaining behind the veil for the rest of this earthly cycle. It would have stayed that way, had it not been for the night of her thirtieth birthday.

A ghost in the humble home, I'd settled into a familiar corner and waited for her breathing to change to indicate a peaceful slumber.

Tonight, it didn't come.

The moment her husband began to snore, Caoimhe slipped from beneath the quilts they shared and tip-toed across the room. She ensured her son slept soundly before grabbing a tartan cloak and quietly grabbing the lantern from its resting place on the windowsill. She eased the door shut, stopped by the woodpile propped against the home, removed the top two logs, and fetched a small basket hidden within. Hastily replacing the logs, she was off before I fully absorbed what she was doing.

She put a safe distance between herself and her home before lighting the lantern.

In my two years with this human, she'd never exhibited deceptive behavior. Was she meeting someone? And if so, how had she made friends, found a lover, planned to run away, without me knowing about it?

I followed silently, brow furrowed.

She stole from the house with muted steps, covering her lantern as she passed the village homes so as not to stir her neighbors. My frown deepened, curiosity growing, as she lifted the humble flame the moment she made it beyond the township.

It was a ten-minute walk to the river, and three minutes beyond that to a flat stone along the softly murmuring stream where she'd once screamed at the mysterious phantom of a man.

My heart clenched.

My hand flew to my chest. I couldn't explain how I knew she was waiting for me, but I knew.

She lifted the lantern as if it might reveal things unseen to mortal eyes as she peered into the darkness. The crescent moon ducked behind a wisp of cloud, plummeting her into darkness once more.

Maybe it was nerves, or perhaps my reluctance to be the source of her fear once more, but I needed to know for sure before I made a move.

I waited.

I'd only been in Hell for a few minutes that day, but it had been enough to give her time to herself. Perhaps that's why I hadn't known what was in the basket that she gently rested near the river. The lantern's buttery glow illuminated one small jar, then another. She uncapped them and set them on the dry surface of a large, smooth stone that belonged neither to the river, nor to the shore, as clear water ran on either side. It was large enough for two, should we choose to sit atop it. She procured two simple goblets and a waterskin, but it was not water that filled the cup. The vapors of sweet, strong cider popped and sparkled as she poured one glass, then another.

Caoimhe slid one goblet to the far side of the stone and held the other.

She lifted it to the night sky.

"I know you're here, Spirit," she said. "I've brought you an offering, though I don't know what you favor."

The deluge of her acknowledgment did something inexplicable. I understood the urge to drink until drunk. I saw the temptation, were I another. One god might say, "The favor of one feels good, therefore, the favor of one hundred will feel spectacular."

And for some, they'd be right. Quantity over quality was the preferred method of most.

I sat with a thought I'd had when I knew my human as Shala.

But I was not born to need humans, nor they to need me.

Human prayers didn't source my power. I had no requirement for offerings or temples or books written in my name. I was beginning to forget what I *did* need, as I struggled to remember why I'd come into this world, if it weren't for this indescribable feeling.

It was so novel, so unlike anything in the undying worlds, to possess mortal affection, to put your heart in hands, knowing they would perish, to experience the world on lips that tasted it for the first time over and over again. Every life with my human was a new form of new after new. An argument could be made that I was addicted to newness, when immortals so rarely experienced it, but I knew any such defense would be a lie. This was an intimacy that couldn't be done through excess. As it were, it could barely be done through one. I certainly hadn't mastered it.

She loosened her cloak, soaking in the unseasonably warm night. The fabric made no noise as it hit the soft heather beneath her, all sounds drowned by the river's steady babble. The moon reappeared, catching the pale curve of her cheeks, her chin, her collarbone, the curl of her ginger hair, the slope of shoulders. She lifted the goblet to her full, pink lips, but she did not drink.

"Spirit?"

"Yes, Caoimhe, my love?" But my response remained behind the veil. She wasn't Love yet. And despite my phonetic struggle with her language, I knew better than to misname someone, even in my own head.

I wasn't ready. She could neither see nor hear me. I didn't need the drink she poured. I was intoxicated by the moment.

"I've felt you many times since that day," she said, speaking over the cider. "And I feel you now."

My staggered inhale did nothing to steady me.

I hadn't been surviving on crumbs, after all. My hope had been real. My human remained mine.

She lowered the cup. "Will you toast with me, Spirit?"

She was offering me the chance to speak on a silver platter, but trepidation consumed me.

What would I say? How would I explain this?

The pressure on a single moment, particularly after I'd scoured the world for her for twenty-nine years only to blunder our first encounter, was frustrating beyond words.

There was no answer that would appease her, particularly as I had no answer that had satisfied my father, my sister, my kingdom, or even myself. I was caught in an anomaly, spared only by my father's obsession with free will that I should be able to follow curious flights of fancy regardless of their logic.

I sighed to myself. *Now or never.*

I settled onto the stone and slipped my fingers around the goblet. I kept my eyes on the drink, too nervous to see the horror in her eyes, as I peeled back the veil and revealed myself.

She made a noise, scarcely intelligible over the stream, something akin to a swallowed scream, as if she'd choked on pushing down her call for help. I kept my eyes on the goblet as I took a swig. It would be impolite to make a face, but the mortals had not mastered alcohol.

"Do you like it?" she asked.

Should my first words to her be a lie?

"I like that you offered it," I replied. "The intention means more than the drink."

She flashed her teeth as if it were the funniest joke she'd ever heard. She wiggled her fingers for the goblet. "Give it, then."

I held the goblet out of reach. It was mine. She was mine. None of this could be taken back.

She rolled her eyes as if we were longtime friends, sweethearts, lovers. The ease with which she fell into me was sweeter than any wine she might have poured. "I have something else," she explained. "Cider is the village favorite, but I thought it might not be to your liking. Don't drink it."

Now, this was a peculiar turn of events. How odd that even in a life where she didn't know me, one wherein she was neither spiritually attuned nor romantically available, that she would regard me with such informality. Gods above and below if she wasn't curious.

My human never failed to mesmerize me.

I held the goblet across the bit of water that separated us as if she were the phantom.

She snatched it from me, draining the cup in two gulps. She procured another waterskin, and a third small jar that I hadn't noticed before. "Do you like mead? Or would you like to try something wicked?"

It was my turn to smile. The joy at her relaxed nature, the pleasure of her presence, the relief of finally being together, and of course, most immediately, hearing this teasing question on her lips when speaking to a demon. "And what, pray tell, do you consider wicked?"

She opened the jar, and I could smell the spirits from here. The fumes alone could kill a man. My grin was one of open-mouthed shock. Gods almighty, these humans went out of their way to die. I snatched it before she could pour the drops.

"Drink this and go blind," I said. "Humans have yet to perfect the distilling of spirits. Let's stick with mead, as I'd prefer you live."

Her strawberry blonde hair caught on her shoulder as she tilted her head. "It's no good? I got it just for..."

Just for me? She thought she was letting me down.

"This," I said, lifting the goblet, "is on the right track. I admire the balls on whoever sipped the liquid and enjoyed the sensation. But it's meant as a topical medicine. It will burn through your innards. Your..." I watched her face. She was neither confused, nor did my words make sense to her. "I'll take the mead," I said. "And please, don't drink these spirits. Keep the jar, though, and dab this liquid on cuts and wounds to keep them from souring."

"Put drink on my cuts?"

"Only this drink. Or else I'll have to work twice as hard to keep you alive."

The humor returned to her expression. "Keeping me alive, are you? Shouldn't a ghost want me to join the other side?"

Thirty years without speaking, and then all at once, she was Love again.

It was my turn to look contemplative. I could tell my expression unnerved her, so I did my best to rein it in. "I wouldn't mind your company," I said honestly, "but it doesn't work like that. Your death would only bring me pain."

Ah, there it was. The wrong thing.

I knew I'd said too much before the words left my lips. The humor faded from her face as she set the mead-filled goblet on the flat stone upon which we sat. "What are you, then?"

Perhaps she was done drinking, but I wasn't. I was glad for the cloud that reappeared to douse the thin moonlight as I spoke into my sip of mead. "No answer would satisfy you."

It wasn't the first time I'd said it to her, though it was the first time she'd heard it in this cycle.

"And what about me?" she asked. "I'm Caoimhe, by the way,

though I suspect you've known my name for some time. My luck turned the day I saw you on these shores. My family has flourished. We're the wealthiest in the village and haven't had so much as a scrape in two years. Would no answer satisfy me there, either?" When I said nothing, she pressed, "Do tell, then, what answer would satisfy *you*?"

Oh, for fuck's sake.

This was my Love. This was the soul that cut to the heart of things, who saw through my bullshit, who spoke her mind and advocated for herself and pierced the veil time and time again. This was the perceptive question that carved out the center of the apple and handed me its core.

The alcohol was nowhere near strong enough for me to be drunk, but my lowered inhibitions came from something. Perhaps it was the reckless thought that if I fucked up this life, I'd do it better in the next. I didn't know. I thought of Brigid's warning and desperately wished the knowledge would appear on my tongue. But I looked deep into the eyes as emerald as the grass upon which she sat and said: "We'd both be happier and better off if I knew the answer to that question."

She chewed the inside of her cheek, considering.

I half expected her to ask about our first meeting.

I had a fleeting, wild fantasy wherein the night ended with her asking to leave her family and return with me to Hell. But instead, we settled into an odd, companionable silence. The small smiles she offered between her drinks almost carried the weight of pity, as if she felt sad for me.

I was reckless with Shala's life.

Eleni would have joined me, if given the chance. She'd been stolen before I'd been able to ask.

Yuka knew better. She saw a greater vision, a bigger purpose, and chose to return to the earth as a human.

And what of Caoimhe? I'd never spoken her name—not to her, anyway. Not on this side of the veil. I heard it on her son's tongue—her Little Rabbit. I heard it on her husband's lips, though he wasn't nearly as offensive of a presence as one might hope, given my desire to hate him. The man was kind and cared for both his wife and child in all the ways a human should. I heard her human name on the mouths of friends and villagers on more than one occasion.

But she hadn't asked mine.

She gathered her things into her basket and readied herself to leave before the moon's sliver dipped below the horizon. She fidgeted as if waiting for me to say something. Perhaps to ask her a favor. To request something. To beg her to stay.

"If I may......" I started.

She looked at me expectantly.

"Why 'rabbit'?"

The question caught her off guard. Her nose wrinkled, head shaking as if it were the most absurd thing she'd ever heard. "Is there a man born without a love for rabbits?" she laughed, tossing her hair back. "He may as well reject the stars."

We were Eros and Psyche once more, and Cupid's arrow pierced my heart.

To her, the words had meant nothing.

Obvious, unimportant, as common as breathing.

But Yuka had been right. Her mortal heart didn't possess the conscious thought of an immortal, but it tucked away things time and time again like a treasure hunt for only her and me. I snatched the diamond of her words and held it breathlessly against my chest as she walked away, a woman in wool abandoning her phantom in the moonlight.

*Stars.*

We wouldn't be lovers. Not in this life. I wasn't her savior. I wasn't her spirit guide. But I held tight from my place behind the shadows, noting every time she poured a glass of mead and left it on the windowsill, knowing it was for me.

Spring flowers, summer heat, autumnal leaves, and winter's snow came and went.

Every year on her birthday, she would return to the riverbank, and we would share a drink. She kept her health and fortune and was too clever to ask how or why she'd been chosen. Her words were a careful dance, and one I respected. Her message was clear: her obligation was to her child, and for him, she could love or serve no other.

"You'd never serve me," I'd chided quietly.

She'd smiled. "Then, you'd be a step up from motherhood."

I fought the answering smile. She was not born to be a mother, rather, became one as a product of her time and culture, and excelled within it. Perhaps she would not have chosen to give birth if her paths had been laid before her, but her Little Rabbit was here, nonetheless.

And while I could count my days with her on two hands, I learned as much about her story and mine as I had in every cycle before.

Brigid was right.

We had not been thrust together to learn a lesson.

We were history in the making.

# Chapter Eleven

**ANOTHER AND ANOTHER AND ANOTHER**

I melted into the silken luxury of royal silks, blankets, and pillows. I'd nearly forgotten what quality bedding felt like, given that I was laying in a bed I'd famously vacated. No one seemed to reject their crown with the same flourish as Hell's least grateful prince. I folded my hands behind my head, eyes open, but unfocused, as I gave myself a rare moment of solace in my room.

"Your Highness?" A quiet voice sounded from beyond the door to my palace rooms.

So much for my solace.

The royal chambers were ostentatious, which made walking to the door a chore. I sat up in bed and threw it open with the flick of a wrist.

"What?"

Two members of my father's legion stood in the doorway. He commanded seventy-two, with two thousand in each, all wispy, smoke-like beings, all eyes and shadow and bowing apologies. They hardly inspired the sort of trembling and fear one would expect of one hundred and forty-four thousand clad in weapons and tooth and armor when brute force was required, but for everything, a time and place. I preferred my legion work in whispers.

"Out with it."

"The King requests an audience," said one.

"Your sister is present," said the other.

The tight, thin line of my lips conveyed enough for the pair to scatter. Their message was not unexpected. I'd awaited an intervention for some time. I'd prepared myself for a larger discussion with my father.

Izi inserting herself further into the narrative, on the other hand?

It was a struggle to keep my fists unclenched and my expression unbothered as I made my way past the ancient architecture, beyond the fountains, through the dining halls and modern wings and galleys of such and such grandeur before I approached his throne room to the most horrid thing Hell had to offer in the loveliest package.

The Soul Eater.

The first emotion to replace my ire was loathing.

I hated the woman-adjacent horror who sat outside his office. She sat prettily behind a desk, though the tiny barrier was to make visitors feel comforted by a false sense of distance, rather than any sort of administrative duty. She was the most terrifying security the courts had to offer.

Her golden hair belonged in wheat fields, not on a living being. Her blue eyes should have been set in a doll's face, not on hers. She had the sort of innocence that tipped the scales beyond uncanny and into threatening. She was the absence of scent, of sound, of air. It was a quality of all Soul Eaters. Crafted by something from the Primordial Monster Realm and loyalty sworn to our court's royal family, she was of no direct threat to us. Blood oaths prevented her from turning her abilities on my father or me.

The spelled shackles did little to put me at ease.

"Your Highness." The Soul Eater, no name beyond her formal title, stood from her desk and clasped her hands in front of her pale blue gown before offering a curt bow. So ladylike. So unrepresentative of her ability to dislocate her jaw and prolong razor-sharp teeth and devour anything before her into utter annihilation, ending worlds and dynasties and any immortal being that hadn't attained the sovereignty of godhood.

Honestly, I needed to verify whether or not godhood would stop her, should her sworn chains one day break. Was she a god-killer?

I brushed past the Soul Eater, suppressing a shudder.

If the conversation between Izi and my father went south, I'd keep such deflecting questions prepared. It was never a bad idea to have a topic change or two at the ready.

I pushed open the double doors to see the figures poised beneath rows of opulent chandeliers. Izi was seated with uncertainty on a settee on the far side of the room. My father folded his wings behind him as if they'd just been flared in the heat of battle. Both of their rigid postures and tight expressions told me I'd interrupted a heated exchange. Izi's scent of amber and heat splashed against his pomegranate and spice the moment I stepped between them, as if I'd plunged my head beneath an ocean of perfume. The assault on the senses was almost too much after my prolonged time with the humans, but I was not the only one suffering.

My sister's tucked position suggested that she was on the losing end. Good. Whatever the fight, I was on my father's side.

"I was summoned?" I asked.

I had exactly one guess as to the topic at hand, and I didn't want to hear it. Apparently, my grace period had run out. It was time to defend myself, and I was in no mood.

Izi opened her mouth to speak, but my father went first.

"Word of your human has spread beyond our walls," he said. There was a sympathy in his voice that I didn't appreciate. I clasped my hands behind myself, widening my stance and planting my feet, but said nothing. He went on. "We've established relations with numerous pantheons. You've kept your word as emissary after our discussion. But prior to that? The realms who feel you tore through their people before dignifying them with a greeting? This was not the best way—"

Ah. This was the angle. I was brought into the kingdom to fulfill the obligations of a monarch, and my crown was ill-fitting? Sure. I could work with that.

"I disagree," I said coolly. "I was there in a way that posed no threat. They had a chance to see Hell in a companionable light."

"There's no power in what you've established," Izi snapped. "We look chaotic at best and weak at worst."

Our father shot her a silencing look. She'd clawed her way into our meetings, but would do well to remember which, between the two of us, was set to inherit the throne.

"This isn't about the other gods," I said. "Why don't the two of you come out and tell me what you've called me in to say: you don't care for my human."

My sister's terse laugh earned her a second silencing glare.

"If I'm the first to keep a human, do tell me," I said. "For it would be news to me."

He sucked his teeth. "Of course, you're not the first. Gods, demons, cryptids, fae…lore of such dalliances lives in infamy."

I'll admit, I was too offended to lean into deference. It wasn't my most respectful of moves, but I buffed my nails against the cloth pressed to my collarbones, then examined my handiwork as I recited text from the pantheon that had banished our kingdom. *"The sons of god found the daughters of men beautiful and took them for wives as they chose."*

Quoting a passage from the King of Heaven's book earned me a glare from them both.

"Angels falling in love with human women is why half of the dukes and counts and marquises in our realm were kicked out of Heaven in the first place. So please, lecture me as to why I am not permitted. Forbidden love is a pillar of our fall."

He lifted his hands as if soothing a wild horse, but whether the gesture was for me or to calm himself, I wasn't sure. "It's not that you have a human."

I clapped my hands together. "Excellent. Then, we're done here?"

Izi got to her feet. "Claiming a mortal is not the problem," she said. "It's that you have *one* human. And you're making choices that put her interest above Hell's."

I opened my mouth to respond.

Izi stamped a foot over my first syllable, speaking over me as she pushed. "The Hellenic pantheon turned a blind eye when their nymph wound up dead, but there isn't an immortal soul who doesn't point silent fingers at you. What was her crime? Seeing you with that girl? What was her name?"

I waved it away.

"Eleni. That was the one."

She must have caught the way my face tightened. She'd gotten to me and, from the way she relaxed her weight into one hip, berry-dark lips twisting up in a wicked, charcoal smile, she knew it.

"How do you..."

She sneered. "I could fill tomes with what you think I don't know."

I kept my expression bored, though it was merely for show. "Your kill count is as long as your body count, sister."

"Mortals!" she gasped. "I do not kill gods."

"You *can't* kill gods," I bit, planting a foot forward as I stepped toward her. "And a nymph hardly counts."

Candlelight from the chandeliers reflected her hate as her glare bore into mine.

My father cleared his throat. "Your sister makes a point, indelicate though it may be. Word continues to grow of your fixation on a singular mortal soul. The Hellenic pantheon has cause to retaliate, should they wish. The Celts and the Innuits—"

"With whom I've established good relations," I reiterated through my teeth.

"They are the exception," he allowed.

My sister's eyes narrowed. Black hair billowed behind her as she approached. "And if the bear god had attacked your human then? If he'd wanted her thrown into the sea? Would you have permitted it? Or would we have another dead god on our hands."

"If you have to invent a fictional scenario to prove your argument, it's a poor defense," I snapped back.

Our father regained control of the room. "Are we to expect that your newly established relations will hold their tongue if Heaven presses them for information? For weak spots? If they offer allyship? How confident are you in these 'ambassador missions' that cover your proclivities?"

Even Izi wrinkled her nose at his final question. Heaven had many tricks up its sleeve, but it would not side with a rival pantheon, no matter the cost. It had no allies.

"You threaten the realm," Izi said firmly.

Histrionics bored me. "Unless you know something I don't, find something to do with immortality beyond my eternal agitation."

They exchanged glances—an act that disquieted me more than I cared to admit.

"Do you?" My voice dropped. I pictured Brigid and her vague warning as I eyed them now. "What have you heard?"

Our father's expression was gentler. "We all have our role to play in the war. You are the heir to our throne, should I fall. As such, you have my trust. Let's put the issue to bed. We can do away with the sorts of rumors that come from other realms and their soothsayers. They aren't our citizens. We aren't beholden to their fates. Tell me what it is that you see in this soul, son. I'll listen. Perhaps if you could articulate your connection with this human..."

I wondered if he saw the pieces of me—a minute twitch of the eye, a tendon in my hand—that betrayed my reaction to the cavalier reference to Love. *This* human. *My* human.

I stood, Hell's Prince. The Hope of the Realm. The Kingdom's Future.

If the Celtic pantheon had shared an ominous vision, I had to believe they weren't the only one.

I didn't see her as a threat, a weapon, a crack in Hell's armor.

To me, she was simply *Love*. To articulate our connection in a way that would answer all questions and reassure the kingdom I left exposed?

A defeated huff came from the hollows of my lungs. "Let's hope for all Hell's sake that I can't."

# Chapter Twelve

**0 ADE**

Avirgin birth, they called it.

Word trickled down that Heaven was curiously divided on what it meant for the theology they dispersed among the humans, but the new host was a win for their realm, nevertheless. Heaven's King would receive the recognition, the energy, the worship, whether sources were to be believed, and their god had taken on mortal flesh, or if the presence was merely a divine teacher.

Hell saw what was coming.

The specifics were negligible.

Facts carried little weight with the faithful. Details and methods and practices were fuzzy among the humans in every pantheon. Intention was the only thing of consequence. It was the aqueduct that funneled the power to their deity.

Love was thirteen when the news of Heaven's development reached our realm.

It was another life on the surface. I weathered the side-eyes whenever I returned to my kingdom, then returned topside, remaining anonymous as I navigated the human realm. I hung behind the veil, helping her in whatever ways I could, as she grew up in a small Syrian village that did not lend itself to the presence of mysteriously white wildlife or marble-pale men. I heard the news at roughly the same time she did. It was mildly interesting, but it didn't change the way we lived our lives.

At least, not at first.

And something odd happened over the next century.

Stories of the now-dead teacher spread. Well, his death was under investigation and hotly contested, but for all intents and purposes, he no longer walked the earth.

He was the heir to Heaven's throne, as the rumors went.

The stories caught fire, the likes of which we'd never seen.

A man called Paul—born Saul of Tarsus, author of many famous letters, a human who loved the new Messiah, as he called him—believed the end was near. So near, in fact, that he was quite sure it would happen in his very lifetime. Word rippled amongst Heaven's mortals of a new message. The end of the world wasn't unique to their worldview. I had a handle on the cosmic Grand Finale and its comparative broad strokes, with or without the nuance. The Nordes had Ragnarök, Buddhists had Shambhala, the Hindu had Kalki's arrival. The similarities were an offensive stretch when connecting paradoxically opposite pantheons, save for a common theme: nothing would last forever.

Heaven procured the concept of Armageddon. In 96 ADE, John the Elder wrote the book of Revelation. In it, he declared that the world's end would be preceded by a figure whom he called the antichrist.

Lore rose and fell every day. Legends, myths, stories of gods, their children, and their prophecies, occurred by the hour.

This one was different.

There was a lure to it, an urgency, a seductive violence that turned stories of the humble carpenter-turned-teacher and his messages of love, charity, and acceptance, that took root among the kind and bloodthirsty alike.

The tension throughout Hell was palpable. The heavy silence as the breathless kingdom watched and waited. We didn't know what this would mean for the stalemate of our cold war, but the tides were turning. We had to be ready, whatever that meant.

Speculation regarding the world's end was fascinating and new. Guesses became accusations. Beliefs became wars. Heaven and Hell left the spiritual realm as Heaven's faithful took up swords, spilling blood across the land in the name of their god.

Some of Heaven's believers proposed the antichrist would be a political figure. Rome's next leader, perhaps. But given John's creative imagery of the Beast, lore took a strange, new shape.

This antichrist was to be the child of Satan, some said, though who or what 'Satan' was remained unclear. By definition, a satan is an adversary—anyone who stands opposed to the one in power.

Ba'al of the Phoenician pantheon was appropriated and bastardized as Beelzebub, one of many to be twisted and contorted as a lesser, as an opponent, rather than a deity from another pantheon.

Satans and devils of the emphatically lower-case noun variety found themselves with new, insulting monikers as time marched on. Sometimes one would be given descriptive titles, like the mocking bastardization of Baal's name, as the neighboring culture adopted his name and Ba'al became baal– a pile of dung in their language. Stripped of his dignity whenever the people spoke of the powerful Canaanite storm deity, they birthed "Lord of Flies" as a name for the Devil (now proper noun—a singular entity). Sometimes satans became demonized through other anomalous appropriations, like the fallen angel cast from their Heavenly King's grace, Lucifer. Azazel, literally translated as "scapegoat," was an autonomous entity until they shifted sin and its blame. Moloch, once known by the Canaanites for ideological sacrifice, such as giving up temptations, donating wealth, abandoning pleasures for the greater good, to a shameful bastardization of a once-beautiful practice. What was once known for its moral humility twisted throughout Semitic polytheism. A curse upon the deity's name came from the King of Heaven himself. Moloch's name was slandered. Pure offerings of self-denial became rumors of child sacrifice by the neighboring nations. Holy defamation swelled as a million brushstrokes painted the final image: every deity, entity, or adversary who stood in opposition of Heaven was conflated with this infamous "Satan."

And so, the merging continued.

Who, then, would be this electrifying enemy? Who would be worthy of the ever-growing hype as humans crackled with excitement at the very thought that their enemies might be tossed into the flame, punished through eternity? After all, who didn't want to see a nemesis squashed? And what better excuse than to say that such a sentence was divine, rather than twisted, unhealed human pleasure at another's suffering?

◆

As with all lore, it's hard to know where the story began.

Occasionally, prophecies come from a singular source, like the booming voice of a flaming angel to a shepherd on a starry night.

More often than not, it's the legion who spreads the word. A message disseminated between lords and gods and pantheons so quickly that it's challenging to know who started it or where it began.

And such was the whispered lore of the antichrist.

The Christ was born of a god and a virgin.

The antichrist, so they said, would be the spawn of Satan and his whore.

Hell's heart fell with collective emptiness as all eyes turned to me and the inextricable pull I'd had to one mortal soul from life to life to life.

I, the demon, and my human were to be their missing piece.

We were prophecy in the making.

◆

I'd never experienced panic or struggle like I did in the moment of seeing the global wheels turn. Pantheons at large understood Heaven's ever-growing expansion was a threat, and Hell was their only chance to save their people from colonization.

This god, this King of Heaven, did not respect borders. He was a war deity, and he was bent on conquering. He overthrew kingdoms, lands, peoples, and minds. Temples were destroyed, holy texts were burned, priestesses were slaughtered, and for the first time, we were united against a common enemy.

The war was no longer Heaven versus Hell.

If the King of Heaven had his way, it was Heaven versus everybody.

My days of speeches and diplomacy were coming to an end. Centuries of building connections across the globe had built to a moment we'd hoped would never come.

I never traveled unarmed, but a visit to Hell's armory

ensured that whether I needed steel to slay a member of the fae, or something stronger to end a god, I was ready.

Hell's Prince was now on the frontlines. The kingdom braced ourselves for our new reality: life would never be the same for demons. Now, it was kill or be killed.

Distant gods allied themselves with Hell at unprecedented rates.

Inter-deity relations thrived like never before.

My father was overjoyed. He looked at me with new eyes, ones that brimmed with hope and pride and compassion. My human, once a source of royal shame, was now Hell's greatest treasure.

I felt as though I was gripping at the thinnest part of a waterfall as I tried to take hold of a flimsy prophecy, to battle it, to fight against it. I didn't want it. I didn't believe it. I wouldn't accept it.

Though I'd loved my human fiercely before, my need to protect her expounded a thousandfold. Prior to this, I'd feared her exposure to the world. Now, her soul was left to ravenous wolves, and many of them had fates in mind far worse than death.

The gods had their prophesized demon.

The only thing they needed was to make his human a whore.

# Chapter Thirteen

**112 ADE, 140 ADE, 149 ADE, 155ADE, 156 ADE**

My knuckles were bloodless from centuries of gripping the throne, unmoving.

I would not participate. She was safer if she was no longer my human.

I wouldn't let them turn her into a bargaining tool, a method for leverage, a pawn.

I had remained in Hell for hundreds of years before, and I'd do it again. I'd shove Love aside. Every excruciating minute of every day was spent in relentless rejection of the prophecy and its gods-dammed ramifications.

Superstitious deities had banded together to ruin my existence and the lives of my human? I wouldn't let them play the role of puppeteer. Trafficking Love into unwilling cycles of whoring was fruitless if there was no demon to impregnate her.

The only thing more painful than staying away from her would be knowing I was responsible for her destruction.

Without me, she was just another woman, free to live a normal, mundane life.

I would grind my teeth into a pulp.

I would clench my jaw so tightly that the knot never released.

I would clutch the arms of my royal seat until my fingers cracked the stone beneath them.

I would remain among thick velvet curtains and marble pillars and latticed windows of my tomb. I would glower at feasts, each forced bite turning to ash in my mouth, as I paid no mind to the world of men. I would hold audiences with ambassadors, carry out my duties, and not sully myself with the ways of mortals.

I. Would. Not. Let. This. Prophecy. Happen.

◆

True to my word, I remained amidst the cities and incense and royal obligations of Hell.

I did not return to the surface for my human's next life, nor for her death. I'd hoped no one would identify her. That they wouldn't know which soul had come and gone from the mortal plane. I'd prayed my secret of the mortal with the mother-of-pearl aura would remain locked in the vaults of Athena and Nanook and Brigid. I remained in the underworld, shoulders forward, face a mask of indifference when news came of her death.

It would have been a mistake for anyone or anything who crossed my path to report who she was, or how she'd died. I would give them nothing to work with. My apathy was my gift to her. The forced cold of an uncaring façade would give her a fighting chance at normalcy, untainted by gods and their folly.

Word came again.

A member of my legion—the fractal of my energy charged with my bidding—heard the word of Love and her passing disseminated among Hell's citizens. Knowing word was on its way, they opted to tell me before someone of higher rank arrived to provoke me with the information.

Twenty-nine this time. A significant number to me alone. My lip twitched as I thought of the Celts, but I forced my expression to remain neutral as the trembling legion told me how she'd died. From the creature's shiver, I knew it expected to die for what it said.

And it was right to be afraid.

The torture it described was unspeakable, quartered and drawn in the Carpathian Mountains. They spared no details when painting a picture of the throng that had surrounded her, nor of the terror she'd felt, the things they'd done that made her inhumane execution a comparative relief.

I would look bored. I would politely listen. I would dismiss the servants. I would not let them know how I seethed within.

And yet...

My covert visits to the mortal realm to end the lives of all involved in ways that would make Czars of Torture tremble. The general of the mutilation realm would have taken notes of the things I did, of the ways I made responsible parties suffer.

My retribution was in secret, as apathy was my outward expression.

The message to the Slavic deities who allowed her death on their soil was bloody.

But they weren't meant to know it was me. It was war. It was an ambush. It was a usurper. It was someone else. Something else. Hundreds of witnesses could attest to how profoundly unbothered I'd been each time news came of her passing. Surely, I had nothing to do with the slaughter.

Until her third death.

She was only eight years old.

"*Don't shoot the messenger*" is a trite platitude, relevant only to those who've never had to watch a messenger report atrocities about the one they loved. A messenger was meant to be a neutral party. There was nothing neutral about their words. No unbiased third party could return to Hell's palace and walk to my room and say the things they'd said and expect to live.

Killing the messenger, as it turned out, was a mistake on more accounts than one.

It hadn't been difficult to guess that I'd been responsible for the entrails strewn about those responsible for the death of her previous cycle. Murdering the legion who'd reported on this death in front of infernal courtiers was the confirmation they needed: Hell's Prince was not indifferent.

Hell had an established weakness, and no matter how I tried to hide it, its Prince was coming apart at the seams.

Whether Izi had legions of her own stationed outside my room or if she'd heard rumors of my mental state and responded, I had no idea. She intercepted me as I burst from my bedchambers. She shouldn't have been in my palace at all. She lived with her mother, Queen of Shadows, in the Nightmare Realm. It was threatening in name only. The nightmare belonged to anyone who stood against them. She, her mother, and the citizens of their court thrived within. But as she looked at me with soot and coal in her black eyes, I positioned myself as an enemy welcoming nightmares.

"This is a mistake," she said, jumping to her feet before I'd turned to address her.

I stormed past the couch on which she'd been lounging. I didn't want to know how long she'd been there or what she'd heard. I needed to speak to the King.

"Don't tell our father," she urged as if she heard my thoughts.

As much as I hated it, her words gave me pause. It was like a physical tripwire brought me to a halt. I regarded my sister, pinch and curve and smoke and shadow, as the First Daughter of Succubi looked at me with true desperation in her eyes. She looked at me with eyes that understood the mortal realm better than I could hope. Despite my better judgment, I remained planted in the hall. The wispy tendrils of her hair coiled and vanished as she stepped toward me.

She clasped her hands like a monk in prayer. "You're standing on the precipice of something terrible," she said. "If you involve him, you'll throw Hell's weight behind your cause and validate their efforts. He will take your side if you stand with this human. Do you see what that means for the realm? We'll be at war with too many battlefronts to count. We cannot win."

I looked down the hall, thrusting my hand to its empty corridors as if her opal soul shimmered in its vacant space. "Because leaving her alone has served us?"

"It has," Izi insisted.

My jaw dropped open.

"You are suffering because you still care," she pressed. "You opened yourself to human emotion, and it can be glorious. I am not without sympathy, brother. I adore sipping from the human cup. But you cannot drink to the point of drunkenness. You've lost yourself."

"But they—"

"They're hurting *her*," she insisted. "Not you. Stop tipping your hand. Every time you react, you give them power."

"And who is *them*."

She threw up her hands, gesturing to the palatial ceilings as if every pantheon rested atop the pillars. "Everyone! You've handed Hell's power to every god, every immortal, even every man who dares push you in one fragile area. If you hadn't slaughtered those men—"

"I didn't—"

"Your lies insult me," she bit. Her voice contained the snarl I'd heard in wolves and polar bears from my time in the Arctic. She bared her teeth as she said, "You can't hear of that mortal's death without leaving a massacre in your wake. The rumors might have been extinguished in a lifetime or two if you hadn't reacted. Three, perhaps, but no more than that. Each retaliation buys your precious mortal's soul ten more murders, ten more lifetimes ending in torture, ten more—"

I broke her locked gaze, jerking my head to the side. "Stop it."

"They're drawing you out, and you're falling for it in spectacular fashion." She planted two small hands on my chest and pushed with the force of a queen. "You are the only one who can stop this. You've doomed our realm. Let her go, or—"

"Or what?"

Silence became its own shadow. It was a lingering darkness that puddled at our feet. After a quiet eternity, she said, "Or become what they hope, and give us a champion."

The fight leached from me. My arms fell to my side as I looked at her with true disbelief.

"I don't believe it either." Her dismay was a breathy whisper. "But they do. Every god, every fae, everyone who wants Hell to act and take down Christendom and its cockroach-like infestation. Those of us in the Cradle of Civilization were the first to fall. The Hellenic gods? Their Roman counterparts? All deities too powerful to believe something like this could happen to them. Rome's only mission was to conquer, and for years they did it under Ares and his banner. Now?" With a snap of her fingers, she gestured to the wide, dark nothing. "Heaven and its armed militia marches on the regions Rome once claimed, destroying temples, pillaging holy sites, erasing every holy book and name and practice that doesn't belong to Heaven. Everywhere they go, the region's mortals are forced to abandon their gods and convert against the tip of a blade."

I grinded my teeth so hard I nearly felt a crack.

Her voice pitched, hands animated as her intensity swelled. "Deities need to hear from Hell. The gods have a vested interest in this prophesized antichrist. They see you and your human as the conduit for their grand hope. Their belief is more valuable than any truth."

"...they..."

I hated it.

Whether I believed it or not was irrelevant. The world was acting upon it, each step manifesting the reality upon two unwilling participants.

"We're talking about *everything*, Amagi. Not just the mortal world, but the countless realms while our sworn enemy usurps their power. Heaven's reach continues to expand. Do you know what this means for us?"

I knew my sister well enough to understand that this was not a dialogue. I didn't bother speaking, knowing she'd scramble over me with her next outburst and finish her thought.

She tensed, practically wiggling with excitement. "They're all looking to Hell, brother! Every pantheon has turned its eye to us. They see our value. They need us. And what's more: they see your human's role in ending Heaven's colonization of their land."

My silencing hiss did nothing to stop her.

She leaned in. "They're provoking you to return to her."

"And if I do?" I bit off the question.

Her small shoulders lifted. She looked at me with too-large eyes as if all her fight had evaporated. "Don't. Not unless you're ready to commit and give them what they demand. Birth the child that will end the world."

I shut my eyes.

After a long sigh, she said, "I know you've already decided."

My brow furrowed. My eyes opened, locked onto hers as I said, "I won't facilitate their superstitions. I won't be a pawn in this lore."

"If you return to her," Izi said, "you won't have a choice."

And Izi won.

Her victory lasted six mortal years—a little more than a week in Hell.

This messenger expected to die, and I was almost sorry to kill him.

Almost, but not quite.

He had to receive the report about the things that had been done to a child, internalize them, walk to my room, and report them while expecting he had no culpability. It was ludicrous to see him as innocent.

It would have been unfair to kill the messenger alone, however.

I found the one who'd given the report and smiled while he'd backed into the nearest wall. He'd lifted his hands in a placating gesture, doing his best to remain amicable until I punched through his chest cavity, puncturing his sternum, grabbing his spine, and ripping it from his body. I'd hoped for a little more relief when his lifeless form slumped around my arm, but there was no satisfaction.

And then there was the moment that turned me into the true Prince of Hell.

I realized then, that my life was not a three-act play. There was, in fact, an encore. And the fourth act would be bloody.

I was the demon of lore, the thing of fangs and poison and horror. I was the bringer of torment, the final tribulation, the pain from which they'd never awaken.

She was four months old.

One hundred and twenty-one human days.

She'd been alive for fewer than three thousand hours.

They wanted to draw me out? They succeeded.

A mortal could die of exposure, of lack of nutrition, of disease, of failure to thrive.

These were tragic, and I would have mourned, and I probably would have killed her parents and the village doctor and anyone else who'd failed her, but they were not unspeakable horrors that deserved true wrath.

Some things are too heinous for repetition even in the mind's eye. Maybe that's why I couldn't be bothered to monologue, to explain myself, to reiterate what or why or precisely how they'd earned my fury, but I made Hell's stance for the kingdom.

Mortals were not alone to blame.

I razed their gods, their fae, their creatures of night as I raked them over the coals, declaring open season on anyone who touched my human from that moment forward. Pantheons held council to which we were not invited. I would give them a war on all fronts.

Summits were called. Gods and their beings gathered from all corners to hold counsel with my father, demanding accountability against his terrorist of a son. I'd committed unforgivable crimes to which retribution was demanded.

Hell's courts united, begrudgingly as it were, as the realm prepared for battle.

◆

Casualties were expected in war, however, and the enemy of one's enemy is quite famously their friend.

Those I killed—human and immortal alike—were unfortunate, so word came down. Losses were tragic, but they were nothing compared to prospective victory. It was noise, an acceptable loss, if Heaven fell. If the Prince and his human facilitated the prophecy, all would be forgiven.

The disgusting summit of minds and powers made it sound so simple.

My punishment was worse than my head on a spike. I was free on one condition: I return to my human, and I play my part in this unholy legend.

The screaming matches within my father's throne room were privy to none but Hell's innermost sanctum. No fight had divided the realms like this, and the courts cracked at our disregard, our selfishness—*my* selfishness.

All was forgiven, so long as I brought about the end of the world.

Go back to the surface, he advised. Embrace the human, just as I desired. Find her. Woo her. Love her. Together, create a child of two realms; one who might take down the enemy that united us all.

They were wildly unsatisfying terms.

"Son," my father had said beneath his breath. "You will never receive a proposition better than this. The rest is on you, and I will stand beside you. It's this, or your head."

"Death or torture?" I'd repeated, the hate of my words

sticking to the back of my throat like tar. "That's meant to satisfy me? This treaty is an insult. It's a spit in the face. It's—"

I could feel my sister's wrath from across the room. She stood, and it was enough to make me bite off my tirade in a snarl.

The Queen of Nightmares, Mother of Succubi, must have had opinions of her own, but unless we learned she had *not* sent her daughter to speak on her behalf, I had to assume the worst. The Nightmare Court, as with the others that crafted Hell's many factions, preferred the shadows, knowing they'd prevail from Hell's victory one way or another. The other pantheons saw their active role in conquest when it came to triumphing over a pantheon expanding with rapid colonization, appropriation, and erasure. If I held the key to the global tyrant's undoing, they'd work with me.

And that's how I won the war of gods while feeling like I hadn't won anything at all.

# Chapter Fourteen

**TEN INFERNAL MINUTES**

The impending conclave was a tomb of marble and power. The coliseum of black, glistening stone, shimmering, ornately-carved seats that could fit tens of thousands, eternal lanterns flickering blue at every outpost, had been crafted for precisely this moment.

Our open veil snapped and pulsed with newcomers far and wide. A Celtic goddess clothed in fire and sunlight. A four-faced god of Canaan standing twenty cubits tall. A Grecian clutching a bolt of lightning. Bare-chested, staff-clutching androgynous gods with white loin clothes and animal heads. A god for this, a fae for that, a cryptid for the other.

Demonic attendants rushed to meet newcomers from around the globe.

Electric slits continued to snap and pop as welcomed guests opened gashes in our realm.

After all, every pantheon was invited, save for one.

Sharks can smell a single drop of blood from a quarter of a mile away. Cut yourself on a boat near shore and pray for death. Human noses showed a shocking evolution to the trait, with their senses picking up the geosmin of fresh rain at concentrations of less than ten parts per trillion. Some of us, in our idlest of chats regarding the mortals, wondered if evolution helped them find fresh water, should their gods forsake their barest of needs.

And then there were the gods and the suffocating perfume of their overlapping scents.

"Can someone bring me a cloth?" A member of my legion appeared at my side an instant later, fresh linen in hand. Its vapor took the form of a temporary hand as it extended the drooping rectangle. "No, I'm sorry. What I meant was: can someone bring me a cloth soaked in enough opium to render me unconscious until this comes to an end."

The stadium commissioned for the shiver-inducing meeting of storm, love, torture, soothsaying famine, debauchery, seaworthiness, conquest, and borderline innumerable major and minor deities whispered, cried, sat, stood, clustered as they waited.

Gods brought their energy, ranging from hate, lust, raw fury, to the sudden domesticated urge to find a soft animal and stroke its fur while it purred in your lap.

My legion crackled with uncertainty, which I didn't appreciate.

There were no double agents, no mistrust, when it came to a demon and his legion. They sat in a space that vibrated between self-possession and lack of sentience, as each demon's army of smoke and shadows belonged to only its leader.

My bed chambers were crowded as Hell and its royal members awaited our unholy symposium.

Smoke-like figures changed me in and out of robes and royal attire until I lost my patience. I would wear black pants, a black shirt, and a structured long, black woolen coat jacket tailored mid-thigh. Unfortunately, I didn't have the luxury of being left alone with my legion.

Pale blue dress, blonde hair, doll eyes, and the Soul Eater's rows of razor-sharp teeth breezed through my room to secure entries and exits. A gray-skinned wall of muscle and metal had been posted outside of my door.

So many had paraded through my room that I may have missed the newcomer were it not for her stark contrast to the Soul Eater's sky-blue gown as they bumped shoulders during the golden-haired nightmare's exit. The Soul Eater blinked her large eyes with genuine surprise that anyone dared to touch her. The newcomer, on the other hand, didn't stop. She treated the exchange with seeming unimportance.

Before this moment, I hadn't met a god or demon, royal or otherwise, who had no regard for the Soul Eater. An imp—one of Hell's citizens—had worked her way into a high-ranking position through competency and the rare sixth sense of social intuition.

Ruby skin, black lips, dark hair slicked into a tight bun, and a forked tail slithering through the slit in her sharp attire made her a splash of color in a brooding room of black floors, black walls, black hearts. She stood far enough behind me that I could make eye contact with her by glancing into the mirror.

Her deadpan, hovering presence was one more irritation on an already-unstable trash heap of chaotic decisions and tenuous relationships.

"I need a few of your minutes, Your Highness."

I stood in front of the full-length mirror, casting a glance over my shoulder to where she hovered.

Hell had created a role, then promoted the imp to oversee it, specifically to prepare me for today's events. She was a speech-writer, a crafter of outward appearances, a reputation ambassador, and today, more than anything, she was a pain in my ass.

"Prince." She repeated the prompt, but not the tone. Her eyes slitted. She put a hand on her hip. It was the sixth time in under twenty minutes that she'd called for my attention. "I'm Tzipporah. And I'm going to need you to take that temper down a notch if you plan to make it through the day."

"For fuck's sake, what?"

I looked at her reflection over my shoulder while buttoning my woolen coat, running fingers through my hair and readying myself for the final moments before Hell made history.

"First, I'm glad you took my advice on the event's attire. I sent it down the pipeline a few hours ago. Rigid, royal—"

The blotch of red remained over my shoulder in the reflection while I straightened my outfit. "Get to it...I want to say... Uzella?"

"Tzipporah. We met roughly six seconds before you misremembered my name. It's in your best interest to pull it together and do four things for me."

I choked on my laugh. I turned my back on my mirror, if only to gawk at her. "*You* need me? Tell me, imp, how can I serve *you* in this unprecedented, history-in-the-making assembly of global deities as I get up to defend why I've dragged a human into the end of the world?"

Tzipporah was unruffled. Bored, even. Her scroll dropped to her side as she sank her weight into one hip.

"Yes." She put her hand on the popped hip. "For me."

The kettle of my irritation had begun to whistle. I saw the

shift in her expression as she watched my internal scream, no matter how level I kept my tone. "The implication that I, as Hell's Prince, would report to an unknown imp on the most important day of our legacy is an insult I hadn't expected. Did my sister send you?"

"Your father," she said, still a mask of indifference. "He believes in my impartial delivery, even if he isn't privy to this particular council."

"Thanks for the vote of no confidence, Father," I mumbled.

Her black-painted lips twitched. "This is a 'lose to use' ratio, Your Highness. I have a gift we can both use, and nothing I care about can be taken, should you retaliate. Strip me of my title, should I fail, I have none. Should I provoke you, would you murder my partner and children? My singleness precedes you. Kill my parents? My family? I was an orphan on the glass-shattered sidewalk of an infernal orphanage. Kill me? I'm an imp in a kingdom that claims to stand against Heaven, yet who is the highest in power?"

My entire body clenched, tensed, readied, against the insult.

"The King of Hell is a fallen angel. Half of the demons with a royal title are fallen angels. Heaven still has a vice grip down here. You were born in Hell, and spared from Heaven's stink, Your Highness. So, listen to me, or don't. We'll both die if I'm wrong. And I'm not interested in dying today."

I felt my brows knit. My shoulders moved. My lips flattened. My fingers twitched at my cuffs.

"Say your piece, then leave."

"Before you roll your eyes—" She was right. I'd begun to cuff my jacket as she caught my expression. She continued, "We're sure you love your kingdom. But the lasting, respectful, loyal, deeply-felt love you have for Hell is at risk against the erratic, passionate, dangerously irrational love for your human.

"You hate the politics and strategy of it all—no, don't bother denying it. You're an unwilling participant. So, don't do the political song and dance for you. Do it for me. Because I'm about to help you get what you want, while appeasing a room of vultures from dozens of pantheons calling for your head."

My eyes narrowed.

"Or don't. Let them kill the Prince of Hell. Let them murder your human. Never see her again. See her, but only in secret, and watch as they catch you. Ignore your human, and see which gods are willing to risk their wellbeing if it means drawing you out of Hell. Be with her, love her, and see how they use it against you. We can fix that here and now."

I don't think I'd had a staring contest before this moment.

The imp relished the unblinking challenge. Her moxie won me over. I relented. "You think you've solved it?"

Tzipporah exhaled. She lifted her tablet. "There are four things I need you to do."

She awaited a second wave of obstinance. Instead, I gestured for her to continue.

"First, you offer no apologies. Not at any point. Not to any god. Not to any other members of the Infernal Court. Not even to your father. They want you to feel like you're on trial. We can't let them have that."

A strong start, I had to admit. I headed to the desk and motioned for her to take a seat. She gave the chair the same bored look she'd given me earlier. I perched on the wooden ledge and nodded for her to continue.

"Second, you'll acknowledge the prophecy. It doesn't matter how you say it. Tell them you've heard the legends. Tell them you understand the lore. Explain that you're on the same page, conceptually. Find those most affected by this new religion and its spread: the Phoenicians and their usurped land, the Romans and their smashed temples. The Gauls, Franks, and Bretons have been watching this monotheistic faith spread. Everywhere it goes, it tears down temples, builds houses of worship, leaves robed monks, and erases centuries of power and tradition from the regional deities. Look them in the eye and tell them you understand their outrage. They've watched pantheons fall and they're afraid."

I looked toward my chamber door as if staring into the stadium.

"Who's out there?"

"All of them," she said. "The angry. The fallen. The usurped."

I drummed my fingers against the desk. "So...eight, nine pantheons?"

"*All* of them," she repeated. "A representative from the Shinto pantheon, an ambassador from the Orisha, a spokesperson for the Mayans. I even believe Nanook is in the audience, should you spot an enormous bear."

She continued to list gods and names, the likes of which I'd never heard. Those personally impacted by the new religion's spread, like our friends in Canaan and the enraged Grecians, had come for their pound of flesh. Deities from other corners of the world, or at least the appointed fae spokesperson from their pantheon, were a surprise.

"What's the third thing?"

She looked down at her scroll, then turned it around for me to see.

Five blocky words took up the entire page.

Tzipporah anticipated my visceral response. She took a casual step out of the way as I pushed off from the desk.

I had one low, growling, argumentative syllable out before she lifted a finger.

She, a Hell-born imp with no title, no family, and nothing to lose, shushed her Prince. My anger evaporated, if from sheer amusement. She was all backbone, no panache. It was winsome as fuck. If I survived the day, I'd give her a full-time job as my court advisor, solely for the knowledge that she'd have the biggest balls in the palace.

Finger still lifted, she said, "Let me finish."

At least I was walking into my execution with the coolest imp in Hell. "Give them what they want. That's your plan?"

"This religion they fear—their Christ—it came with a predetermined adversary. Gods went from revered and thriving, to discarded and banned overnight. We've never seen anything like it. They're clinging to this legend—"

I scoffed. "It's barely obscure folklore."

"They're clinging to this *lore*," she amended, though the irritation as she emphasized the supplemented word was enough to win me back, "because it is the hope they need. It doesn't matter if it's lore, mythos, or prophecy. They have no options without it. So, go. Be with her. We all know what she looks like, now, anyway."

Every muscle in my body contracted in a visible flinch.

"Her soul has quite the aura. Out of, gods almighty do they breed, how many are there now?" She folded her arms, tapping her foot as her gaze went up and to the side. "Three hundred million? You couldn't have picked an emerald soul? A sapphire aura? It had to be this cloud-bright shimmer? That's on you."

I took to pacing. "So, I *am* on trial."

"No. And that brings me to my final point."

My steps slowed. I stopped a few feet away from Tzipporah, meeting her eyes. "Get on with it."

She went to the desk and slipped her crimson fingers around the scroll. She rolled it tightly, then stuck it into a compartment somewhere on her back—a bag, a pocket, for fuck's sake maybe she was holding it with her forked tail—before settling against the wooden lip, just as I had mere moments before.

She shrugged. "Kill them."

A single, breathy chuckle. I wasn't wrong to like her. "Excuse me?"

Only one shoulder lifted and dropped this time. "Get out there. Remain unapologetic. Tell them you understand their fear. Reassure them that you'll be with your human from this point forward, as your presence in her life is your wish as much as theirs. And then explain that, now that you've complied, anyone who hurts your human will face whatever wrath you see fit."

I pressed my fingertips into my temples. "They won't..."

"They will. Have everyone press their fingertip to the treaty before they leave."

"Tzipporah, not to be rude, but—"

"But I'm just an imp." She headed toward the door. She yanked it open with one swift motion, then plunged her hand into the pool of shadow within the hallway before someone standing guard handed her an object. She jerked her head toward the corridor for me to follow, then disappeared into the hall.

I was several paces behind by the time I reached the hall. I could scarcely make out the flick of Tzipporah's forked tail in the torchlight as I jogged to catch up to her.

I followed her, as if she was the palace's resident and I was the stranger. She remained silent as we crossed the length of the grounds.

We heard the cacophony of noises long before reaching the stadium.

Perfumes, oils, musk, inborn fragrance, handheld incense, balm, hit me like a wall. Too many gods, too many smells, too many sounds, too much energy, too many beings who didn't belong in Hell.

I was suddenly grateful for Tzipporah's smooth gait as she led us to the dark chute with one dim light at the end of the tunnel. Through there, we'd reach the stadium. Through this tunnel, specifically, I'd bypass the audience and march directly to the center, alone and on display.

"Ready, Prince?"

I shifted my jaw from side to side. "I hate this."

Her apathy cracked for the barest of moments as she gave me a glimpse at underlying amusement. At last, it was time for me to see what she'd retrieved from the hall before marching me to Hell's funeral.

The object remained behind her back. "Do me a favor."

"To one day walk in the shoes of someone with your boldness..."

She procured the object. A black, thorny ringlet. A crown.

I took it from her, frowning at the circle.

"It's an emblem for them." She waved to the nebulous *others*. "Their prophet wore one for his martyrdom. It was brown, earthy, and—"

"And I'm no martyr."

Babbling languages splashed over one another, a river of energy splashing down the hall as the throng awaited me.

I looked at the circlet, then back at the imp. I settled it onto my forehead, unflinching as a thorn bit into the flesh at the crown of my head.

"Kill 'em," I said.

Her smile was bigger this time, though her teeth remained behind her tightly shut black lips. "Give them Hell."

# Chapter Fifteen

**TWENTY INFERNAL MINUTES**

"A virus is spreading."

The spotlight made it challenging to look into the eyes of the gods who stared back. A splotch of white caught my eye as I scanned the audience, each slow, careful step turning me until I could soak in the sheer scope of attendance.

Tzipporah was right. Nanook had come to hear what Hell had to say.

"Some of us existed before time. Conceptual, nebulous power shimmered in the nothingness before the first mortal atom exploded. My father, the King, was one such being. His song of worship became one of equality, of independence, of freedom, long before the first mortal fish flopped upon a muddy bank. We've carved out places for ourselves in their world. We sliced up Pangea, then partitioned the continents that followed. We found our people. We discovered the power of worshippers. We sampled the glory, the flavor, the heartache, the pleasure, the newness of mortality when we made a name for ourselves among the humans."

The stillness, given the staggering power contained in one room, was unsettling. They offered me silence. Not even an answering murmur.

A tickle at my brow distracted me. A finger went to my forehead as I wiped the offending liquid from my skin, then inspected the tar-black liquid on my finger. I stared down at what the crown had done, and it was my turn to smile.

"The faith that threatens it has chosen an emblem who was murdered for his message. He taught peace, charity, and acceptance. He destigmatized the woman who sold her body, holding her as she washed his feet with her tears, her perfume, and her hair. He yelled at those who claimed to be holy. He flipped tables in the temples of the immoral. He advocated for kindness toward foreigners, hospitality for strangers, and told the wealthy to give away all of their money, believing that no human with riches was capable of morality."

Another smile, though this one was born of sadness. "Our Kingdom, Hell, was born out of a fight for fairness. For equality. For respect. We would not be subjugated. We would not be slaves. As such, I don't think anyone in our realm sees their scapegoat, their teacher, as a nemesis. These thorns I wear today don't mock their sigil. But the wounding crown does come with a message: you made a martyr out of your champion. Hell has a martyr of its own."

◆

An ocean of sound lapped at me from all sides. Uproarious applause, shouts of victory— premature celebrations of those who thought they'd get something for nothing. Swirls of starlight, golden glows, turquoise and feathers, gnashing teeth, animal heads atop chosen mortal torsos, metallic shimmers, wings, smoke, and countless other shapes, sights, and sounds awaited me.

I'd done the impossible. Everything, everyone, from everywhere. Worlds collided as the far reaches of known reality and beyond broke barriers to attend my proclamation: nothing in this world or the next came for free.

I hadn't prepared for this speech, nor did I need to.

Slow, rotating steps allowed me to drink in the holy gathering.

In their silence, I spoke the only truth I knew.

"Friends, new and old. Our welcome has been cut short. Many of us were robbed of the luxury of meeting under times of peace. War is at our door. Some of us are already living the smoldering ruins of this new reality. Powerful gods have been overthrown, threatened, shoved into corners."

Greek and Roman gods spat, muttered, sneered in heated agreement. Heads across the stadium watched their reaction, bracing for what came next.

"The King of Heaven outpaced us when he adapted to culture. He found a new avenue for his war before we knew what happened. And right now, he's winning."

Pregnant, choking silence descended upon the divine throng.

I plucked the crown of thorns from my head.

"We're immortal. Our hubris kept us from considering how many ways a god can die without being killed. We didn't even realize we were at war. After two thousand years of toying with humans, flourishing in his role among his people, watching over bloodied weapons and overflowing graves, he turned his sights on something new. The Kingdom of Judah defeated high gods across the map whether or not he bothered to lift a sword."

A dissonant reaction from the crowd.

Agreement. Questions. Anger.

My eyes adjusted as I peered past the beam of light into the shadows encircling the stadium in time to see a flare of black wings. The King of Hell abandoned the ornate throne carved to accommodate his wings. He got to his feet, turning on the crowd behind him.

They were in our house.

*And*, I reminded myself, *I was not on trial*.

I spotted a blue-skinned man with an ornate, feathered crown forced to resemble a hummingbird. Huitzilopochtli, the Aztec god of war, had left his throne in the lush jungle for this meeting, despite the oceans that separated our mortal territories. He realized I was peering directly into his eyes and held my gaze. A feathered serpent flicked its tongue beside him.

Their winged snake had a gift shared by few in each pantheon.

Their god could see the future.

Across the stadium's sandy floor, shrouded in darkness halfway up the terraced seats, my father settled back into his throne, nodding for me to go on.

Years ago, I'd yelled at Izi and my father in his hall, demanding to know if they'd heard something I had not. Now when I scoured the stands, I searched for the faces of gods known for their power to peer into the future.

Every present pantheon in attendance had brought their prophet.

They knew what was coming.

I let the knowledge empower me. My chest swelled.

"Maybe this new faith has yet to touch your region. Perhaps you're here out of politeness, or curiosity, or to delight in the suffering of the fallen. But..." Another slow rotation as I spotted other unfamiliar pairs—entities who'd never interacted with Hell before this day. I recognized them through reputation only as I spotted gods of the rainforest, of the dunes, of the snow. Their king or queen of battle, each accompanied by their soothsayer.

"You already know."

The eerie silence returned. My eyes unfocused.

"That's why you've come. The deity we face isn't just conquering, he's colonizing. Your gods of guidance, those with premonitions, those who directed your actions as they peered into the horrors to come..." With an open hand, I motioned to the Aztec deities.

"This virus has spread from the Cradle of Civilization to North Africa, to the Mediterranean, and northward. I've spent more than one hundred mortal years on the ice of the Bering Strait. It will take centuries, a millennium, even, for this infectious faith to poison the people, sully the temples, and overthrow the gods across the sea. And yet Huitzilopochtli has attended today's conclave. Whatever Quetzalcóatl has seen, showed them the future. This faith, this sickness, it may not have reached your pantheon yet, but..."

I was able to ignore the spotlight altogether as I made yet another slow rotation, this time truly seeing how many immortal prophets, oracles, seers had come.

"You already know."

I planted my feet as my circle came to its end.

If they had seen me and my human together, they wouldn't have needed to arrive, to push me into the legend, to beg for Hell to play its role in overthrowing the rapidly-spreading faith.

Their future had told them that, whether tomorrow or a thousand years from now, this new god would be at their doorstep. Jerusalem's war deity was certain, and as such, his future had solidified. He would keep fighting. He would keep winning.

As of yet, I'd remained undecided. As such, no visions soothed their panic as they watched their gods, their people, their kingdoms fall with no one to challenge Heaven's King.

They were here because they needed the prophecy to be real.

My performance had come to an end. There had been no cries for accountability. No one had arrived to see my head roll for what I'd done on their soil.

I was their only hope.

I could work with that.

I rallied my vestiges of diplomacy and made my final proclamation. "This is our first time meeting, but it won't be our last. We're united behind a common enemy. They have their virgin birth between a god and the purest of his mortals. You want your demon and his—" I stopped short of the word.

*The antichrist would be born of a whore.*

My expression flickered. Through the shadow, I saw my father learn against the ornate arm of his throne. His elbows rested on his knees, fingers over his lips, as he waited to see if his son's next words would save Hell, or damn them all.

"She is my human." I shot a scathing look to the top of the stadium where a single Slavic deity had sequestered himself far from the rest of the pantheon. "*Mine.*"

The war deity's lips pulled back in a snarl.

Mine split as well, in a grin, as my speech reached its climax.

"I'll remain at her side in the lifetimes that follow. I'll play my part in this prophecy. On one condition."

The babble of disquieted whispers and muttered objections were expected. But this was the nature of compromise. Everyone loses.

"I return to my human, and in return, none of you touch

her. Not in this cycle. Not in the next. Never. You, your people, your gods, will not bring harm to my human."

The hush was cord-taut as they waited for the inevitable *but*.

I adopted Tzipporah's cool, smiling apathy.

"If harm befalls her at your behest—if you or anyone in your realm orchestrates pain, torture, death, or the cruelty you've attempted to lure me out of my kingdom and back into her orbit —I will kill you."

The uproar was instantaneous. Gods on their feet. Raised fists. Incoherent shouts.

I waved a quieting hand but didn't wait for the full cooperation of their silence. My apathetic smile cracked, a white row of teeth shining as I stripped emotion from my voice, save for calm, assured amusement.

"I will kill any god, any servant, any fae, any one of your faithful. I will smite them on your soil. I will watch them die, and there is nothing—" The cries of outrage nearly drowned the speech, but my cool certainty kept the corners of my mouth turned upward. I raised my voice, but there was no anger in my yell. The loud, booming threat clashed with my unsettling smile. "And before you leave, you will press your consent to this treaty to our scroll. All who participate have made an ally in Hell, and no harm will befall you, as long as you don't lay a hand on my human."

A sizzle from one end of the stadium sliced the veil as three goddesses slipped out of the symposium, making a show of their non-compliance. A swirling black crack in the world allowed a few more to escape. Dozens departed. Thousands remained.

The moment my father stood, he commanded the room. I held fast, anchoring myself to the axis between pantheons as he gave his final decree.

His wings flared once more, all eyes on the tall, regal freedom fighter in a simple, silver crown. They watched the deity whose act of rebellion began a civil war that would ripple through the world.

"I will add an addendum to the treaty. Gods will not be responsible for favoring or protecting this human. They will not be punished for natural mortality, nor for the actions of godless humans acting outside of the will of the region's deity."

*Semantics.*

"You may stay, you may feast, you may drink Hell's finest wines and luxuriate in palace suites reserved for gods. Discuss what you must with me and my retinue. Before you leave, touch your finger to the treaty. Sign and have an ally in my people from now until the prophecy between my son and his human has been fulfilled." The King flicked his wrist and a scroll hovered inches above his upturned palm. "Stay as long as you'd like and read, reread, study, and make your decision. Your regional entities known for wisdom and counsel are welcome, and Hell's veil will remain open, should you call them in to examine the treaty. For once you've agreed to it, the contract cannot be broken."

From the upper corner, still snarling, a guttural voice spoke to the King rather than me.

"We're supposed to sign a binding contract that allows him to kill our gods at will?"

It was the King's turn to smile. "You avoid hurting an individual every day. Jarovid, is it? Tell me, have you ever harmed, or have you commanded a friend or worshipper, to harm Perun?"

His question was laughable. Had the Slavic god of anger ever tried to murder the highest god in their realm? Their tales were still too fresh and sacred for their people to put their legends to paper, but their pantheon's supremacy was without question.

The King didn't wait for an answer. "No? So, it seems you're already an expert at avoiding killing a single entity. Simply... continue doing that. If you cannot comply, you are free to leave."

Jarovid split the air beside him, but before he stepped through the veil, I commanded the floor once more.

"Tell them."

Rippling muscles, full beard, and a ferocity for the ages stared me down.

I leaned toward him, one foot in front of the other, challenging the god of rage, war, and fire before the convergence of deities. "Confess to every god and goddess sitting in Hell's stadium today the role you played in this blood oath."

The veil remained torn at his side, but he returned my threatening posture, leaning into my threat. "I didn't lay a finger on her."

"How many missionaries had reached your mountains? Three? The faith we battle wasn't even a threat to you. Not yet. Not when you captured her. Not when you tortured her. Not when you tied her wrists and ankles and sent your horses in four directions."

Words like tumbling gravel, he snarled, "I. Didn't. Lay. A—"

"Mastislav. Yaropolk. Zbiginew. Vojin. Your men. Your faithful. They wore your sigil as they invaded her home in the night. You ensured the beer flowed freely that night as they passed her around. Her death was a welcome relief after what was done to her in your name."

He reached for his weapon. If I hadn't been frothing with hate, I might have laughed.

"They're dead now, of course. Along with a handful of your spirits, cryptids, and what is it that *you* call demons? That's right. Aitvaras. They serve you by haunting your enemies in the afterlife, right? Well, served. Good luck finding a single Aitvaras in the mountains you've cursed."

I'd spent a long time topside—enough to know how this information would land on human ears—but I'd been with gods before we conceded to the mortal concept of time. As such, news of a god harming a mortal garnered little reaction from the deities intently listening, save for a few soft gasps from the tender-hearted.

Maybe they didn't care that an immortal being had tortured a human.

But they *would* care *why*.

"You chose her because you knew she was mine."

This had the stirring effect I'd been expecting.

"You didn't even have a quarrel with Heaven. Hell was nothing to you. You'd heard of the woman with the opal aura, and in a pissing contest between realms, you took something that didn't belong to you, *simply* because you believed you could send a message to a god."

The murmurs swelled. The remaining members of his pantheon had their backs to me as they'd fully turned to stare at the perpetrator.

"Did it work, Jarovid? Do you feel powerful now? Do you feel safe?"

His face changed as he looked into my eyes. Fight turned to flight, and no parting battle cry could cover the truth of his disappearance. Jarovid stepped through the veil, disappearing from the stadium. A coward, running from the consequences of his actions.

He'd made a powerful enemy.

And I was on the precipice of receiving permission to act on my wrath.

Mokish, the Mother Earth of their realm, got to her feet. She straightened her dress. Cleared her throat delicately, then addressed the King.

"And if we sign this treaty, then someone"—she cast a glance to the empty space where Jarovid had been only moments prior —"violates it, is our entire realm at risk?"

My father turned to me for the answer.

"Only the perpetrator and those they used to facilitate it, Goddess," I said. "You're binding yourself to non-retaliation, so you cannot call for vengeance if I kill the god who murdered my human. Her life for theirs. If you'll allow the indiscretion: I'm pretty confident saying that if Jarovid harms her, I'll toss his head into the snow, and leave the rest of your gods, your people, and your land in peace."

The skin around her eyes crinkled with her smile. "In that case, I'll be the first to sign your treaty."

✦

Many left.

Many stayed.

Many signed.

Many didn't.

Hell gained unimaginable allies, though their terms left something to be desired.

They didn't agree to battle on our behalf. We weren't to call on them for aid in battle. But those who remained swore to stand firm against Heaven. They would not touch my human. They would stand with Hell, should Heaven bring bloodshed to their soil. They were no longer strangers, and certainly not our enemies.

The mass of oath-wary heavy-hitters left semantics for future negotiations.

Even some of the deserters didn't quite set us up for battle-ready caution. They could return and sign the treaty at any time.

They could refuse to sign it and still know better than to harm my human if she was on their soil.

The toppling stones of destiny had put things into motion long before my compliance. After today's formal declaration, global eyes were on me, for better or for worse.

Despite how hard I'd fought against it, despite how much I'd loathed grandstanding before lords and ladies as they waited for promises I was unwilling to keep, despite the reaction when I'd calmly promised death to beings, mortal and immortal alike, I left the night with one, lone certainty.

Come the infernal sunrise, I would head to the surface, and I would find my human.

# Chapter Sixteen



Baking heat and the sizzle of street meats wrapped their arms around me, embracing me in my long-awaited return to mortal streets. Save for my brief and bloody missions for vengeance, my last full cycle spent with my human was overseeing a healthy, happy life in a small Syrian village when news of "the miracle" trickled through the grape vine.

I wished I'd savored those days.

I longed to go back, to commit every breath to memory, to hear her happy, unbothered heartbeat before the world changed. I wished I'd slept beside her, if only to experience joy each time her eyes began to move beneath closed lids. I wanted to see the moment she left this world for astral dreams. I craved the small joy of a loved one's restful sleep.

It was a lesson in taking things for granted, and one I didn't intend to repeat.

Years of denial, followed by a history-altering treaty, were the final shackles of our distance.

I paused beneath the wilt of a tent between two barking merchants. I flicked a hand, instantly conjuring a member of my legion. The dark, wiggly lines, the vaguely human-shaped extensions of my will, had grown uniquely useful. Before our relationship had gone untameably public, I'd closed off the parts of me that had maintained one foot in Hell, leaving my legion woefully underutilized.

"Yes, my Prince?"

I frowned at the spiderweb of narrow roads, then back to the wisp as human bodies brushed through him, completely unaware that they were touching eternity.

"Byzantium is much larger than I remember it being. Take a dozen or so and report back with her location. Last reports had her working at her family's stall for the day market. If she's gone home already..." I checked the sun, contemplating what I knew of Byzantine and its work culture. It seemed too early to retire.

"Certainly." It fizzled, presumably relaying my message, then reanimated. "It should be noted, my Prince, that you last visited this city before it fell."

There was a reluctance to his delivery that held a mirror to my increasingly human emotions. Whatever he had to share was something I didn't want to hear.

"It's now called Constantinople."

"The etymology...no. Constantine? But if he's a Roman Emperor! I had nearly left Hell's conclave when that man was in power." I shook my head like a dog trying to rid its ear of a fly. My words poured out faster. I'd stayed apprised of the earthly powers as they moved every moment I was away. This couldn't be happening. It was too soon. "Nearly every Roman deity was in attendance in protest to Rome's conversion to Christianity. That was only, what, sixty-five mortal years ago? He can't have gotten this far! And then after passing the Edict of Milan he declared the local people newly-minted followers of Heaven, and didn't let the ink dry on his decree before capturing Byzantium?"

I could hear my frown as I argued—a fruitless endeavor. They were incapable of lying to me. That was, of course, unless the lie was one I was telling myself.

"There's more, Your Highness."

The tendons in my hands flexed as I channeled my impending horror into my fists. I knew what he was going to say before it left him.

"They call her Damiane in this life."

A nail in the coffin. My fists went slack. In Byzantium—the now-Christian Constantinople—her parents had cursed her in Latin. The name had been brought to former Byzantium on the backs of Roman. In this life, her name meant, "to subdue, to tame."

All at once, the meats, the spices, the city sounds and colors and smells were too much.

I pushed through my legion, vaporizing his shape as I picked an alley on blind faith and marched toward what I hoped would be her home.

The four-limbed legion appeared in front of me again as I marched over the large limestone slabs paving the road, nearly tripping on the packed dirt from one gray, flat rock to the next.

"Your Highness—"

I continued to walk, feeling nothing as his shape burst and reformed.

"My Prince, please, I must tell you—"

Just then, I caught the sharp, clean scent of the sky above the clouds.

*Her.* I had to be close. I'd followed my heart, and the unseen cord that tethered us drew me to her, even without the help of those who were created to serve me. A burst of red—terracotta roofing tile—fell from overhead, shattering into a million pieces at my feet. I squinted into the sunlight to see the undefined shadow of arms and legs as one of my legion grabbed a second tile and chucked it into the space before me.

The first appeared on the far side of the faux-danger, curved ochre pieces of someone's home tossed for no gods-damned reason as they stood between me and my human.

"Wait! Wait." He held up a pleading hand.

"You think clay will hurt me?" Heat flowed through me. I pointed at their sham attempt to wound me—a father who'd lost the last vestiges of patience with his children. "Unless I've been relieved of my crown and formally dispossessed from the royal family, you will stand down, *now*."

The legion atop on the roof ceased his feeble attempts to delay me. The first member trailed me, his ever-shifting plumes of smoke taking up space in my periphery as he refused to obey a direct order.

"But, Prince. The conclave. Our meeting. The treaty. Those that left, sire. The ones who departed... They didn't keep our... Told... Knows... Guard... There... Sire... Heaven..."

I hadn't listened to a word he'd said from the moment I'd caught her scent on the wind.

The painfully clean lungful of air grew stronger. I rounded a corner, dragging my fingers along the pale bricks, counting the windows of the long, single-level building as I angled for the modest two-story home at the end of the street.

I skidded to a halt.

There, in the midday heat and light, seeped the shimmering glow of something ethereal from an upstairs window.

I began to run.

One stride for home.

A second for love and Love alike; the emotion, the compulsion, the person.

A third for our reunion.

A fourth—

I rammed into an unmovable wall long before I'd reached her front door. I collided with the object with such force, it sent me sprawling onto my back, head bouncing against rock. I blinked up at the white-hot sun, head spinning. There was no time to process the impact before a weighty pillar crashed into my chest, pinning me to the limestone.

Reality flooded in from all directions. Every devastating revelation crushed me, some more literally than others.

It was no pillar on my chest; it was a foot.

The obstruction hadn't been a wall; it had been an unseen man. No, not a man. This was no human. It was the heated glow of metal yanked from the forge, pressed against my throat. A mountain of beige leather and tanned meat glared down at me with blazing, golden eyes.

A wave of brown hair blocked the sun as he leaned toward me.

"The mighty Prince of Hell," chuckled my assailant. "I was wondering when we'd meet."

He'd had one singular advantage: the element of surprise.

I didn't know who he was. I didn't care *what* he was. He was in my way, and he'd lost his upper hand. Literally. No one stupid enough to launch into a villainous monologue deserved a fair fight.

I twisted to my left with explosive force, my right hand grabbing the ankle on my chest, rolling toward the blade as my left, open palm shoved the broad side of the blade. The stranger lost his footing, the tip of his sword driving into the gravel as I turned my roll into a forceful sweep of my legs. Already stumbling from my shove, my legs against the back of his calves landed him on his ass.

The second it took him to gather his bearings was all I needed. He threw his weight into his sword in a two-handed arc, but rather than eat into my flesh, the metal hit stone, for there a new shape planted four enormous paws where only seconds earlier, a man had stood.

Frothing lips pulled back from fangs.

Ears flattened against scalp.

Claws extended.

I caught the reflection of piercing white fur, jagged black stripes, and a half ton of an apex predator.

I unhinged my tiger's jaw, snapping down before he'd regained control of the sword. He scrambled beneath me as I bit into his face with every drop of strength, satisfied with the pop as my incisors pierced his skull. The sword clattered to the ground as he continued to twitch beneath me, hands grasping for nothing as he tried, and failed, to latch onto my fur. The hot, bitter rush of myrrh. I yanked my mighty head to the side, tearing the assailant's face free.

He strained to stay upright, swaying as exposed brain tissue, the ripped dangle of a tongue, and gold, shimmering blood oozed from the stump of his neck. I stuck out my tongue, dropping the angular jaw, straight nose, and popped eye sockets of someone who had either been very brave, or very stupid, to take on the Prince of Hell.

Glitter oozed between stones for all who had eyes to see what stood just behind the mortal veil. A young boy ran by, dirty feet passing straight through the attacker's legs, our realms meshed, yet wholly separate. I wrinkled my nose at a familiar scent. It was sweet, and minty, and though I hated it, I couldn't quite place why.

The oils...the perfumes...the baked in smell of—

The staccato slap of flesh on flesh tore my eyes to an imposing figure leaning against the clay wall. He took three loud, slow, resonating claps. Somewhere in the back of my head, I was nearly impressed that three notes of percussion conveyed such clear mockery without saying anything at all. The man pushed away from the wall and strode toward the fallen assailant. He kicked the leg, carefully avoiding the pool of metallic sparkles.

"Shame." The newcomer rested a heavy hand on the hilt of his sword. He feigned a protruding lower lip in the briefest show of performative sympathy. "His first day on the job, too. You think after a millennium of training, you'd know better than to leave yourself open to so many points of vulnerability."

I took one step back, claws still extended, teeth bared.

A shrug. "Oh well. Eliminate the weakest links in the chain."

The snarl sat in my throat, an unrelenting rumble.

He looked me up and down, eyes sleepy, as if he found the interaction tedious. "You're outnumbered, Your...*Highness*."

My ear twitched with the sound of a new set of footsteps. The big cat's body was mighty, but its muscular neck prohibited a quick glance over my shoulder. I twisted to see two men emerge from either side of my human's home, all dressed in pale neutrals, all armed to the teeth.

"Come on. Step out of that tiger. Let's have a talk. Man to... well...whatever we are."

Even with my shapeshifting abilities, I didn't think I could take three of them at once. The first takedown had been fresh blood to chum the waters. Between their swords and untested skills, my best bet, at least for the moment, was negotiation.

The terracotta roofs slowly populated with shadow as my legion congregated. Dozens became hundreds, became a darkened sea, two thousand deep. They stacked, piling, arcing overhead until they blotted out the sun. Perhaps they didn't exist in corporeal form, but they were no more smoke than I was tiger. I could change my being, as could my fragments.

I liked our odds.

Another step back, and I shifted onto two legs, black on black, and hair as snowy as the newcomers' rich glints of sand.

From over my shoulder, one of the others called, "We're not here to kill you, for better or for worse."

The last scoffed. "Your lucky day. Don't fuck it up."

I was no longer snarling. I had a legion, the patience of a hundred lifetimes, and the nonchalance of a god-killer. They had...sparkles.

I pointed to the third speaker. "I'm going to call you Lucky." Rotating slightly, I jabbed my index finger toward the one in the center, announcing to the second speaker, "BW. Better or worse. It's cute. I bet it'll catch on." Then, tapping my chin, I sized up the one posturing as their leader. The vanity required to build structured shapeware around your bulging muscles really was something. "And you, rippling pectorals, will henceforth be known as Tits. You've got a nice rack."

Lucky chuckled. BW hissed at his brother in arms. The leader's boredom evaporated. Tits lit up, as if truly enjoying the shift in energy.

He planted a foot over his fallen comrade. I matched him step for step as he moved, keeping the space between us equidistant.

"My friend here wasn't lying. Today's little meet and greet isn't an attack. Consider this...a courtesy."

We'd paced until Tits was poised between Lucky and BW. I wanted to be comforted that I'd corralled my enemies into one corner, but for all I knew they had a new set of armed meatheads wrapped in leather ready to storm in from the market behind me.

I was skilled in hand-to-hand combat, I had thousands of other-worldly loyalists ready to throw themselves on a sword for me, and should I need to live to fight another day, I could turn into a bird and dart from the scene before they'd even comprehended the unexpected flutter of wings.

I didn't recognize the entities as native to Byzantium. They were too polished to be cryptids. Too confident to be fae. Too informal to be gods. I faced soldiers, to be sure, but the swords, the leathers, the hauntingly familiar perfume...

The memory connected to the smell hit me all at once.

My father's old clothes.

His leathers, the white feathers he'd plucked from the ground, the weapon he'd encased in his office.

He spoke seldom of his past life, but the visual reminder strummed at my heart strings as I watched him move through the realm. He was kind, self-possessed, powerful, respected. He was a dreamer. A visionary. But the display reminded me: he hadn't left from hate, or corruption, or anger. He'd been cast out, rejected by his King, abandoned by his people. I was certain some vestige of him still held a candle of that love, or the armor, the feathers, the reminders of a life he would never have back, would have been cast into the fire long ago.

Angels.

I slipped one foot behind, shifting my weight to the balls of my feet. "Ah, Tits, you came all the way down from Heaven to pay your respects? A letter would have done just fine."

Lucky seemed to find me funny, which I appreciated. What was a comedian without his audience? BW shot him another scathing look, but Tits had no idea as to the disorganization in his ranks.

There it was.

Over the gore of spiced angel blood, stronger than the food stalls, more powerful than the old scents of Byzantium and the new odors of Constantinople combined. Clean air, higher than the mountain tops. Her soul's shimmer had moved away from the topmost window, but she was in there. I knew it.

I clapped my hands, then rubbed them together in parting. "Well, Gents, I wish I could say it's been a pleasure, but why bother with the lie? Now, I have business in the city, and unless you wish to be mauled by a tiger, I'm going to need the three of you to step aside."

It was BW's time to laugh, though the drip of sarcasm at every forced note added a piece to a puzzle.

Heaven had found my human. Three angels were here. They claimed to be here for a courtesy. BW found the idea of me walking toward the house amusing...why?

Unless...

My self-assuredness fractured. My hands went limp at my side.

Tits cracked into a self-congratulating grin the moment my face drooped. The men behind him exchanged meaningless, performatively masculine gibberish. I hated their delight in my suffering.

I looked up at the interlocking wire of scribbled arms and legs of my legion. The alley darkened with their shadow. I gave them a slow, single, shake of the head. "No."

I understood now why Tits had moved back with his men. I was in no place to ask favors, but I was so close. She was right there. It was unfair. It was cruel. It was downright diabolical.

Tits exhaled. "I'm afraid so. Hell has a weak spot. And Heaven wants you to know that you've shown your hand. Your human?" His laugh wasn't even cruel this time. A quiet huff, no performance, no need for frills. "Our human."

My eyes unfocused. She was within spitting distance. I could have wrapped my arms around her. I could have helped her, guarded her, loved her, begged her to see me. But she was a snow hare trapped behind a fence.

"Can I touch it?" I asked.

He hadn't been expecting this. Perhaps they didn't realize how quickly I'd put it together.

Lucky spoke for the retinue. "I think it'd be easier for you if you did."

The others made a habit of chastising him, but he was unruffled by their judgment. He wasn't here for their approval. It wasn't very *angel* of him.

I took a few careful steps forward before lifting my fingertips. Each step grew smaller, as I closed the space between myself and the host of heavenly soldiers. I was less than an arm's length away when my fingertips hit the shock of bottled lightning. Pale tendrils spread from my gentle touch, spreading and disappearing like clear ice cracking and filling, as the snaking, electric lines revealed the dome surrounding her house.

Tits strode forward, inches from the unseen protective layer. He could easily reach through and grab me, unaffected by its voltage. I'd have to learn their real names to see if this handful of angels could put up a good fight, even if they couldn't kill a god, or if I was facing archangels.

My legion had uncoiled, but remained on the roofs around us, as if prepared for how desperately I wanted to hold the broken parts of myself together.

She was right there.

*Right* there.

My legion, trying desperately to stop me, plucked sharper memories from the muffled remnants of disregarded advice. Those who had departed Hell without signing the treaty had put their money on a champion horse. They'd scampered off to Heaven, ready to suck the cocks of whoever would be the most powerful.

"She's not at the market today," I said slowly, "because it's the Sabbath. She and her family..."

"She's ours," BW was quick to interject.

"The prayers are hers," Lucky said. "She, specifically, is praying against all who stand against her God."

In the twisted tangle of paths laid out before me, how hadn't I considered the single, most obvious obstacle between myself, my human, and the prophecy? It wasn't the interference of meddling gods. It wasn't their fae, their agendas, their vendetta against my vow for bloodlust, nor their shortsightedness, as we decided how to handle the viral pandemic that was Christianity and its spiritual contagion.

"You could just kill her." I heard the deadpan words as if they happened somewhere beyond myself.

"If she dies, we get rid of the immediate problem. What if she's reborn somewhere that hasn't been exposed to our King's message? We kill her, and we roll the dice. You may get your shot at her, after all." The piece of information Lucky volunteered might have been comforting under other circumstances, but here? Now?

She wouldn't be harmed.

No torture, no puppeteering, no...anything.

Tits took two long steps toward me, abandoning the safety of his shield, forcing me backward toward the dead soldier.

"I could kill you today, you know," he said. He dropped his voice so only I could hear. "It would be so easy. Hell's Prince gone"—snap—"just like that. But Hell would retaliate, of course. We'd win. It's been predestined. But who would we lose in the process? See..." He puffed his chest. I stood my ground this time, eye to eye, chin to chin, as he leaned as close as he dared. "We've been racking up victories before the world even knew we were in the fight. And this prize piece you've been hiding up your sleeve? We really appreciate you exposing the wildcard. We can't tell you what it means that you gave us everything we needed to win without spilling a single drop of angelic blood."

I kicked the body behind me, shoving it with my heel, but didn't break eye contact.

"A single drop of *important* blood, anyway. See, Prince, you were born in Hell. You don't share memories of The Fall, of the Watchers, of our brothers who once knew what it was like to be on the winning team. You've served your kingdom, you've loved your people, and I'm sure you will try your hardest."

He stretched his sausage fingers toward me as if to pat my head. I scowled, swerving out of the space before he could touch me.

"Your father kept you from the real enemy for as long as he could. Either that, or you weren't important enough to register on our hit list before now. Hell's Fraudulent King probably knew what it would do to you when you realized: you're outmatched. There's no triumph for you. Not when you go toe to toe with Heaven."

He punctuated the point with a final bolt through the cage that separated us.

His cronies walked up to the edge of the dome but remained on the safe side.

BW's forced smirk was more annoying than if he had been truly amused. "Finally, you're grown enough to play with the big boys."

Satisfied with their taunting last words, it seemed our interaction had come to an end.

Tits turned to leave with BW close on his heel.

Lucky loitered just long enough to say, "You didn't want her to be in the prophecy either, right? This is her best-case scenario. If you love her, maybe you'll let yourself see that."

A high-pitched whistle bounced off the clay walls. Tits barked his command as they departed.

"Hey! You coming or what?"

Lucky meant to convey something with the weight of his last look, but I couldn't fathom that there was anything he could say or do that would make this situation better or worse.

She was alive.

She was safe.

And for as long as her family worshipped our nemesis and prayed over their home, she'd be close enough for me to touch, while being a lifetime away.

I experienced a new kind of loss as I watched the three men disappear.

I settled onto the clay shards and stared up at the window, hoping for a glimpse at who she was in this life, a sense for her smile, her health, if she was happy. I sat for a day and a night, but she did not come to the window.

What if this was it? What if, in this cycle, her faith carried her to an afterlife in Heaven? What if our story was over before I'd gotten the chance to say goodbye?

The clear sky was pink with morning light. The angels did not return, nor had I moved, threatening the boundary they'd set.

I detached from the hope I'd felt in Hell's stadium, surrounded by almighty beings willing to press their oaths into our treaties.

My heart hollowed, its beats echoing in a tinny, absent way as I stared.

I could rally the pantheons.

I could make history with unforetold treaties.

I could be one half of a legend that belonged to the two of us alone.

I could get the support of my kingdom, of the gods, of the world.

And it still might not be enough.

# Chapter Seventeen

**450 ADE**

I drowned in an ocean of tedious exhaustion.

Every available resource went to the endless labor of my search.

My legion wasn't alone in the hunt to find my human. My father's seventy-two legions— one hundred and forty thousand entities—set a precedent. Duchesses, counts, presidents, and marquises donated portions of their legion as we scoured every inch of the humans' insufferable ball of water and dirt. So, so, so much water.

A sickly-sweet self-loathing rolled on the back of my tongue when I'd heard of her death—healthy, loved, and surrounded by a family who prayed she'd make it safely to Heaven upon her passing, even if she hadn't lived to see her fifth decade.

Part of me feared that she'd done exactly that.

We dove through caves, we overturned boulders, we burst through the doors of every home from pole to pole. We scoured pastoral nomads, warring Visigoths, the frost-bitten Samoyedic peoples, the mountains and plains and rolling hills of the scattered Rouran Khaganate. In our desperation, we were on the precipice of coming to the most reluctant of terms that she'd transitioned into Heaven's kingdom after her death, relinquishing her soul to the enemy.

As the mortal years of our search stretched onward, the legions and our allies were crestfallen at having lost a spark of hope. As each year chipped away at our fragile optimism, so too did it chisel through whatever it was I had that passed for a soul. The thought of her loss shattered me. Day after day, my legion watched as I became unmade.

Thirty mortal years into tearing the earth upside down, news came of a speck of sand in the center of a deep blue nothing. Green trees, fresh coconut water, nutrient-rich fish, vitamin-dense fruits, and thousands of leagues away from the marching horde of Heaven's reach, a soul was found. A woman, fist-size circlets of black curls for hair, hourglass shaped, and a month before her thirty-third birthday, contained the only pearly shimmer in the world.

Intrepid mortals, with their insatiable thirst to know, to do, to move, had little regard for their fragility when they launched from the tip of mapped civilization into the blue horizon.

Hell was fully aware of the divine ancestors and principal gods of Tangaloa at the time of our summit—Havea Hikule'o, Tangaloa 'Eiki, and Maui Motu'a—all notably absent from our assembly. My father had made a comment at the time about the hope we should glean from those who had chosen not to come: perhaps they'd seen the future spread, and their kingdoms remained unthreatened.

We didn't find her among the first peoples who'd found island homes. Or in the second. Or in the sixth.

Her nearest populace clan, the Teva'i Tai, was two islands away.

*My* human, for the graces and blessings of every deity from every pantheon, had been born into a village that *believed*. There were gods for peace, for rain, for fertility. War, lava, the sky. The ocean, of course, and the regional storm deity, reigned supreme, but belief in the spirit of the trees, of the rocks, of the creatures that roamed the earth, was my first exposure to animism. The belief that supernatural powers organized both inanimate objects and natural phenome alike shook them from the inhibitions I'd found in every other culture.

They told me what they'd uncovered.

They repeated the information.

They watched as I processed a dream too good to be true.

There was no veil when we landed on her shores.

Even my legion, all fizzle and froth, had been spotted when scouring her village. Her pot had shattered as she'd yelped at the jumping shadow, more startled than frightened, as she saw the creature for what it was.

In some ways, this knowledge rose the stakes to unspeakable heights.

Unlike my struggle with Yuka on the ice, my legion was now deeply integrated into my pursuit of my human. As they lingered in the shadows, absorbing her language, so did I.

I lurked offshore, learning of her culture, understanding her words, practicing the new way vowels and consonants rolled together, for the better part of a mortal week, gazing at the light of her soul. I could see her, yes, but what would it mean to be seen *by* her? There'd be no gradual introduction. I couldn't be the hero. I would just be...me.

On the eighth day, I watched the pearly shimmer of her soul separate from her tribe. It wasn't unusual for all genders to take walks, to fetch fruit, to spend time communing with nature, and this was the first time I could catch her alone. The bright orange sun turned red as it dipped toward the horizon. She lit a torch as she padded down a well-worn trail.

I stopped breathing as I stepped through the space between things. I shifted from a league offshore to the brush only a few arms' length from my human, lungs burning against the lingering fear that a single inhale might shatter the dream.

She snapped to attention the moment I arrived, though I'd been silent.

"Hello?" she said.

My head spun, lungs laboring against the spike in my pulse.

Had I already fucked it up? Was she afraid? Was she—

She stuck the torch carefully in the soil, then slowly lowered to the ground, one leg folded over another. Tall, unruly grasses obscured the lower half of her body. We were in a cave of inward-bending branches, of obfuscating bushes, of walls of vines behind which I could hide.

She spoke first.

"My village has been haunted by spirits. Are you one of them?"

*Shit. Shit shit shit.*

I opened my mouth to answer, but only dust came out.

"Are we being visited by spirits of our ancestors? A god who seeks our attention? A—"

"No," I said, perhaps too hastily. I remained tucked behind the slits of a broad, green leaf as I softened my tone. "I'm no god, and I'm not of your people. I'm only here for you."

She went perfectly still. "Have I brought a curse upon us?"

I stopped short of smacking my forehead, only because I knew she was astute enough to hear the sound. I thanked the

195

stars I had no prophets scribbling down my clumsy legacy, as I wasn't sure I could relive this encounter.

"You have not," I said. I didn't have to feel calm to play the part, and I couldn't risk scaring her.

"Are you here to claim my soul?"

*Great. I was the fucking Grim Reaper.*

I realized I'd overlooked an important detail in my days of hovering. I'd learned about her people, her village, her culture, her language, but I had not asked my legion of her name. After all, in many lifetimes, she'd asked me not to use it.

In this one, however...we needed a balance. She needed to see me as curious, not all-knowing, nor all-powerful.

"What do they call you in this life?" I asked. I cleared my throat. "Your name, I mean. What name did your parents give you?"

She brushed a circlet of dark curls from her face. "Rauana. It means—"

Those sounds had been strung together by pale people from mountaintop regions and grassland shepherds, each forming their own names. But among this branch or offshoot of Tahitians, I recognized the combination of words and their meanings.

"Many stars and caves."

Her star in the cave. My human on the earth, no matter how far, no matter how hard, she was mine, and I was hers. As much as I wanted to fight the horrors the world wrought upon us, we were destined.

Gods and their tales of omnipotence had nothing on the power she held over me.

I was immobilized, mind, body, and soul.

How could she know?

And what was more: what would it take for me to trust in our connection and believe in my human, if not this?

Leaves scraped against bark, wind masking the unnamable thread that tied us.

*Speak, for fuck's sake. Say something.*

"Rauana. I am not a god. I'm not here to hurt you. I'm not here for your people. But...you are not beholden to me." I battled against the power imbalance inherent to the implicit bias of animism. A godhood granted to everything would place me above her. It was an inequity with which I was unwilling to contend. "You owe me nothing. Think of me as a man who would like to speak to you as an equal. And when we do...you have the power to send me away, if you do not wish to see me."

She wrapped her fingers around the torch's shaft. "If you're a man, you should know: I'm unmarriageable."

I swallowed. "Oh?"

"I was born under the lonely star. I am not to bear children."

Gods, I could cry. I wished she could reincarnate here forever.

It was I, not she, who needed time.

In my panicked years of fearing she'd left her cycles for Heaven, I'd nearly abandoned hope. In my time studying her island, I hadn't dared to *truly* believe she'd hear me on the first try, despite animism and its evidence.

I was overcome.

Another first.

Tears in my eyes, I kept my composure as I said, "In three weeks, I'll meet you here. If it rains that day, as is common in your village, I will be at that cave just atop the cliff. And until then, I will appear to you three times."

Her eyes sparkled at the challenge. "And how will I know you?"

"I will be a white turtle on your shores at sunrise. I will be a white bird on the thatched roof of your hut. I will be the white shark whose fin you see just beyond the safety of your reef. And then, I'll return."

◆

As the storm gods of the Great Sea would have it, the winds howled that night. Rain doused Rauana's torch before she made it five steps beyond the village. Her friends, her advisors, her relatives begged her to take shelter, to stay home, but she'd seen the turtle, the bird, the shark fin, and had come at last to meet the man.

I didn't wait in the cave.

I followed closely, terrified she'd slip and fall, that she'd break an ankle. Thorny branches sliced at her forearms. She tripped and stumbled over exposed roots. She felt her way forward on memory alone, determined to make it to the cave.

The rain was too harsh. The wind was too loud. She lost sight of the trail. She could no longer distinguish the mud of a well-trodden path from the treacherous squish of unfamiliar forest. Rather than turn back, I watched in slack-jawed horror as she abandoned the trail altogether and marched for the wall of sheer limestone.

My shouts of protest were stolen on the wind.

The ocean waves broke against jagged rock with incessant, thunderous booms.

Rauana's fingers bit into rock, teeth gritted, hair plastered over her eyes, as she scrambled up the rockface. Knife-like shards jutted from the cliff, carving a deep slice down from her knee to her inner thigh.

I flashed from the place below her through the cut in mortal space.

I thrust one blue flame over my shoulder, illuminating the

cave, and one outside, too dim to startle her, but just enough to let her see one handhold over the next. She grunted as she pulled her weight nearly to the top before we both heard the flint-like scrape of stone on stone.

Her footing gave loose.

Her fingers couldn't hold her weight.

She barely had the time to scream before I had her forearm in the vice-like grip of my fingertips. I held her away from the cliff as I hoisted her up, trying to ease her onto sure footing before I released her, but there would be no releasing her.

She crashed into me, first arms and hands and fingers, an embrace, gratitude, incredulity.

We didn't have time to be mortal and immortal.

We didn't even have time to be different.

We were just creations, cursed to loneliness, who had only each other.

We stumbled backward into the cave, me touching her wounds, healing them with each step as our hands moved. Our lips didn't touch. Our clothes remained intact. But the scrambling, wild way with which we explored each other's faces, tugged at one another's hair, stared into each other's eyes, belied a recognition that transcended time.

We made it to the blue flame before she pulled away, gasping for air, eyes wide.

"Who *are* you?" She asked.

I shook my head uselessly. "I've never had a name on mortal tongues. None, save for yours. You called me—"

Her breath caught. Her fingers flew to her chest. She finished my sentence with a word. "Star. You were my Star."

I could count on my fingers the number of times my eyes had watered, and each belonged to her. "Star."

She knew me.

She. Knew. *Me.*

The rest be damned.

◆

Even in the moment, I knew these touches would replay in my memory for centuries to come. Her mouth found my neck first, her soft lips on my throat. My fingers clutched the plumb, perfect cinch of her waist, pulling her into me. She tore at wherever she believed my shirt to be, though the clothing of my kingdom and time left the undoing of tunics and sarongs a little unfamiliar.

She's never known the touch of a man.

I'd never known the touch of any human but her—and *never* had the intricately woven frond of our story unfurled like this.

Our lips fused, tongues drinking honey, hands on fire. Her back flattened against the cold cave wall, bare before me as I was before her. She went on to her toes, wrapping one leg around mine as she pulled me closer. She breathed out as I breathed in, absorbing one another as we faded from two beings into one.

"Rauana—"

She paused, hand against my chest. "No."

I froze. "I'm sorry. I—"

"I see you," she said. "I see past the chipped moonlight in your eyes. I see beyond the starlight of your skin. I don't see the animals who visited me. I see a woman on the ice and a beast twice her size. I see a palace, a bed of unimaginable colors, a love beyond words. I see a woman who nearly bled to death along the sea, and the Star who rescued her."

I flickered, awareness struggling as I fought to make sense of it. Everything came crashing to a halt. The heat between us chilled as she stared into me.

"I am your Love. And you are mine."

No mortal word sufficed.

The warmth of the sun. The permeating soak of treasure at the bottom of the deepest ocean trench. The frenzied grip that rivaled fingers clinging to a storm-drenched cliff. The down-soft press of naked skin. The explosive pleasure beyond anything a god of debauchery might pour.

There was sex.

There was fucking.

Then...there were the universes born when I entered my Love.

♦

When I came, the shimmering gloss of my seed coated her belly, her ass, her throat, her mouth, or sometimes the arc of my own stomach. My oath agreed I'd find her, I'd love her, I'd bed her. No one would invade the sanctity of our lovemaking to see the way I refused my role in the prophecy.

In this life, Love was no whore—a word born of sanctimony and otherness that I rebuked with every fiber of my being—but even if we weren't evading the prophecy, she'd made one thing clear: she was never to marry, nor to bear children, in this life-time. I'd honor her culture, her people, her wishes.

I found purpose in her ecstasy.

When she came, I was the one who saw god.

♦

Flesh and need consumed me.

She was the mortal, but I was the one consumed with our cycle of loss. She remained in the present, while I craved her every atom, knowing the fleetingness of each perfect moment.

There was a rabidness to our carnal connection that was best left to the cave. I struggled to let her leave and begged for her return. Gratitude over her existence dried my tongue into something unquenchable. She stole away to the cave as often as she could. No matter how many times a week, then how frequently per a day, it was never enough.

No discretion could excuse her absence as she ran to me, her ache growing for a need only I could feel.

Rauana told me—not asked, *told*—that she planned to inform the village first of my presence, and second, that she'd been born under a lonely star so that she could fall into the arms of a living star.

Given her unmarriageable status, the announcement was met with interest rather than rejection. Whoever, and *whatever*, I was, threatened no one.

She spent weeks preparing them for my appearance, and when the time came for me to walk upon their sands at her side, I was met with little resistance.

Rauana, now one who walked with spirits, was granted the privacy of her own hut within the community.

She would bear no children. She would take no husband. She would continue her roles as they moved between aiding the fishermen with their catch, gathering fruits and vegetables, weaving, storytelling, and all things expected of her prior to her brush with starlight. They accepted my presence as I helped her with her tasks, and I avoided using any powers that would perturb them. I caught her fruit. I helped her dig trenches. I gathered fresh rainwater. They were gendered roles in her village, but my presence was not questioned, because whatever I was…I was hers.

She would allow the spirits to take her on the journey meant for her. She would live her life as normally as she could, save for one difference.

This time, for the first time, we lived as two mortals might.

We were us.

We had a home.

Our love was known.

And in a world of newness, I, an immortal being, was able to experience the day-in and day-out of what it might be like to live a normal, mortal life.

# Chapter Eighteen

**510 ADE**

"Please. I beg of you."

Bright red mud washed into the murky river that separated us. Mami Wata perched on the far shore, her bright red cloth stark against the rolling green of the countryside behind her.

I had never met a member of the Orisha. Not formally. They'd sent a loyal ambassador to our summit many years prior, but the gods themselves had no need to set foot in Hell. Nor, would it seem, would I be allowed to set foot in Orisha territory.

"We're a closed pantheon," she said. It wasn't cruel. It wasn't apathetic. It was simply a fact.

Given my years of passion, of intimacy, of devotion beyond the veil with Love, my grief at her death, and then joy at the knowledge that she'd been reborn in a land beyond the reach of Heaven's conquest, were short-lived.

I hoped she valued honesty, for I knew how desperate I sounded. "You sent an ambassador to Hell's meeting. You have a seer, yes? Orisha Orula? Surely, he saw what the future holds as the war deity from the Dead Sea spreads his rule. He infiltrated the Roman Empire, and their mission is one of colonization. You see it coming to your soils, yes? You see the threat he poses?"

The river was too large to babble. It moved noiselessly between us, the occasional tuft of green floating by as a fallen tree made its way between us.

"Is he here today?" She asked.

I hedged. "Well, no, but my human—"

"Is with us. He is not welcome here. Nor are you."

My frustration boiled. "But I pose no threat to you! I won't infringe on your gods, on your people—"

"We are a closed pantheon. It is true today. It will be true tomorrow. It will be true in two thousand years, no matter what colonizers trod upon our soil. I'm speaking to you now as a kindness. I advise you to see it for what it is, and leave."

A broken body in a cave who asked me not to leave.

A wealthy Grecian who loved me, heart, body, and soul.

A spiritual advisor on the ice.

A superstitious mother among the misty, emerald hills.

A believer behind an impenetrable wall.

A seer on an island who enveloped me in her passion, her insight, her clairvoyance, her power, and made me certain of our fate.

"But I belong to her as much as she does to me." It sounded pathetic even as I said it. "She should be the one who gets to reject me. It's her right."

"Are you not used to being told 'no,' Prince of Hell?"

I let the stare last a lifetime, for I knew that when this conversation ended, so would my time near my human.

"But...I love her."

"Love is water. Yours and mine, everyone's and no one's.

Nothing worth loving can belong to you," she said. "Possession is not love. And obsession, wearing love's mask, is no different."

Love was within Orisha territory, and it was vaster and more thorough than any electric angelic cage I'd experienced in Constantinople.

If ever I was to return to Hell, it was now.

# Chapter Nineteen

**A SINGLE NIGHTMARE**

Uncomfortable glue stuck my lashes together. My vision was foggy. I stirred as if from a drunken stupor.

I was Hell's Prince, and as such, could come and go from any court or location of the realm as I pleased. I expected cobbled streets. Architecture, old and new. I expected my palace, my home, my bed.

My title, my power, my being was older than mortal years.

The gods, as it was, were eternal. Their ideologies, squabbles, and partitions existed long before atoms split, and the physical universe rolled into organic life. Humans were late toys in the game of gods. It would be inane to anticipate anything out of the ordinary when stepping into my realm.

But this wasn't my court.

My vision, my sense of smell, my thrash of heightened awareness spiked at once.

Thick opium, silken drapes, lungs full of involuntary oxytocin, and the endless pitch of onyx where walls should have been alerted me that I was somewhere I'd heard of but gone out of my way to never visit.

I knew my sister was to blame before I could articulate her role in my arrival. As half siblings, she came to the Royal Court for a reason.

I drowned in an ocean of thick, inescapable tar.

The blue-gray crackle in a cloud illuminated a cluster of snakes off to the left. Another thunderstrike illuminated a horrifying silhouette, this time of someone bound by chains and thrust into a bottomless ocean.

I knew where I was, and it was the last place in the multitude of realms I wanted to be.

The Court of Nightmares was for succubi, incubi, and things that went bump in the night. This wasn't for fallen angels. This was for blood suckers, parasites, and creatures beyond and before the veil that struck fear into the heart of the mortals on whom they preyed.

◆

Fighting for sobriety in a land soaked with sex was like swimming up from the murky depths of the deepest lake. I blinked to clear my head as I looked for the culprit.

A deep, disembodied purr seeped through the haze. "This is your fight."

It wasn't my sister. I was quite certain I'd never heard the voice. Given its gravity, I had a singular guess. Izi's mother, the

First Succubus, Queen of Nightmares, had broken through the haze.

"She's talking to me," Izi sighed.

I felt her before I saw her. She yanked my hand, pulling me onto a silken cushion.

The jump caught me off guard, but the shock had passed. I shook off the cloud to glare at her clearly. I was on my feet before she had the time to prop an elbow against the pillows and pout into her hand.

"You have ten seconds to explain yourself."

"Consider this your intervention, Amagi," she pouted. "You've failed."

We'd surpassed sibling rivalry. I'd sooner start a war with her court than let her taunt me when it came to my Love.

"Nine. Eight. Seven."

Her lower lip protruded. "The prophecy really bummed you out. I get it. Then for Heaven to hear about your human? Uff. They really forced your hand, huh? But then..." She sat up, gesturing to the isolated blackness around her. "You were handed an opportunity on a silver platter. Fulfill your duty a million miles away from Heaven's touch. A willing bride. A human with open eyes. No one to stop you."

I hissed through gritted teeth. "Four. Three. Two."

"You aren't going to do it. You think you weren't watched? You think just because you were in the middle of the fucking ocean among gods that all eyes weren't on you? You didn't question once—not *once*—why not a *single* Samoan god showed up to confront you. When did you lose your curiosity? Fuck, love really does make you stupid, huh?"

Her timer had run out, but a new rage tethered me to the ground.

"What did you do?" I spit the question through my teeth.

"Me?" She batted her lashes, feigning innocence. "What did I do that hundreds of deities didn't do? We interceded. We asked for a reprieve. We made promises. We bartered on your behalf. We let you fuck around under the oath that you would get the job done."

I stared at this creature—the only being I'd ever deigned to call sibling—as the inky tendrils of her hair floated around her. The sultry chaos she offered the world focused on me.

"Finish it," she said.

I thought only humans could teach me new emotions.

Here, in the Court of Nightmares, a new insidious drip began within me.

I repeated my question, tendons flexed, jaw clenched. "What did you do."

She rose to meet me. Within her own court, she could distort her shape and amplify her voice at will. She doubled her height, bending as she yelled, then tripled her size as she towered over me. Her voice boomed across the obsidian.

"You could have left her alone!" The shout was half accusation, half maddening cackle. "The day I wandered into that shitty, clay hut, I told you, brother. Play with the humans. Have your fun. But to focus on one? To protect her? To *love* her?"

An iridescent glow reflected off the draped silk, and I knew it was my rage personified. I vibrated with it as I waited for her next words.

She laughed, her towering form pacing the endless land of terrors. A crackle of thunder in one corner. A scurry of spiders in another. An ooze of blood, a fanged beast, the gleam of a weapon, all crackling in their respective nightmares.

She tilted her head back this time, opening her mouth, unhinging her jaw like a snake as a wicked, belly laugh reverberated through her court.

"But I didn't," I said.

"But you could have!" She snapped back to my size, my equal in all but rage. "You could have stopped in the hundreds of years before the motherfucking prophecy! You knew better than every other deity? You were wiser than the beings who walked among the humans? You and your hubris, your attachment meant more?"

She was drunk on her own monologue. I let my fury grow, light banishing the shadows, forcing nearby residents to scurry to the comfort of known darkness.

"So then," she drawled, "phase two. Heaven, spearheaded by a war god, found sheep's clothing. You can only conquer so many lands through weapons and body counts, right? After all, every pantheon has a war deity, and they all use the same play-book. It's why they stick with their own people, give or take a neighboring kingdom or two. But *this* guy? Our nemesis? Holy *shit*."

I'd cut off my nose to spite my face if I grabbed her by the throat now. She was on the verge of telling me something. Yet the brighter I grew, the smaller she was. This may be her court, but she was no god. She could control her shape, but whether my land or hers, she did not hold my title.

Izi flipped her hair over her shoulder and walked toward a blank, black wall. She thrust her hands toward the darkness and flung a map of the mortal world amongst its nightmares.

"He almost deserves his victory. The first war deity to realize there was a new frontier to conquer: consciousness. He fought with emotion. His weapon became hate in the shape of peace. His blood-soaked agenda wore a kindly teacher's face. He claimed victory over minds! Cultures!"

The blue-black crowd spread to show the expanse between the Dead Sea and the Tigres and Euphrates, the birth of Heaven and Hell. A blood-red ink blotched above and below neighboring seas, further west than Rome, all the way to Hispania, further north than Britannia thanks to the Plague of Justinian, further east than my sorrowful visit in Constantinople.

"Do you know what our soothsayers predict?"

The blue-gray expanded higher and wider than any nightmare I'd yet to witness. The red spread to lands neither I nor my legion had visited. I watched the fall of the Aztec Empire, understanding their presence in the summit, though I knew neither when nor how. The crimson blotch smothered continents on all sides of the globe in shapes that had yet to be mapped by any earth-bound scholar.

"You could have stayed in Hell," she sneered. "You didn't listen to my advice the first time around. You didn't listen to my advice after their motherfucking prophecy when I begged you to stay here, to wait until desperate pagans thrashing for relevance stopped pressuring you to sire their champion. You could have waited, been silent, taken my advice, allowed the gods and their schemes to grow bored."

Her map vanished, but the full moon glow of my silver rage continued.

"You decided, brother. You chose. You'd fulfill their prophecy. So, where is it? Where is the evidence you're holding up your end of the bargain? Show us the fruits of your labor, Treacherous Prince. I'd hate to believe this infertility is intentional."

My lips pulled back from my teeth. "What was your role in this?"

She plopped onto the silks once more. "I was on your side, even when you weren't, Amagi."

I studied her silhouette and had an epiphany that winked my starlight into blackness.

"Izi," I said, fists clenched.

"Amagi," she replied automatically, taunting, bored, ever herself.

"I owe it to you to tell you: this is the last time I will see you as my sister. With the resources at my fingertips, it will be hours, nay, minutes, before I unravel the fateful threads you've knotted in my life. You believe you're wiser than me? You know better, you have Hell's best interest, you're worthy of puppeteering?"

Her throat bobbed without swallowing.

"I have a single piece of advice for you."

Her brows pinched. Her back straightened at the unforeseen turn.

"Don't come back to the Royal Court. That said, I expect we'll see each other, whether in the mortal realm, among the infernal, or in another pantheon. I want you to understand the grace I'm giving you with my warning."

The clouds ceased. There was only black as Izi stared up at me.

"I don't care if I'm visiting a pantheon in a royal capacity, if I'm undercover behind enemy lines, if I'm simply listening to a harpist with my father in the Royal Court..." A light chuckle. Her skin blanched as hate blackened my eyes.

"The next time you see me: run."

# Chapter Twenty

**1060 ADE**

Adrenaline's metallic prickle filled my veins.

I rolled onto the balls of my feet, eyes wide, ready to run.

An incomprehensible clash of fire, finger-painted smear of warpaint over pale skin, screams, the high clang of weapons and a flash of white-gold braids swarmed to my right. Frigid wine and ice blew from my left, swelling with the staccato slapping of saltwater against anchored, wooden ships. Seaworthy vessels burned, ornate dragon-heads smoldering, the air reeked with the putrid melding of rotting corpse, burning hair, and fishy stink of salted cod as it fell from drying rods, curling into briny dust among the ash.

*Love, where the hell are you?*

Electric tendrils cut through the snow as a lightning bolt doomed a thatched roof to join the flames.

Mountains.

Sea.

Ice.

Thunder.

This had to be the Nordes. I looked to the sky for Thor's fabled lightning. I spied the peeling paint on a fallen shield as Yggdrasil, the Nordic tree of life, sizzled and popped.

And if so, I'd landed amidst the Vikings. The rise to power had been a flash in the pan, and if this was any indication... another in a long line of short but impactful peoples, and not the least of my worries.

The tether that bound us didn't pull me to the smoldering huts or the ships that succumbed to slate gray waters. I scoured the sheer cliffs, the moss, the trees, the very clouds and the relentless god who rained his white blaze of explosive fire and destruction upon the village.

*"Where are you?"*

I was here for a reason. Someone knew where she was.

What did I know of the Nordic fae? Their trolls were infamous. Their skosgrå, beautiful, nymph-like entities, were renowned for their beauty. If Thor was preoccupied, then someone, *something*, had to know where she was.

I could have laughed my relief when I spied a bipedal puff of smoke. I scooped the shadow as it neared, squeezing the member of my legion by a tendril.

"You brought me here, right? Explain yourself."

"We were only tasked to find—"

I could separate the fizzle of its throat from the rest of its body with a single, furious pinch. I had no patience for excuses. I bared my teeth. "What's happening?!"

"The collapse!" It sputtered to relay a message as information poured in from hundreds of its counterparts. "She's here, Sire, but the people, the village, the nation—"

Another flick of pressure and I'd smite it where it stood.

"Speak!"

It was spared by the first pair of eyes that grinned at me through the veil.

A woman with hair that matched the flames—no, it had to be a goddess, given the way she looked into my core—threw her head back in delight. With deer-like movements, she crossed the space between us in two strides and swatted my legion from my hand with an irreverent, backhanded swat.

My legion evaporated to join the throng before I locked onto doe eyes alight with a wild sparkle.

"Save that for later. This is a party!" She whipped her head to the side, a flash of red curls obscuring her face as she gestured for me to follow. "Join the chaos!"

Who the fuck was this person, fae, god, *being*, and what business did she have interfering with—

"Hell, right?" she asked. She pointed somewhere over the charcoal. "Demons are all about the war until it's time to burn shit to the ground. Your friend is somewhere over there."

I reached for her wrist, missing it as she danced away. "My human?"

"Ha!" I didn't understand the joke. I had no say in whether or not our conversation continued. She'd already turned on her heel, giggling as she disappeared against the sparks. Just before the bonfire road overtook her, I could have sworn she'd shouted for me to *make myself at home.*

The others...how many of them were immortal?

Whisps of my legion traveled down the smoke. I caught the second closest and shook it for the parts of me that could understand what the fuck I'd fallen into. These fragments of my power, these extensions of my will, they could only tell me what I, on some level, already knew.

"My human!" It came out in a bark.

"She's alive," the shadow insisted. "We know she's here. There's so much power, Your Highness. The gods, the immortals...they walk among the people. We..."

It continued to speak, but my shoulders slumped as I took it all in.

This was truly the end, and Love was lost amidst the ruins.

The Viking age, it seemed, had come and gone in the time it had taken me to fight with a succubus whose moniker no longer deserved breath. The seafaring people, it seemed, had enjoyed their powerful bedlam as they exploded onto the scene, establishing trade routes from their frosty land of Nordes to Britannia, then Constantinople, on to the Caspian Sea, and eventually, the Silk Road.

From what I gathered, their gods were nearly as close to their humans as I was to Love. The Nordes answered the Viking calls, carving impossible paths, facilitating their progress, disregarding known possibilities, and laughing in the face of tradition.

I released the legion's arm, absorbing the cinders, the inferno, the trees, the mountains, the gust of chilled, salty air swirling off the fjords.

I knew these gods, didn't I?

The Nordic gods had wisps of power at the conclave.

One thousand years later, Odin, Frejya, Thor, and Loki laughed, swords drawn, as I joined their Valkyrie on the battlefield. A demon was just another spirit in a slew of chaos as their experiment toppled. Yet this was not the air of a defeated people. There was a thrilled cackle, an unrequited power, an unkillable delight to burning it all down.

I watched the city crumble, fascinated by an energy that said: we have nothing to lose, and everything to gain. Try, try, try again.

I brushed past the highest of deities in the pantheon as they answered the songs and dances of their people. I didn't understand the circumstance, nor the custom, but holy shit, the people called, and their gods *answered*.

And for the first time in my existence, I was surrounded by gods who fucking loved demons.

I would have marveled forever, but I was on a mission.

I was here for Love.

If the milling chaos of deities were unbothered by my presence, then I wouldn't trouble myself with proper introductions. A tip of a hat, a squeeze of a bicep, but my presence was little more than a fraternal passing amidst their calamity.

A chuckling soothsayer rolling on psychedelics met me outside of Love's village.

"Fire at our door in more ways than one?" The human pulled their lips back to reveal blackened teeth, rattling in rotten sockets. She rattled the necklace of pearly white canines and incisors to replace those she'd forsaken to practices I had yet to understand.

Could the humans see me here, too?

Disoriented, I put one foot in front of another. I listened for a familiar voice, scanned for a shape, a color, a scent. My time within Northern Europe gave me a head start on their language, but before finding my human, I found something else entirely.

In a crowd of six-foot-something raiders was a taller figure. He was muscled, black of hair, with a strong jaw that could fit in with the crowd, but this was no human. In a sea of pallor stood a man made of slate with charcoal horns curling upward from his tousle of hair. He wore a thick, black fur coat, and a silver chain around his neck marking his sigil.

Amidst a sea of Nordic humans, bustling, unfamiliar fae, and gods I had yet to meet, for the first time in my years of traversing the soil, I met one of Hell's own. A house collapsed behind him, kicking up a pillar of smoke. He nearly disappeared against the plume.

He clocked me before I'd finished processing the oddity of seeing one of my Hell's own outside of my realm.

Black eyes wide, he dropped to a knee amidst the calamity. "My Lord."

A demon? When the chaotic goddess had told me Hell was welcome, could she have meant...whatever it was, it could wait.

I grabbed him by the shoulder, fingers digging into the muscular swell of slate-gray shoulders. I forced him to his feet. "You're my citizen?

He was nearly taller, if only by the horns, and perhaps more bewildered than I.

"Yes, my Prince. I'm Farefax—" He cleared his throat. "My partner is...no, I'm here for my practitioner. I mean—I'm going by Farefax. A woman, a nun from Britannia was captured in the Viking raids. Instead of calling on Heaven, she asked for—"

"Hell answered," I said, cutting him short. Surely, this would be a fascinating story on a different day, in a different life, but for now, the clock was ticking, and Love's environment seemed ferociously unsafe.

"I'm looking for a soul," I said, gaining his full attention. "Help me now and gain my favor, Farefax. The Nordes and their might have confused my legion. I need a demon's help. If you've been here for a while, surely, you've seen my glowing soul. Pearls. Opal. Starlight. She smells like the air above the mountaintops. Do you—"

"Yes! Yes." Black eyes shone. An iron finger pointed to a house on the far side of the fjord. "She—"

I squeezed his shoulder as I pushed away. "You'll be rewarded!"

The air before me split as I stepped through the veil, jumping from one side of the fjord to the other, throwing an off-handed command to my legion to ensure that the demon was both recognized and rewarded for his invaluable help. I trusted that they'd see to it, as the world around us fell, I had eyes only for...

The door opened before I reached it.

The storm and glacier steel-blue of a gown scraped the snow as soft, leather boots stepped from the threshold. A woman—a girl?—no older than nineteen hugged a fur shawl tightly against her shoulders. Pale hair hung in a loose wave down to her waist, taking on a life of its own as the wind whipped from the water.

A man's voice wafted through the darkened doorway.

"Sigrid? Is it done?"

I stepped backward, perched on the edge of the cliff as she lifted her chin. Piercing blue eyes gazed at the village below. Unfeeling, she replied, "It'll be gone by nightfall."

"Excellent," replied the man's voice. "Come back to bed."

*Fuck that.* The gods didn't care that I was here? They danced in the city's destruction? Then surely one more life wouldn't matter.

I pushed past Love without drinking her in. It could wait.

By the time she returned to the pile of furs warmed by the fire, the nameless warrior, husband, owner, male, *presence*, was relieved of his ghost. I was still holding him by the throat, savoring the final hiss as his eyes went glassy, when she returned.

She left the door open as she made slow, intentional steps toward the lifeless body, as if she knew what she was approaching. A pale slice of gloom created a perfect rectangle around the man's slack-jawed, limp frame. Her blue eyes had the dispassionate whitecaps of an unfeeling sea as she looked down at him.

She didn't check him for signs of life.

She didn't even call his name.

One long emotionless minute was wasted staring down at his

corpse before she drifted toward a barrel beside the ornately carved table. She fetched a lathed cup from the table, examined the remnants within, *humphed*, popped the barrel's wooden top, then plunged her entire fist beneath the liquid. Her fingers dripped with sickly sweet mead as she brought the drenched cup to her lips, sucking down the entirety of one cup, then returned her forearm to the barrel for another.

The honeyed alcohol ran dribbling down her chin, soaking the fur, dripping onto her feet as she finished a second, then a third.

She smacked her lips, wiped her face, took two wobbly steps towards the man's corpse, then flung the empty cup at his skull.

It struck with a dull *thunk*, bobbling on the floor unceremoniously as a thin dribble of blood seeped from the shallow wound.

I didn't need a mirror to know my breathy, grinning laugh set my eyes ablaze.

Gods above and below did I love this woman in all her forms.

She was fierce, she was a force, and she was aggressively, bizarrely, uniquely *her*, no matter what shape it took.

Her unceremoniously liquored-up disdain for the dead man who'd shared her bed was simply sugar atop an already perfect dessert.

Sigrid—Love—my perfect, magnificent, incredible human, left the house and walked toward the cliff once more. This time, when she surveyed it, she spoke.

"Claim your offering, Loki," she said with the same disinterest she'd offered her late husband. "Your fire and mischief have done more than I'd prayed. What once was mine, is yours."

A mortal may have jumped at the preternaturally tall figure who appeared upon the cliffs.

The surprise I felt was not for myself, but alarm at my human's nearness to a god of such bedlam. Lithe shape, red hair, cracked, smirking lips, scarred face, the half-Jötnar giant turned to me with glimmering eyes.

"She's a force," he said. The whirl of sleet continued to twirl Sigrid's untamed hair, but Loki's didn't move. He jutted a thumb toward her. "Yours, right? Big meetings, hundreds of gods, pomp and circumstance and all that? This is the one?"

I blinked speechlessly at the god's harsh silhouette.

He shrugged. "I get it. She seems worth it."

We were an odd triangle of power atop the cliff. I had no idea what to make of him as I asked, "What did she promise you?"

He laughed. "I don't care. I'm in it for the love of the game. And for what it's worth?" He made a sweeping gesture to the wreckage below. "We're rooting for you."

"...thank you?"

A wink. "Oh, this is delightful. The wolf-mother would kill to be here. She'd want to do this. Which, of course, means I have to get it done before she gets here. What's life without a little chaos?"

I was impatient enough to grab a prominent entity by his throat and shatter relations between our realms forever. I didn't care for his riddles. I didn't want to know what games they played. I just wanted *her*.

He took a step toward my human. "Wanna see something cool?"

Loki, among other things, was a god of deception. I wasn't sure that I *did* want to see whatever it was he considered cool.

He reached an eerily long hand toward Sigrid's back, slid his unnaturally thin fingers down the golden strands of her hair, and leaned toward her ears.

His lips brushed against her hair, whispered just loud enough to rise above the wind as he said, "Open your eyes."

✦

My sentiment remained: I loved my human in all her forms.

I loved her soul no matter its body, no matter its personality, no matter how life had shaped it. She'd been wise. She'd been compassionate. She'd been patient. She'd been insightful. Some souls needed protection. Some needed guidance. Some needed gentleness. Then holy fucking shit, there was Sigrid.

Whatever had shaped the woman who watched the collapse of the Viking empire had formed a desire I honored. She didn't want a spirit guide, a listening ear, or whatever responsibilities I'd carried every time I'd stepped from beyond the veil.

Sigrid—my human—*Love*—wanted a cock.

From the moment Loki showed her the world beyond the veil, she turned to me with an immediacy, a thirst, an insatiable appetite that no nymph, no goddess, no demon had matched.

We tore each other's clothes to shreds as she shoved me so close to the fireplace that the flames licked my thighs. I was throbbing for her the moment she touched me but hadn't expected the dripping desire between her legs as she commanded me, body and spirit.

I was hers to use as she jumped into my arms, rocking against me as I grasped every unholy sensation. I kissed her neck, then sucked, then grazed my teeth against her throat.

"Bite me."

I sucked harder, teeth sinking into her flesh.

"I said fucking *bite me*!"

I would never cause my human pain—and denying her pleasure *was* pain. I broke the skin, drawing blood as she released an earth-shattering moan.

"Fuck me," she said. "Fuck me like you hate me."

I ripped her off my cock and dropped her to the floor. In a swift motion, I had her against the wall, hand to her throat. Warm blood dripped from the gash I'd left over my fist as I pressed into her arteries, watching her eyes roll until she saw stars.

"Hate you? Oh, my Love..." I crushed my weight into hers, forcing her against the stony hearth. "Anyone can fuck you like they hate you. But me? I can fuck you like a demon."

My free hand went to her head, scraping against her scalp as I took a handful of her hair.

"Yes, *yes*," she pleaded.

I dragged her to the table, and she clutched the far lip greedily.

I slammed into her, salivating over her moans, but it wasn't enough.

She needed more. Deeper. Harder. She rocked backward, ass slapping into my hips until she got the depth she craved.

Cheek pressed against the wooden table, she issued her next command.

"Hit me."

I slapped her perfect, pale ass so hard it left a welt.

"I said fucking *hit me*!"

And so it went.

We fucked in the snow, scraped raw by the ice. She grabbed my still-wet cock, dripping with her juices, and sucked me clean while she straddled the open mouth of her not-yet-cold husband's face. She grabbed my hand, pushed it to her hair once more, then plunged her face into the mead as she drowned with her next climax.

Seven times the first day.

Three times the next.

Twelve times the day that followed.

"You have to eat," I gasped the morning of the fourth, shocked by her stamina.

"Then give me something to swallow," she murmured before her lips swallowed me whole.

There were demons.

And then there was Sigrid.

Love wore many faces. No matter how it looked, one thing remained the same: her life was hers. She could be curious. She could be sweet. She could be violent. And to love her meant to hear her, believe in her autonomy, and embrace her in every form.

# Chapter Twenty-One

**A THOUSAND YEARS OF COLONIZATION**

Blood stained the Egyptian sands in 1217 as I laid waste to Pope Innocent III's bloodthirsty crusades. Horus had his people covered, but we'd been awaiting this moment since this conclave. The falcon-headed god of war locked eyes with me as we unleashed wrath on the chainmail and crosses that dared to touch his faithful, as Heaven and its brainless battalion tried, and failed, to capture Love—Nefru—*my* human.

I was holding six-year-old Colel's hand in 1517 when the first Spanish ship beached on sovereign Mayan soil. I protected a child, her parents, her brothers and sisters, and anyone who followed as we made the most of a life on the run from Cortés and the conquistadors that followed. We found joy in the crystal blue, clean waters of cenotes, we found an abundance of food, of shelter, of sun, but her gods were not my gods, and her people not my people. When twenty-three-year-old Colel dropped my hand to return and fight for her kingdom, she became Buluc Chabtan's.

I watched over Hiso's home, a distant guardian, permitted at arms' length by the Shinto, when Portuguese missionaries arrived in 1599 Shogan territory. The first ships had landed in the foreign nation nearly one hundred years prior. It was foolish to hope they wouldn't find us.

A commotion drew me from her home the day peaceful monks arrived, decades into their studies of the new world and its mother tongue.

I followed Hiso as the family slid open the door, walked past the cherry trees, and watched the newcomers pass under the city's red arches.

White leathers, shimmering sword, and a nearly apologetic slope to his shoulders, Lucky stood in the middle of the road as the brown-robed Portuguese walked around him to spread the word of their god to Hiso and her villagers. We said nothing as the future unfolded before us both.

Golden eyes, rippling muscles, and a longsuffering expression—Lucky conveyed to me what a war table couldn't.

Fool me once, so the saying goes.

Unfortunately for me, it took three lifetimes of horrifying arrivals, combined with the resigned tightness around Lucky's eyes before I understood Heaven's army wasn't just spreading—it was *following*.

The time, the nation, the church's sudden impulse to divide and conquer had a compass of its own, and I was its north star.

Heaven's faithful and its marching orders: the continent, the people, the gods-damned villages, boiled down to Love and the demon that threatened their Book of Revelation. Any emperor, king, pope responsible for the decree was yet another string-tied doll plucked by hidden hands.

I'd known from our first encounter in Constantinople that Heaven would claim her when they could...but to tail me?

The only entities privy to my whereabouts were citizens of Hell.

And there was only one member of the Infernal Courts foolish enough to betray me.

When I'd told my sister to run, I'd been too generous.

It was a mistake I wouldn't make twice.

# Chapter Twenty-Two

**1618 ADE**

Breathe in. Breathe out. Clench your fists. Be still as the drumming stomp of soldiers approached. Don't look away. Don't back down. This is it.

The treaty was mine, and as such, they were my words to regret.

Love was mine to protect.

Every pantheon who had pressed its finger to the scroll had vowed to honor the terms.

I continued to play my part in the prophecy to the letter, evidenced by my faithfulness to her no matter where, no matter when, no matter who. Gods knew better than to make assumptions, and the treaty hadn't specified that I fill my human with the liquid, demonic potential.

True to my oath: never again would I avoid her. From one life to the next, I'd seek her out, woo her, protect her, and know her carnally whenever the cycle allowed. In return, they offered me an unconditional pardon for whatever I had to do for Love upon their soil.

Centuries of baffling impotence was the fault of those who'd assumed I'd take the next logical step in the gray area.

Love and I had a few beautiful lifetimes.

We had a few cut tragically short.

We were thwarted by Heaven more times than I care to admit.

And at last...it was *my* turn for the stars to align.

◆

Orange sunlight peeked through clouds, illuminating snowflakes as they swirled. I preferred when the sun shined on rainy days, but a sunset amidst the twinkle of frost was its own kind of magic.

The snow, the pine, the harsh rock had changed names over the years. Reclusive royals tucked themselves into the stony valleys years before the blood flowed through Wallachia. Vlad III Dracul—a surname destined for legends—impaled, disembow-eled, beheaded, torn, thrashed, violated, burned, plucked, nailed, and otherwise scribbled verbs into the long list of accomplishments of Hell and its Marquis of Torture.

My people were as varied as the humans, wise and respectable, kind and generous, homicidal sadists. Variety was not a mortal quality.

Five hundred years after Vlad's butcherous delights whis-pered through the kingdoms, I found myself on the mortal soil belonging to a pantheon I'd been waiting a long, long time to visit.

Heaven had spent centuries flooding the region.

Reddish-orange light washed the home sheltering a perfect,

mortal soul. Love was somewhere indoors drinking stew from a ladle with her parents. I knew from the legion that found her that Love was only a few years old. I also knew I would not see her face in this life.

I approached her house to leave my mark. A single cut across my palm. A symbol she and I had crafted together in a former life. A formal announcement.

I was here.

It could have been any village among the ever-moving, war-torn borders. The Polish-Lithuanian Prince had fallen to Heaven. Mortals couldn't hear the thousand boots and their distant tremor. They hadn't even received the news that the people beyond the safety of their mountain had been trampled. But I heard the earth's dull roar as foreign royalty marched on territories too far from the Tsar and his army to hold with a closed fist.

Love was here. In nearly two thousand years since the conclave, this was my first reason to plant my feet fully on Slavic soil.

The army would be here by nightfall.

A mutinous god of war carved a rugged path through terrain as he led the colonizers to Love's soil. But he wasn't the only one I was here to see.

A god and a bitch rumbled into an ambush.

Someone would die today.

If I fell on the battlefield to my adversaries, at least my story ended over someone worth dying for.

I soaked in the mortal world as if I might see it for the last time. Eastern peaks shimmered as they glowed in the west. A dozen perpendicular logs in the Baltic highlands smoked with life. I eyed the snow-covered, hay-thatched roof, steep enough for a small avalanche to bury three men in a chilly grave. Oak trees, dense, toxic berries of the rowan tree, and a fragrant perimeter of spruce pressed in from all sides.

Villagers milled about their day. Some jolly, some bored, some grumbling about one thing or the other, all ignorant as to the horrors awaiting them. Three thousand people, some with fair hair, some with a constellation of freckles, some fur-chested and black of hair, eye, and spirit.

I couldn't warn them.

Not this time.

◆

I'd bided my time to deal with Jarovid's bloodthirsty display at the conclave. Perun, Dzbog, Veles, Lada, and the retinue in attendance had watched their sneering brother and pressed their fingerprints to Hell's treaty.

An optimized agreement would have held out for reciprocation in wartime. Hell was offered no such promises. We were bound to their aid in battle. They were bound to ours through inaction.

This was my fight.

Snow hit my cheek but didn't melt against my icy skin.

Ten fingers, and I was nearly approaching both fists when it came to the number of times tears had lined my eyes. Today was such a day as I stood, and I waited.

Thunder rumbled overhead—rare enough for wintry days that it startled the villagers to dash into their homes—as the first deity stepped through the veil to see who had disturbed his people. I savored the last glimpses of sunset before clouds rolled in from over the mountains. This was not the gray of a late-afternoon and its snowfall.

The village vibrated as the sky darkened to a shade of iron.

Axe in hand, beard to his chest, clad in armor, the divine being of war, storms, and the chief of the mountain cults, appeared on the far side of the village. Perun watched as his people scattered, unable to see his shape, but obedient to the sound of his presence. His eyes blackened, a reflection of what could have been a night-dark sky.

I extended my still-dripping hand, dropped my blood upon the snow, and lifted my chin.

His knuckles flexed against his weapon. In a low rumble, he warned, "You offered us protection, Prince. Your legions have arrived throughout the mountains to fight with us, and yet the foreign god spreads. The oracle says this village will fall. She says the bloodshed will end only when we relent our faith."

I tracked his line of sight as he spied the wobbling shadows in the trees surrounding the village. My legion was here in full force, but not for him.

I spied the shades of other legions mingling with my own. I had not asked for backup. In fact, I'd told none of my plans. Yet, I'd consulted the citizens of Hell who peered into the glasses of time and returned with an answer. I suppose I shouldn't have been surprised that word of my intent would spread.

"They'll call it the Truce of Deulino," I replied. "Heaven will win. Your Tsar will concede. This will be their final battle."

The thick bushes of two gray brows clouded amidst his troubled forehead. Another crack of thunder, closer, louder, joined the snow "You believe in an ever-changing future, too, Prince. You speak of this one as if it's in stone. This is only our destiny if—"

The tightening of my eyes, the flex of my jaws, the subtle quiver as my throat bobbed was its own interruption. I couldn't cry in front of their highest god, but he was on the verge of understanding what I planned to do.

A sealed fate awaited this village, their people, and my human within it. I was to blame.

Perun tried again. "Are you saying..."

I did my best to create a few moments of levity, however brief, between myself and the high god. I needed him to remember me fondly.

"Heaven and its false peace has been championed by a god of war for two thousand years. This future was foretold." In my dullest attempt at idle chatter, I added, "At least your people believe in art. Among the colonizers and his places of worship... Your mosaics, the glasswork, the buildings they've erected... beauty is a small consolation."

Perun was not one for small talk. "We attended Hell's summit as this war god was seen among our oracles. The doom you casted warranted attention, and yet, I was reluctant to believe. Futures change all the time."

"And this one?" I asked. I knew the king of their pantheon didn't have a gift for premonition. But I wasn't asking about the fate of our people. This question belonged not to the years, but to the moments stretched before us.

He looked into the eyes of a man ready to die for the one he loved.

Perun dipped his chin. "Your scroll states that we will not retaliate, should you seek revenge. It does not say that we will come to your aid when Hell spills blood upon our soil."

The final wooden shutter slammed shut.

"I understand."

"Jarovid has not yet violated your treaty," he warned. The caution was unnecessary, and he knew it from the water lining my eyes. He lowered his axe. "I hope you know what you're doing."

I could have chuckled. "So do I."

I appreciated the ominous vibrations that shook the world. The sounds, the terror, the tremble of the earth itself, paid a solemn respect to the moment and its gravity. A warm, sunny day would have been downright disrespectful.

Perun was long gone, but he'd left behind the rumbling thunder of a storm that refused to arrive. Those who dared a glimpse through the shutters wouldn't see lightning amidst the gathering blizzard.

He masked the distant cadence of a thousand heels.

His people wouldn't hear the first murmur of war.

I expected I would never again receive a gift from the Slavic pantheon, as he granted me something as kind as it was cruel.

This depended on my predictability, and as such, I dug in to do the hardest thing I'd ever had to do. I tore myself from Love's perimeter, perching just beyond the village, certain that the evergreens would mask my earthy scent as the army approached.

The plated crusade, its prince, the metallic clang of his religious army, believed they sought territory. The humans had no idea who pulled the strings, orchestrating their every movement.

They called their impulses "divine revelation."

This wasn't the first time, nor would it be the last, that Heaven's King could sit back in his chair, fold his fingers behind his head, and not lift a finger as others did the dirty work of his colonization for him.

The land would be his at the end of the day.

The rest was negligible.

I remained between Love's home, hoping she enjoyed her final moments of peace, as the army crested the far hill and the enemy came into view.

To my surprise, Heaven had indeed volunteered a few of its men to stand side by side with a so-called pagan god and Hell's most treasonous citizen.

The angel was unfamiliar—some asshole with a blue-green, scaley, fish-like albacore shimmer—who matched his uneasy strides with the angry, frothing god of wrath, war, and flame.

Heaven's glinting bastard was flanked by one other presence I'd suspected for hundreds of years but needed to see with my own eyes to believe.

An hourglass shape.

A cloud of inky tendrils, floating on a wind of their own.

The smiling, confident stride of a succubus.

◆

Izi had been issued a fair warning.

She'd killed Shala when she thought I'd become too attached to mortals, believing it was her role to nudge *me* to play, rather than manipulate Love.

She'd toyed with my mortal, her culture, our fate.

When the threads of time had begun to weave new tales, she'd become relentless, finding new ways to orchestrate our story.

Her fingers remained in my life, manipulative, self-inserting, jealous, persistent.

Perhaps she'd only meant to teach me about obsession and its double-edged sword. Then she'd kept me from my human for hundreds of years while Love was tortured; convinced me it would undo prophecies projected upon us.

And when I finally returned to the surface, I played along in name alone.

I put no seed in mortal bellies. I fathered no children. I kept the final semblance of our connection to us.

She should have fled.

Instead, she'd fed information to Heaven and Jarovid alike.

Izi loved the sound of her own voice. If I gave her the chance, she'd grandstand before the battalion, monologuing her grand intentions, taking the spotlight one final time.

I wouldn't allow her the luxury. Her intentions were twofold, both boring and transparent.

On the one hand, if she fed information to Heaven and they won, their claim to Love would delay the Apocalypse. In her eyes, she'd save Hell, sparing the civil bloodshed of demon versus angel. If she got her way, she could delay the End of Times and the lost lives that went with it for decades, centuries, or possibly forever, should Love choose their king and his afterlife.

But Izi was too strategic to put all her eggs in one basket.

She drifted between Jarvid and the angel, feet not touching the snow, hair a darkened cloud around her as they grew closer, closer, closer. Seeing her beside an angel was an absolute joke. What honor could they have if they'd allowed their pawns to be moved by the dripping talons of someone I'd once called family?

Her other motive wasn't hard to guess.

If Heaven failed to convert Love, she'd force my hand. I'd attach myself more ferociously, more violently, inevitably jump-starting the prophecy I'd been avoiding.

She was so desperate for relevance that she'd dug herself a grave of delusion.

I almost felt sad for her.

Almost.

A crack of thunder. A stampede of feet. A battalion of—

A feminine shape tore my attention from the looming throng.

A flash of silver and red, a smattering of freckles, and the wicked glitter of wide, doe eyes that delighted in destruction broke from the tree line.

A legion could hide. Their shadowy, spindly nothingness disappeared, undetected, no matter who was looking, but this?

She'd giggled as the Viking age collapsed. She'd welcomed Hell without knowing my title or purpose. I thought Loki was the Nordic god of chaos, but there was something in this entity drawn to downfall rather than mischief.

Who the fuck was she, and why was she *here*?

I knew the Slavic gods, and she was not among them. In fact, I recognized her from the flaming villages along the fjords. She'd been chaotic even then, but here, with her red and silver streaks, her speckled face, her face-splitting grin, there was no hiding. We were too far south from the Nordic empire for her people to pay their visits. But she wasn't walking with the throng. She was walking toward them.

"Wait!" I called out to the flame-haired Norde.

She twirled. "Hey, Prince! Thanks for a shot at the end of the world!"

I coughed through my surprise. "Are you—"

She lifted a dainty hand to her brow in a salute. "Team Ragnorok." A flash of pearly whites, a glint of joy, a swish of forest-green skirts, and before I could guess at her name, she offered her battle cry. "I don't give a fuck about Heaven and Hell. I'm here for the end of the world. I don't know if you've read our Prose and Poetic Edda, but we're not about to let Heaven have the last word. If you help us to the finish line? I'm on your side."

I was ready to fight this battle with my legions. I searched the tens of thousands of hours of tutelage for rhyme or reason an entity from a neighboring pantheon would prance gleefully into a battle that most definitely wasn't hers.

"Norde!"

The bellow stopped her mid stride.

"I'm not here for you. I have no quarrel with the Nordes, but the treaty stands. If you get in the middle of—"

Exasperated, she popped a hip. "The Nordes are among the only pantheons that share your end-of-everything tale. I exist to burn shit to the ground. You're not *my* king. You can't keep me from the action."

"I don't need your help with the Slavic pantheon. If you're seeking some allegiance with Hell for you or your people. I don't know that this battle will result in—"

"Take the fucking win, will you? Let a girl have some fun."

The Norde dashed into the forest. I didn't know her powers and couldn't speculate as to how much help she'd be, but the time had come.

Fine. I'd kill her later if I had to. There was no line I wouldn't cross.

The humans crested the threshold as their invasion began.

The immortals spotted the flame-haired entity before I had a plan of action.

*So much for my cover—*

The thought ended with a crackle as the Norde picked up the angel by the throat, a shimmering arch of teal and shine, and slammed him into the ground.

*Holy shit. She hadn't blown my cover. She was my cover.*

A chance like this didn't come twice.

I sliced through the air, able to ignore Heaven entirely, two fists shooting through the veil before my body landed on the far side.

We sprinted into one another with a resounding clash.

I grabbed a fistful of Izi's hair with my right hand and Jarovid's ear with my left, slamming their skulls together as my legion descended.

Izi fell to the snow, scrambling on the ground with wide, black eyes in the instant it took her to understand how royally fucked she was.

She vanished in a predictable flash, leaving me alone to face the sneering god of war.

Soldiers threw their body weight into doors until the wood collapsed. Husbands, fathers, citizens dashed heroically into the fight, screamed like cowards as they dashed into the woods, or wet themselves as foreigners ransacked their village. Women wailed as their homes were set ablaze, some throwing their bodies on top of their children to protect them, some picking up weapons, some scooping infants against their breasts as they hid beneath logs or under snowbanks. Chaos descended within seconds.

I ran backward, my sights stuck to the enemy.

"You're finished, Prince," Jarovid sneered.

Eyes wild, fists at my side, I backed further and further toward Love's house. "Don't you *dare*."

I watched his pupils as they darted from me to the house I'd marked with blood. His lips pulled back from his teeth as his eyes locked on her home.

"No." I pressed against the logs, arms stretched wide.

A tar-soaked laugh oozed from the corner of his lips.

I forced myself to freeze as he did what I needed him to do.

No words existed for my agony. No vocabulary for my shame. No proverbial hell dark enough, painful enough, cruel enough to atone for what I needed to do. I awaited a binding treaty, shattering at each footstep that brought us closer to its breach.

I didn't deserve Love. I wasn't worthy of her knowing my name after what was about to happen.

*But...*

There was no 'but'.

For me to take my vengeance, for every god in every pantheon to tremble at Hell and its wrath, I wrapped my fingers around the intrusive gaze of every deity who dared to use my human, my *Love*, as a pawn, so across time, across lands, across faiths, no one would dare to repeat the mistake.

But to keep her safe, I had to become unworthy of her love.

My tenth tear—the one that had been dancing along my lids from the moment I landed in her mountain village—spilled at last.

I loved her enough to find her, to fight for her, to spend life after life after life with her.

I loved her enough to call a summit that surpassed kingdoms or geography or politics in the name of our treaty.

I loved her enough to sacrifice my kingdom.

And now, I loved her enough to sacrifice her.

Unseen claws grabbed my heart and ripped it into two. Teeth shredded its remnants. An eleventh tear fell. A twelfth. I couldn't count the salt that spilled as I listened to Love and her family, as venomous testosterone overrode Jarovid's logic. He slashed through the wood-hewn cottage with a point to prove.

He emerged, sword dripping, dark eyes gleaming with his wicked grin to see me standing twenty paces back, arms held away from my body, feet poised for launch.

The second hand of the clock ticked once, then twice before he understood his mistake.

My legion swarmed him, anchoring his feet, his hands, his writhing, bulky worm of a worthless body as I turned into an eagle. Sharp, raptor claws dug into one eye while I dove my beak into another.

The pain was enough for him to burst free, sword swinging. Blood poured from his sockets as he continued to wield his weapon, flailing sightlessly.

A grunt, a step, another useless arc of his sword as my legion swarmed him once more, quicksand immobilizing him in a thousand shadowed hands. He called on his allies, but no one answered.

My body ripped into pained oblivion as I became a grizzly large enough to tear his sword arm from his shoulder. I chomped through skin, feeling the popping of tendon, the snapping of bone, until metal clattered to the snow.

I'd expected more of a fight.

The war raged on around us, tapered only by a nameless ally on a journey of her own.

Despite our efforts, I knew the village would fall.

By morning, the invaders would plant their flag and declare a new god.

But not before I eliminated the one who had brought the enemy to their borders.

I stepped into a man's shape once more as I plucked the sword from its still-gripping hand.

We would have lost, had it just been one demon against a war god, an angel, a succubus, and a thousand human warriors. The village was already in ruins. There was one last battle within its charred remains.

An entity—too powerful to be fae, too chaotic to be a goddess of any order I understood—had taken care of the heavenly problem so I could focus my attention. While she hadn't stood against me, I couldn't be certain she was on my side either. And yet, her efforts left me alone for this final, choking moment. Thousands of wriggling limbs pinned him in place, two crimson rivers rushing down his face, shoulder spurting where once his weapon had been, as I came a breath from his face.

The proud god jutted his lower jaw. "I didn't realize Hell's prince was a god-killer."

I scoffed. "Yes, you did." The screaming began to die as the last of the village's people were slain. I sensed the heartbeats of those who hid or fled, but knew it was only a matter of time before their hope was gone, too. This massacre had only one ending.

"Heaven?" I asked. "Really?"

He didn't have to see me to know where my eyes would be. He maintained his defiance. "The enemy of my enemy, you piece of shit."

It was too bad he couldn't see my eyes roll.

"You've had it out for me before you called your fucking summit." He sucked blood and saliva into his mouth and spat his belligerence onto the snow at our feet. "I'm why you called your fucking conclave, right? A humiliation ritual before every god. All because I'd listened to your cunt of a sister about drawing you out. Fuck you, and fuck that whore, too."

I twitched at the barest of news.

Izi had done...what? Oh, I was already going to kill her, but this was one more notch in her wickedness.

I was a cat with a mouse, and I didn't play with my food.

The war god's time had come to an end. "You know what, Jarovid? You're right. You did motivate the summit. You made history. Good for you. Now," I pressed the tip of his blade into his throat. "Any last words?"

He snarled. "You won't get away with this. I'm a *god*. My

pantheon will come for you. You're nothing. You have no name. No cults. No purpose. Instead, you're wrapped up in these damned ticks, these fleas. They're mortals, you short-sighted fool. They're just humans. And you—"

"Tut, tut," I chastised lightly. "Not just humans. *My* human. She's more special than you'll ever be. And you, once mighty god of war, have just ensured no one will avenge you."

A high, clean ring cut through the crackle of flames and sobs of the few living victims.

The wind howled.

The snow turned into ice.

And a god's head rolled, sockets unseeing, tongue lolling, as I proved to the world that I meant every word.

Iridescent, immortal blood dripped from the blade.

I was a god-killer. The sword, on the other hand, was not.

One day, whether in weeks, or months, or ten thousand years, Jarovid could fight his way back to the surface and reclaim his seat in his pantheon, should they accept him.

My choice of weapon was a tenuous, threatening olive branch to all watching.

I made good on my promise.

My mercy would not be shown twice.

No one would harm my human and live to tell the tale.

# Chapter Twenty-Three

**CENTURIES OF SEMANTICS**

I was a caged animal, pacing against technicalities as I watched the ripple effect of Jarovid's death.

The dramatic uproar wherever I went was obnoxious.

I'd always been respected in the streets of Hell, but there was a new reaction whenever I left the palace for the cobbled streets. Whether fear or disapproval, the whispers of demons on the streets confirmed a certainty: no one doubted why the royal lineage was passing to me.

I'd carried the power of a god-killer for a millennia. Before our battle in the mountains, the strength that came with my crown simmered within me, untested.

Hell greeted me with renewed reverence.

Topside, I had to learn to internalize my irritation. It would serve neither me, nor my Love, if I met every deity for the rest of her cycles with hostility. But the change in their behavior...Did treaties mean nothing? I was annoyed by their shock, given the lengths to which I'd gone to follow our agreements, which both hardened and emboldened me.

As an unforeseen consequence of new reputations: I was met with caution, inhospitality, or outright hostility in new territories.

When a god *truly* smites a fellow immortal, there is no three-day stone that rolls away from the tomb. They aren't reborn as a phoenix. They wouldn't return as a tree. No one awaited their invasion of another body, their burst from the bottom of a lake, their appearance in a dream, or any of the etched texts of slain deities who returned with powerful theatrics.

The luxury of poetic reemergence that granted the epic ebb and flow of gods and goddesses came to an end.

My act of grace—a god-killing entity killing without a god-killing weapon—seemed to have been lost as word spread. I might as well have finished him once and for all.

As it stood, my presence couldn't be risked.

◆

I tolerated regional animosity during Love's Christian cycles, particularly in the years following the world and its theological tilt in the centuries following Jarovid's death.

Whether or not I was allowed to be with her, our agreements remained:

Don't harm my human.

Don't even touch her.

But just as I found loopholes, so did the gods.

Our treaty said nothing of nudges, of prompts, of whispers. I was helpless against their pushes, their encouragement, their malignant guidance as they lured her toward a title that would facilitate the prophecy in one lifetime after another. They beckoned her out of churches, goaded her out of her home, bribed her to step into brothels, to sit down next to Madams, to sidle up to a desperate man with a pocket full of gold, all without touching her.

I followed Love's soul as humanity—too disorganized to be a colony of ants, too wicked to be a swarm of wasps, too complex and beautiful and nuanced to be the animals I was already bored of comparing them to, and too fleeting to worry about the lasting impact of their sins—filled every corner.

The mortal world was mapped, known, conquered.

Heaven had, as I'd said from the conclave, done exactly what I'd said it would do.

I, on the other hand, did not rise to the occasion.

I was not my father. I had not once served Heaven's King, loved its ruler, or shared the blood of the covenant with angelic comrades. I had no bias as I watched a war deity be the very best of his kind. I had a raw appreciation for the black and white fulfillment of his purpose, but my heart turned cold against thoughts of the war, its strategies, its stakes.

My father fought with me once, and only once, on the topic.

Exasperated, he'd pleaded, "You are my son! You are Hell's Prince! This is your birthright! You must—"

"Have to disregard all Hell stands for, forgo my free will, fight blindly for a king whether or not I consent?"

◆

He forewent swords and blood and kingdoms and borders while the other pantheons remained stuck in the past. An innovator, he began conquering culture, consciousness, minds, dreams, and every deviation of war long before the others knew they could expand their definitions.

He won.

Yet even his own book had an antagonist and thus continued my usefulness on the global stage.

No one had seen him in four thousand years. But if I got the chance...

I popped my knuckles at the thought.

Cryptids, fae, lesser entities, inter-realm parasites, discarded heralds, spirits, beings of battle, creatures of the garden, wights, omens, lurkers, dream-feeders, relics, saints, nameless miracle-workers, witches, warlocks, wraiths, beasts of elder names, unseen governors, the half-divine, stray seraphim, lesser angels, the vast majority of Hell's citizens, royal or otherwise, and the a rambling litany of preternatural beings too long to bother spewing, none of which could land a killing blow, even if they had the gumption.

They'd already believed in the champion we might conceive before witnessing how I'd ended a sovereign member of the undying. Now, global eyes turned toward me, convinced their role was more important than ever, even at the risk of their immortality.

One piece of the prophecy remained. My caution, in theory, would have been unwarranted in her lives as a mother, a seam-stress, a shaman, a basket weaver, a military wife, if she'd ever wanted to have children. We could have sired a cambion—powerful, magical, and utterly irrelevant to Heaven and its games.

Those days were long gone.

All eyes focused on the missing technicality: Love had to be a whore.

✦

In the hundreds of years that followed, many lost their lives.

Humans to be sure.

Fae in the dozens.

A bold god or two.

But most were subtle with their coercion. Those who came with silk, coin, and a purr, were usually allowed to keep their lives, as long as she remained safe, comfortable, and happy.

Love found herself with Madams, sometimes in the plush of red-velvet brothels, then serving amidst the smoke of opium dens, after that, a Bavarian village making house calls until I ensured she was hired by a foreign dignitary as a live-in mistress on one's dime.

American boots marched into Port-au-Prince in 1915, which took the pressure off local deities. Gods needn't get their hands dirty when invading soldiers were so efficient at violating land and body alike.

My wrath earned its own ghost story as the streets ran red with vigilante justice for more than a decade. I was single-handedly responsible for more dead Americans in that cycle than the Haitian resistance.

Death, sex, money.

In some lives she knew me. In many she didn't.

I was as bound by the treaty as they were. I couldn't retaliate if she was unharmed. Once the die had been cast, it was too late. The best I could do after she'd been led down the path was facilitate the highest-ranking position, the best pay, the most comfort, and of course, facilitate the sudden heart attack, choking on tongue, stroke, aneurism, and any other instant death to a man who made her feel disempowered, even for a moment, while she worked.

✦

I waited roughly fifteen hundred years before Jarovid paid for what he'd done when he'd overseen the men who'd tortured her, brutalized her, then tied her hands and feet as she was pulled in four directions.

The years I'd refused to participate in the lore were long behind us. The days of gods egging me out of Hell had come and gone. The conclave, at long last, granted me the retaliation I craved.

Vengeance lingered as I hunted the missing traitor.

In 1947, a twenty-one-year-old named Winifred bore a thick Irish accent, a round, happy face, and the daily chore of salting and dying cod in the cold, North Atlantic island of Newfoundland. I caught wind that the rocky settlement was disproportionately plagued with a night demon they called "the old hag."

Sailors, mothers, babes, would awaken to a twisted woman sitting on their chest, paralyzing them as it terrorized the island.

In thousands of years, I'd learned the stack of tricks played by the succubus.

And it was here, in this cycle, I knew I'd find my sister.

# Chapter Twenty-Four

**1947 ADE**

Jellybean homes dotted an endless coastline as fishermen took the reds, pinks, greens, yellows, and blues from their boat and painted the rest of their lives to match.

Winnifred—Winnie, according to the three hundred or so in their cove—lived in a mustard home, with a mustard boathouse against their dock to match.

Hers was one of many isolated inlets that dotted the shores, most inaccessible by road, cut off from the world, save by ship. Many outharbours kept to themselves, while others sent their sailors on months-long journeys—some through the Northwest Passage, cutting through ice, trapped for months as they harvested seal, whale, and cod. Others went south, returning with rum, conches, and a tan.

She was tasked with skinning, curing, and otherwise preparing the cod when they were available. She milked the goat. Hid the shame of lobster shells—cockroaches of the sea eaten only by the poorest of families—and had raw, pink fingers from her nearly impossible time with crops, save for the potatoes, turnips, and beets that could survive the weather.

Cruel winds kept trees from growing more than a few feet tall, as the bluster ripped their roots from the shallow earth if they stood above a man—with pockets of inland exceptions, of course—though if she wanted reprieve from the wind, she and the rest of her family hunkered down in the living room against a roaring stove, hoping the chopped wood would last through the storm.

She enjoyed the sailors' tales but was not one for the sea.

The men, women, and children kept the world turning on rural beaches, their Celtic roots taking on a life of their own, Emerald-Isle tongue developing its own in-speak, and lore birthing new superstitions. Gods, fae, and powers, were no strangers to people who experienced blessings and curses in their rawest forms among the unforgivable rock.

With the crack in the veil held by their belief, came the inevitable darkness.

If Izi wanted to hide, changing her motive of operations was a half-assed job. Sexuality was a preferred form of draining, but for the most part, only worked on men.

She had someone else to torment, a brother to evade, and a death sentence to dodge.

✦

I didn't dare take the form of a sea creature amongst a people who were sustained primarily on root vegetables and marine life.

A bird might do the trick, but given the circumstances, it didn't quite fit.

The island, though too southerly for natural apex predators, faced an annual parade of icebergs as they broke free from Greenland and floated down the Atlantic current. At least once a year, an iceberg would make landfall somewhere along Newfoundland's rocky shores, delivering a starving polar bear, or any other creature that had the misfortune of living adrift for weeks or months without food.

Love left bowls of milk out for the fae. She avoided circles of mushrooms. She wove interlocked crosses made of grass. And at night, she kept her eyes peeled for signs that the hag might visit her family.

It was late spring when I finally stepped out from behind the veil.

It was high tide, and the rhythmic lapping of waves breaking against rocks covered the sounds of my approach.

Love was shuttering the goat well past sunset when I saw my chance.

She closed the doors to the barn and turned to see the only form I could think to take that was special enough to affirm her belief in the otherworldly, but small enough not to startle her.

I curled a white tail around my paws, sat tall, and waited with wide eyes to see if she would know me, accept me, love me, as an arctic fox.

Her back flattened against the barn, and for a horrifying heartbeat, I was certain I'd frightened her. Then, as she slowly sank to her bottom and set the lantern gently beside her, I realized that the move had been so she wouldn't startle *me*.

"Are you a ghost?" she whispered.

It was a shame she couldn't see me smile. I shook my head, and she nearly choked.

"You understand me?" Thin fingers flew to her chest. "You are no fox."

Bowing felt too stiff. I laid down, legs stretched toward her, head tilted toward the side.

"Are you a good spirit, or a bad one?"

*Hm.* She hadn't exactly set me up for success with such a complicated ask. I chewed on the answer as she readied herself for her next question when a scream sliced through the wind and waves.

Love knocked over the lantern in her haste to her feet. "Mother!"

She sprinted for the house. I cast a wasted look at the flame before remembering where I was. The soaked grass didn't have a chance of catching fire. I twisted to follow her into the house, pushing through the door she'd left ajar, as she crashed into her parents' bedroom.

Her father had been gone for months, and her mother, unable to move, was panting, frozen, while a twisted ghoul straddled her.

Maybe Love had the ability to see through the veil in this life, but I doubted it.

Mortals caught between sleep and consciousness, paralyzed by spirits, however, were cursed with the ability to see.

*So much for my time as a fox.*

I wasn't sure if it was Winnie, or Love, whose hands flew noiselessly to her mouth as I burst from my fox shape and leapt for the hag. The succubus ripped me from the mortal realm as we tumbled through time and space, through breath and suffocation, through poison and venom and hate and terror as she snared me in a nightmare.

# Chapter Twenty-Five

**ETERNITY**

I landed, panting on my hands and knees, on the edge of the Dead Sea.

Heat scorched me. My hands burned. I winced against the blinding sun, an endlessly blue sky. A stampede of men stormed over me, trampling me underfoot. My mouth was forced into sand, jaw twisting, choking on dust, as their accusations filled the air.

I struggled to my knees, spitting sand onto my forearm, as the memory yanked open a door I'd closed, forcing me to watch an innocent woman beg for a god who would not answer. Somewhere, on a distant cliff, Gula would be watching. I felt the cuts and bruises of a mortal body, shoving as if I was just another man, as I forced my way to the front.

The sentence was issued, and the stoning began, but it was not Shala on the shore.

Yuka looked up at me, wide eyes forsaken and wet with

betrayal as she spied her protector, complicit in her death. In her silence, three pained words pierced me:

*I trusted you.*

Watching, when the first rocks hit. The Qawiaraq word for "Fluffy" barely escaped her lips, the pleading cry of the abandoned.

The air escaped my lungs. I shoved men out of the way, the impact of their rocks exploding against the back of my skull, bruising my spine, cracking my ribs as I threw myself over her.

When I landed, there was no one beneath me.

The sun, the sands, the crowds, were gone.

I shivered against the cold, shocked by the smell of manure and unwashed fur. The strained hiss of rope was a unique noise, but one I'd encountered before. I scrambled to my feet once more, knowing I'd left my mark on the realms and their challenges. Jarovid threw back his head in a cackle as he gave the order.

I'd never met the swollen, battered woman at the center of the quartet of horses, but the shimmer of her soul was enough to shatter me.

This was a life I'd evaded—a death that had haunted me even when told by a legion while I seethed from my palace.

Four men slapped their horses at Jarovid's count.

I cried, throwing myself upon her once more, but this time I was not spared the violence.

I held her body against mine as she screamed, clutching her as arms and legs were pulled in four different directions, sobbing into her hair, promising her it was okay, that I had her, that I would save her, as she was ripped in quarters.

I cried into the bloodied stump of her torso before it evaporated.

A single light illuminated an infant at the center of the room.

I stopped short.

I turned away from the infant only to see it appear in the opposite direction under the same spotlight.

"This isn't real," I said, first to myself, then to the room. I closed my eyes but knew it wouldn't be enough. Nightmares didn't work by closing your eyes. Not when your vile bitch of a sister came from the Court of Nightmares.

"Izi," I seethed, "You are almost clever."

I knew what was happening, but I was still losing.

She'd never outrank me in the Royal Court. Only the heir to the throne would inherit the king's powers. Her royal blood was useless while I lived. Even if she could take me in battle, she wasn't a god-killer. A thousand years of perfectly honed skill, and even my beheading would see me knitted together to return and seek vengeance. She couldn't best me on mortal soil, nor in Hell.

The air left my lungs.

A crushing weight suffocated me.

I scrambled for reason, for a foothold in logic, as I searched for my assailant.

A cough, a gag, and my knees hit the cobblestones. I braced myself, hands clutching rock as I choked on something horrible. A rope? No, it was moving. I heaved, puking the head of a cobra as it twisted backward, its body still invading my throat, fangs dripping as it poised to strike.

I grabbed just behind its jaw and ripped it out, esophagus raw as the scope of our battle seeped into me with horrifying clarity.

The Nightmare Realm, however...I was ready for swords. Give me fire, fists, warriors. Roll me in storms, drown me, burn me alive. But I'd spent so much time with my human that I was nearly mortal, myself. My nightmare was singular. And this...this was a trap I didn't know how to escape, unless...

The infinitely black room.

The single light.

A helpless infant in a life I hadn't gone to the mortal realm to protect.

I couldn't cry. I couldn't rage. I couldn't save her. I couldn't break.

I looked toward the ceiling and tried the only thing I had left.

"If she dies," I said, letting my voice quake, "I'll still love her."

The light reappeared on the ceiling, the baby upside down as the nightmare tried to force me to look at it. But terrors fed on panic, on urgency, on suffering.

I looked down, hands clenched, and said, "She'll die. She always dies. She's mortal. Sometimes she dies of old age, happy, loved, and safe. Sometimes she dies because you're a cunt. Sometimes I feel guilty...but do you know what I learned about those times?"

The infant again, this time deep underground, as if through a translucent floor. The single spotlight flickered. The infant itself wobbled, struggling to keep its form.

"I felt really fucking guilty when you convinced me to stay in Hell," I said. "Turns out, I had nothing to feel guilty for. Her deaths are on *you*. I didn't intervene because I trusted you. Briefly. You're an absolute disappointment. You know why you never earned father's favor?"

The light flickered until it strobed in and out of visibility.

The baby appeared inches from me, but the unstable dream had no face as the lighting disintegrated.

"You enjoy your jaunts on the surface? It was fine, the same way we let cows graze in the fields, Izi. It's fine when the cow stays in the pasture. But you're a cow who's broken out of the fence. You're incompetent. You're an embarrassment. You became a fucking liability."

Her voice crackled through the darkness.

"You don't know what you're talking about." The sentence wobbled, much like the image of the infant, but I grabbed hold.

I sneered. "I've called the only summit of gods in the history of immortals. I've murdered major deities for disrespecting something I care about. I'm the linchpin to a prophecy that will save the world, but do you know what's better, *sister?*"

Only the flickering spotlight remained in a sea of darkness. No children, no imagery, no versions of love assaulted me as I peered into the nightmare's core.

"*None* of that was true before I became father's favorite. I'm the Crowned Prince. I was granted a kingdom, a realm, a world, before proving myself in the slightest. He had two children, and what did you get, again?"

"Stop it."

"He. Gave. You. *Nothing*."

"Stop it!" Hurricane winds blew through the nightmare as she appeared, screaming at me amidst the crackling clouds of the Court of Nightmares.

I took a step toward her. "He gave you his time, his patience, his love, because *he* is good. But you? Izi, you had to slurp your worth to pretend you had relevance."

"I'm his only daughter," she hissed, matching me step for step. She pressed her face so close that her nose was nearly on mine. "He won't even *let* himself be disappointed in your monumental failures while your essence remains. All that wasted potential. All the citizens you put in danger with your selfishness. I'm the heir you'll never be. The best thing you can do for our kingdom is die."

I looked at the cloud crackle overhead, witnessing the blue-gray rumble as electricity silhouetted godly shapes who pointed and laughed.

I took one step forward, forcing her toward the cloud.

"No one with power needs to scheme, needs to manipulate, to lie. Power doesn't steal. Power simply *is*."

Another step, then another.

She extended her hands, mouth in a snarl, still leaning toward me, but unwilling to let us touch. "There is more power in words, in knowledge in the battles that exist within the mind than you—"

"I am humiliated that I ever called you sister, you amateur. You led *Heaven* to our doors. You were so desperate for relevance that you spent cycles upon cycles snitching to the only realm that could take us down just to remain in the game."

One more step.

The lightning crackled again, this time so close I could taste its ozone.

"It should have been *me*," she cried. She jammed her finger into her chest, snarling as she rolled onto the balls of her feet. "I have the fight! I have what it takes! I'm the heir that should have ascended!"

I could barely exhale through my laugh.

"Yeah? Then prove it."

I exploded with energy. Two flat palms against her chest, I used my final steps to push her into her crackling nightmare and watched as the cell of lightning bolts crackled around the cloud, trapping her in the cellar of her prison.

I stood and watched the silhouettes as she cowered, as she raged, as she fought.

She ran, she cried, she ran, she battled, she ran, she ran, she ran.

I'd been prepared to kill her.

I had no idea how much time passed as I watched Izi—the succubus I'd once called sister—trapped in her own nightmare, before I knew there would not be escape.

I had one thing she didn't.

In my lifetimes of weakness, I'd experienced the one thing she'd never had.

I knew Love.

# Chapter Twenty-Six

**10 YEARS BEFORE THE PRESENT**

The cramped bedroom was one I knew well. A cross hung over her bed. A framed picture of her family forcing a smile sat upon the dresser. A *Lord of the Rings* poster featuring Legolas ordained one wall—okayed by a deeply religious mother given the Biblical undertones of Tolkien's work—and a Keira Knightley poster in pirate garb from the *Pirates of the Caribbean*, okayed because it was a woman, and her parents couldn't conceive a world where their daughter might be queer.

In this cycle, Love's name was Marlow, and tonight was one of familiar pain.

She was on her knees, eyes closed, hands clutched over the bed, face stained with salt from tears that would no longer come.

I thought I'd seen it all before I'd experienced the acute pain of this cycle.

Born with a drop of fae blood—a great grandmother who'd loved, mated, and created a strained, beautiful, terrible life with a

Norde from beyond the veil—Love had been able to see me from birth, which, if Izi had her way, would have been a nightmare of its own.

The trailer house outside of her Midwestern city was set so deeply within the woods that she was unable to experience anything beyond isolation, no matter how close, or far, I remained.

I hadn't found our relationship complicated before this one.

Prior to this life, the options were clear-cut. In some, she neither saw me, nor asked for preternatural help, and I played the role of helpful spirit, much like every spiritual human knew they had. I protected her, aided, and respected her autonomy without question.

Some cycles I was absent entirely. In others, I found her but was not permitted access.

And finally, in the best of our lives, save for young Yuka and her guardian wolf, Love had consistently learned to see me with the conscious autonomy of someone in her twenties, thirties, or beyond. She'd been spiritual, intentional, and wanted to see beyond the veil.

Even in life where my human had been born and raised to see beyond the veil, it had been with openness, with curiosity, without the guilt, the crushing shame, that came with Marlow.

Our first milestone came before kindergarten, years before her family abandoned the city. She was four years old, nosed pressed against the window of their two-bedroom trailer house as she watched the big kids wash a car three trailers down, dancing to silly music, getting colorful shirts and shorts wet on a hot summer day.

Her mother had given her a red bucket of soapy water, a sponge too big for her hands, and put a red baseball cap atop her head. I watched my brave human approach the children, then felt the painful chill as they stilled, as they paused the music, as they made it clear she wasn't invited. I watched her stand at the end of the driveway, suds flowing past her shoes, as she tried not to cry.

If she didn't, I would.

Her first rejection destroyed me.

I became a fox before I could think. I jumped around, leaping, desperate to make her smile. I darted between houses until she saw me. I darted into the house, desperate to get her away from those who wished to crush her spirit.

I'd be this human's pet, her imaginary friend, the spirit guide that showed up to keep her from breaking. I'd remain that way forever if it would help keep her whole.

I didn't count on the day when her mother opened the door and saw me, too.

Of course, the fae blood ran on her maternal side, and Lisbeth Thorson, woman of god, daughter of Heaven, prayer warrior, four-times-in-church-per-week, knew what I was long before it was appropriate to admit it.

Lisbeth had seen a demon.

Marlow was dragged to the church screaming and sobbing while elders prayed over her, casting out Satan, praying hedges of protection over her.

I braced myself for Constantinople, ready for the domed barrier, for the angels, for the banishment where I'd have to wait decades to see her once more...

But instead, a tearful girl too small to reach the bread with her folded hands had prayed for me—her guardian angel. She'd described me. She'd invited me into her life. She said she knew I was good, that she wanted blessings for me, that she thanked god for me—even if we may not have been talking about the same god.

And though I waited with flinching trepidation, the dome never came.

The years passed.

She read her Bible.

She listened to her mother.

She attended church.

She prayed.

And every night, she cried. I'd come to learn the tears of the clairvoyant—the death sentence cast upon anyone cursed to see beyond the veil in a world that didn't accept it.

When she asked to see my face, I obliged, though as far from her as I could be in the small room. She insisted I was a guardian angel, even when I refuted the title. And when she made the mistake of telling her mother of her angel, the torment of evangelical exorcisms returned.

✦

Tonight, as she cried, her prayers had taken on a different nature. There was a bottle of orange pills in her mother's medicine cabinet, and she wanted so badly for the pain to end, that she begged for her angel to take her hands and give her a sign.

There was church language for such things. It wasn't meant to be literal. It had been six months since she'd seen my face for the first time, and given the revelation's religiously disastrous end, I was reticent to reappear.

But for fuck's sake, she could not die because of her mother's relentless cruelty.

The wooden spoon, the leather belt, the forms of physical, emotional, and psychological abuse, quickly added Lisbeth to a list of enemies that had, until this moment, only been populated by war deities and succubi.

On the far side of the bed, I slipped my hands over hers and spoke.

"I'll protect you," I promised. "Please, trust me."

She opened her eyes just enough to see that I was there, then shut them again. Choking sobs filled the tiny space. She closed her eyes tighter. "Why did you give me an angel, God? Why would you give me one if I would only be punished for having one?"

I squeezed her hands inside my own.

I pushed down the urge to murder her mother. Love—Marlow—my human, prayed for her parents' safety on a nightly basis, much to my chagrin. Besides ignoring Marlow's autonomous wishes, Lisbeth's untimely death would solve little. Marlow was a minor with no relatives, and unlike when the world had only a few thousand humans and a king here or there, I couldn't orchestrate her rise to a better life with ease in a world of red tape. The best I could do until she turned eighteen and could get her the hell away from her mother—when I could finally inflate her salaries, fill her cupboards with food, have every call from her mom mysteriously go to voicemail—was just to keep her alive.

"Love, listen." I began the sentence without knowing how it might end. "I want to tell you that your mother loves you, but I can't see her heart. I can only see her actions, and what I see is this: she's scared. You don't deserve to be punished. You deserve love. You deserve to be heard. To be understood. To share your stories without fear."

Dry tears choked her through a stream of silent prayers.

She waited until she could take full, deep breaths before she opened her eyes to look at me.

"I'm sinful," she said.

I could have thrown the frame against the room and watched it shatter. I restrained myself, shaking my head. "No. *No.* Love, I—"

"You shouldn't be my angel," she said.

"Don't say that."

"Please, go," she said.

And her fae blood had a second, horrid effect. She could see me before she was ready. She could also banish me before I was ready.

✦

Love would graduate college in three days.

She was a complicated, strange, beautiful disaster. She'd given me a new name. A Shakespearean one. In this life, I was Caliban. I quite liked the moniker, though I wasn't sure if she could fully appreciate what it did to me to have a name.

I avoided her seeing my face as diligently as possible until she was in college. Even then, I wanted her to see me as a fox, and to save her as a guardian angel, but with her combination of fae blood and religious trauma, I had no idea how to respect her autonomy while balancing on the razor's edge of impossible situations.

She crashed into the door of her shitty basement apartment in a bandage dress, one heel broken, makeup smeared down her face. If I hadn't been playing a lifelong role in the shadows, I would have assumed the worst, given her state.

Instead, the worst was the depths of her unhappiness.

This wasn't the first time she'd come home too drunk to see, but each time, I pressed a healing hand into her back, disappeared behind the veil, and helped her to bed without her knowing.

Unless, of course, she commanded it.

Being summoned on command was unfamiliar and uncomfortable. I was never her prisoner, but I didn't have the option of giving her space when she called out to me. The combination of her bloodline and our soul tie shifted the power dynamic.

I'd always wanted her to be in control.

I'd just never imagined it would be in a lifetime of pain.

She hiccupped, newly sober with my help, but esophagus still spasming from the blue raspberry slushie she'd painted across the alleyway.

"I'm here," I murmured in the dark.

"Lay next to me?"

It was all I'd wanted to hear in every lifetime. In this one, everything she said sliced through me. Therapy, medication, religious trauma counseling—they were the sort of topics she no longer wanted to hear. After leaving the church, she'd decided I was psychosis. She imagined me to cope, and as such, I was as much a part of herself as my legions were fragments of me.

It was truer than she realized, given her command over me.

I settled on the far side of the bed atop the covers, extending my hands. She stained her pillow with mascara, voice muffled as she said, "What if you're real?"

*What if?*

Thousands of years ago, I'd met Shala on the edge of the Dead Sea and experienced something that felt like empathy. So curious. Interesting. New.

Each emotion, each life, each cycle, she taught me more about myself than I ever could for her. Love was uniquely herself in each life, no matter who, or where, or what.

I hadn't thought I'd ever experience a newness that I'd hate.

"I certainly might be," I said softly. "Would that be okay?"

Another hiccup. A choked sob. "No."

I squeezed her hands, more for myself than for her. "Why not?"

She released my hands, rolling onto her back, staring at the basement apartment ceiling and the cheap, blue-green glow-in-the-dark stars left by the previous tenant. She stared up at the fake constellations and said, "You were my fox, and I got the shit beat out of me for it. You were my angel, and I had a fucking exorcism. I left the church. I take my meds. I go to therapy. And..."

She shoved the heels of her hands into her eyes.

I watched as each moment was a new nightmare. Every drop of her pain was something I'd never experienced before. Something I wasn't sure I could withstand.

"And?" I dared.

It was my duty to remain calm.

Only one of us could break, and these emotions weren't hers to carry.

"If you're real...then denying you? Praying you away? The life I've spent trying to medicate, to ignore, to push down, to pretend...you have to be fake, Caliban. You have to be my imagination. If you're real..."

She rolled back toward me, extending a hand toward where my face would be in the apartment's inky blackness.

Another hiccup.

"You can't be real," she insisted. "I couldn't live with myself if you were, knowing what I'd done to you. Another failure in a lifetime of failures. My biggest, cruelest—"

"Love." I cut her off gently, brushing a piece of hair from her cheek that had been plastered by tears. "If I'm fake, then enjoy me. Savor the imagination. Let yourself have fun."

A hiccup. Her eyes squeezed shut. "And if you're real?"

I had to swallow the shimmering tears that glazed my laugh.

*If I'm real? I would save you from the Dead Sea.*

*I would stay with you when you asked me not to go.*

*I would marry you to a Greek general then banish your husband to years of campaigns and conceal his death so we could be together.*

*I would follow you on the ice, spend decades as a wolf, a spirit guide, a friend, supporting more than a hundred years of your guidance as you lead your tribe.*

*I would find you married with a child in the Emerald Isles and wait for you every year just so you might offer me a cup of mead on your birthday.*

*I'd suffer the unbearable torture of feigned indifference for centuries, over one sliver of hope that you would find peace at my absence if I could just learn to control myself and leave you alone.*

*I'd call a conclave of every god known to man and even those beyond mortal comprehension, swearing them to your protection, threatening their immortality if they harm a hair on your head.*

*I'd lay bare my willingness to shred my reputation with my kingdom, choosing my human over my people, whether they stood with me or not.*

*I'd fight angels, becoming a tiger and mauling Heaven's conquering army for the chance to see you through a window.*

*I'd become a turtle, a bird, a shark, then spend a mortal life on an island roleplaying humanity, just for the chance to see what it might be like had we ever been husband and wife.*

*I'd grovel before a closed pantheon, pathetic, shameless, begging for a glimpse of you.*

*I'd climb a fjord, dance among the embers, and fuck you like a demon until you were satiated enough to last the thousands of lifetimes we wouldn't touch.*

*I'd be there with you through the rise and fall of empires, through colonization, through misery, through choice, through autonomy, through death, in kingdoms and nations that no longer have names.*

*I'd murder a god and paint my legacy with his blood.*

*I'd find you on a windswept island among the icebergs and chase you into a realm of nightmares.*

*I'd trap my only sibling in a purgatory of her own making.*

Another hiccup.

"You're quiet because you're not real. And every time I beg my imagination to talk, I only seem crazier and crazier. I should just go to bed. If you are real, I'm a worthless nightmare, Caliban. I've ruined everything. I would never forgive myself. I've ruined your life. I've hurt you in ways I can't fathom. Caliban, oh my god, if you *are* real? I've known shame. I've known guilt. But the hate I would feel over what I've done, over what you must have felt, over what I've put you through—"

"Love?" The hot spike of emotion rose within me once again. She owned all my tears, both those that fell, and those that didn't. Her eyes were not made for the dark, but I could see her just fine. I watched her still as she searched the blackness for a sign of something real.

"If I'm real?"

A final hiccup. "Yes?"

"And if you believe I love you?"

A small laugh this time. A long pause. A yawn. A sleepy, sheepish, "Yes?"

"Don't worry about what you're doing to me. Let me worry about that."

Her hands slackened. Her eyes closed. Sleep began to settle over her. "If you're real?"

The world around her dimmed. My shoulders softened, her

glow consuming me as I regarded the complicated, fascinating, unpredictable, irreplaceable, perfect, beautiful embodiment of Love.

My hand settled over hers—the soul who owned every one of my tears as I gazed at her through the shimmering haze of my one, unconditional truth. I squeezed it lightly until her lashes fluttered open, eyes locked on mine.

"Then destroy me. I'm yours."

# Acknowledgments

Have you ever had a niece/nephew/nibbling proudly hand you their mess of a finger painting, and with love in your eyes, you look between the fragile toddler, so proud to share their creation, and the brownish smudge on the page? How ever you feel about the brownish blob, we're reaction-bound to the script of: "Wow, that's beautiful!"

(I'm both the uncle and the nephew in this story...and so are we all).

I, your friend/fae Piper, am an established speed writer. (Hang on. This is relevant.)

In dozens of books, I've created a face-paced career known for hyper-fixating on my novels for 12-17 hours. (Thank gods I established these manic episodes and the burnout-inducing rate of production before the age of AI, or else my under-medicated superpower would all be for naught.)

Juxtaposed against my keyboard smashing career stands *Hell and the Heart*.

For context: I wrote my first series, *The Night and Its Moon* as a four-book quartet, in the fall of 2021. I paused in the middle of the third book to write the *Villains* Duology, completing *Chill* and *Pyre* before finishing the fourth and final installation of *TNAIM*. During nap time, I wrote four accompanying *TNAIM* novellas. Then, to "unclench my brain from high fantasy," I decided to tackle my religious trauma by launching into a modern mythology tale about a human girl and her demon "imaginary friend." I had early half hazard drafts of the first three books done in a matter of months.

*Hell and the Heart* began, and something changed.

This wasn't a fictious world I could imagine and create the rules.

This wasn't today, with the Heaven, Hell, cryptids and fae I knew well and could write from memory.

This was thousands of years of faith, language, and history. To tell this story, I needed to slow the fuck down. Hours passed at the library, on JSTOR, hunting down the remaining ancestor of an Indigenous tribal advocate who could help me with the pronunciation of a near-dead language, and it still wasn't enough. I need a bigger team to help me do it right.

In the interim, I continue to pump out stories for fun, for joy, for mania, and because I love what I do, and I do what I love. (I've been known to celebrate the completion of one book by immediately beginning another one.)

Whether you read it to fill out the *No Other Gods* universe, or as a standalone, you're now beside me on the couch (remember, I'm the uncle in the previously established kiddo/art scenario), and at least one of us (me) is stoked to see the toddler (also me) and their mudpie of a painting. I look at what I've created with appreciation of a family member who says, "Sure, bud. That smear absolutely looks like a giraffe riding a motorcycle. You're not crazy for thinking that, and neither am I for seeing it."

◆

Now that I've nearly finished my second novel in the back of the book, it's time to actually begin thanking the people who made this possible.

Kat, my incredible editor, none of this would be possible without you. Thank you for your patience, your tears, your attention to detail in a typo-riddled world, and for giving Caliban as much love as I have. Helena, you've done it again. You brought the cover to life as better than I could have imagined. Letty, you hit the developmental edits out of the park. Luna, I'm so glad you were willing to take on this project independently so that the No Other Gods universe could be brought to life by one consistent voice. Zachary, you continue to be the only one I'll ever go to for formatting. And thank you to the wonderful sensitivity editors who, due to sensitive (ha!) nature of their day jobs, have asked to remain unnamed in indie projects, for helping to tell the best version of the story.

Give us this day our daily goblins: Haley, Lindsey, Bela, Allison, Cera, and Kelley, you remain the first I come to with every thought. Madison, Katrina, and Sarah, you're not only #TeamDemon friends, but wrapped this book in love while helping me remain whole. Thank you to the ARC team and everyone who gave their time, energy, and tears to 3,000 years of love.

I'm grateful for your honest reviews and anything that helps to put Caliban's story into the world. I will remain three football fields away from reader spaces when it comes to reactions and feedback. If you'd like to share or tag things that you feel are appropriate for shared spaces, I'd be so happy to see and boost them. I also look forward to one of the few places it's okay for authors and readers to interact: reactions and conversations (with the "spoiler bars") in the discord—there's a button for it in my linktree.

Cheers to us.
Cheers to late nights.
Cheers to religious freedom.
Cheers to the Other Gods.

# About the Author

Piper CJ, author of the *USA Today* bisexual fantasy series *The Night and Its Moon* and *No Other Gods*, and *New York Times* bestselling series *Fern's School for Wayward Fae*, is a photographer, hobby linguist, veteran sex worker (and online "beducational" SW community member and advocate), and of course, a French fry enthusiast. She has an M.A. in Folklore and a B.A. in Broadcasting, which she used in her former life as a morning-show weather girl, hockey podcaster, and in audio documentary work. Now, when she isn't playing with her dog, she's gaming, binging cartoons, dissecting fairy tales, or disappointing her parents.

Instagram: @piper_cj
Threads: @piper_cj
TikTok: @pipercj
Website: pipercj.com

# Also by Piper CJ

**New Adult Books and Novellas**

**No Other Gods**

*The Deer and the Dragon*

*The Fox and the Falcon*

*The Serpent and the Siren*

*End and Evergreen (2027)*

**The Night and Its Moon**

*The Night and Its Moon*

*The Sun and Its Shade*

*The Gloom Between Stars*

*The Dawn and Its Light*

**Accompanying *The Night and Its Moon* Novellas:**

*A Night Without Whispers*

*Wing and Arrow*

*A Year of Tea and Honey*

*Crown and Crumble*

**Villains**

*A Chill in the Flame*

*A Frozen Pyre*

**Indie Publications**

*This Book Sucks*

*Whoreiffying*

*Cruel Honey*

**Middle Grade Books**

**Fern's School for Wayward Fae**

*The Graveyard Gift*

*The Grim Adventure*

*The Daughter of Death*

*The Hollow Child*

# Content & Trigger Warnings

This is an emotionally tumultuous story, filled with loss, sorrow, and pain. As the author, I cried while writing it. My editor cried while reading it. And hopefully, I can empower you, as the reader, in a mission for harm-reduction, to ensure we're crying for the right reasons, despite our shared pain.

**In these pages you will find:**

Continuous cycles of death, sometimes accidental, sometimes through murder, stoning, torture (medieval, brutal, on-page, but not gratuitous, description of quartering), natural causes, implied harm brought to an infant (murder, emphatically non-sexual), war, death in battle, death of deities, angels, and demons may be deemed unsuitable or disrespectful by some, beheadings, stabbings, and further on-page violence.

A character intends to self-harm, with on-page suicidal ideation, thwarted attempted.

On-page sex, some sensual and titillating, with one life cycle/occasion of BDSM/dark-romance taboo sexual practices, including: consensual rough sex, breath play with water, disturbing a husband's cadaver. Sex work becomes a later theme, as with in the primary No Other Gods cannon, we explore why a sex worker ("whore" by lore quotation) is plot integral.

Gods and entities "humanized" or reimagined in ways that some readers may not find agreeable. Lore and mythology reimagined in ways that some readers may not find agreeable. Major world religions questioned or re-cast in ways that some readers may not find agreeable. God and gods as fictionalized entities, including major world religions perceived through the lens of a demon protagonist (using language some readers may find blasphemous as he makes generalizes or crafts insults).

# Pronunciation Glossary

Notes on pronunciation: many of these entities have Western prominence that have changed certain vowel or consonant sounds, syllabus emphasis, or may otherwise contradict the pronunciation in this glossary. (An easy example: the Catholic Saint, Brigid, used the hard "g", as opposed to the Celtic goddess, where the Gaelic soft "g" was preferred). The goal through this research was to find the pronunciation most accurate to the geography, culture, and time period—with this in mind, the in-text pronunciation may sometimes feel contradictory to familiar, modern portrayals.

Adlivun — AD-liv-un
Aea — EE-uh
Aengus — ANG-gus
Aitvaras — AIT-var-us (EYET-var-us)
Akkadians — uh-KAY-dee-un
Amagi — AH-muh-jee
anjatuq — an-GAHT-kuk
Assyrians — uh-SEER-ee-ans
Azazel — AH-zuh-ZELL
Bacchus — Bah-kuss
Bacchos — bah-KHOSS
Βάκχος — VÁ-koss
Ba'al — buh-ALL
baal — BAY-ul
Balor — BAY-lor
Beelzebub — bee-EL-zeh-bub

Brigid — BRIH-jid

Buluc Chabtan — boo-luc chahb-TEHN

Canaan — CAY-nun

Caoimhe — KWEE-vuh

Cernunnos — kare-NEW-noss

Colel — COH-lell

Dagda — DAHG-duh

Damiane — DAY-me-ahn

Demeter — deh-ME-ter

Dzbog — DAHZH-bog

Eleni — eh-LEH-nee

Gula — GOO-lah

Havea Hikule'o — HA-vee-uh HE-coo-lee-oh

Huitzilopochtli — weet-see-luh-powch-tuh-lee

Igaluk — EE-ga-luk

Izi — ee-zee (easy)

Jarovid — YAR-oh-vid

Kalki — CALL-kee

Keeva — KEE-va

Khaganate — KA-gu-nate

Lada — lah-dah

Lúgh — loo

Mami Wata — Mah-Me wah-tah

Mastislav — miss-TISS-slav

Maui Motu'a — mow-ee mow-too'uh

Melekh — MEH-lechk

Mokish — moh-kosh

Moloch — moll-uck

Nai — Neh

Nanook — nah-NOOK

Nefru — NEH-fruh

Orisha — aw-RI-shuh